Destined for Love

The Bradens, Book Two

Love in Bloom Series

Melissa Foster

ISBN-13: 978-0-9890508-9-0
ISBN-10: 0989050890

DESTINED FOR LOVE

Cover Design: Natasha Brown

WORLD LITERARY PRESS
PRINTED IN THE UNITED STATES OF AMERICA

A Note from Melissa

Rex Braden is one of the most loyal heroes I have ever created. His heart has always belonged to Jade Johnson, the one woman he cannot have. Everything in their lives has kept them apart, including a long-time family feud. Jade has just moved back to Weston, and the white-hot chemistry between her and Rex is impossible to ignore. The high-spirited, stubborn rancher has no choice but to follow his heart—even if that means walking away from the family he loves. Buckle up for a wild ride as Rex and Jade fight for the happily ever after they deserve. I hope you enjoy their emotional journey to coupledom as much as I enjoyed writing it. If this is your first Love in Bloom book, all of my love stories are written to stand alone, so dive right in and enjoy the fun, sexy adventure!

The best way to keep up to date with new releases, sales, and exclusive content is to sign up for my newsletter.
www.MelissaFoster.com/news

About the Love in Bloom Big-Family Romance Collection

The Bradens at Weston are just one of the families in the Love in Bloom big-family romance collection. Characters from each series make appearances in future books, so you never miss an engagement, wedding, or birth. A complete list of series titles is included at the end of this book, along with a preview of the next book in this series.

You can download **free** first-in-series ebooks and see my current sales here:
www.MelissaFoster.com/LIBFree

Visit the Love in Bloom Reader Goodies page for downloadable checklists, family trees, and more!
www.MelissaFoster.com/RG

For all the women who dream
of handsome cowboys

Chapter One

REX BRADEN AWOKE before dawn, just as he had every Sunday morning for the past twenty-six years—since the Sunday after his mother died, when he was eight years old. He didn't know what had startled him awake on that very first Sunday after she'd passed, but he swore it was her whispering voice that led him down to the barn and had him mounting Hope, the horse his father had bought for his mother when she first became ill. In the years since, Hope had remained strong and healthy; his mother, however, had not been as lucky.

In the gray, predawn hours, the air was still downright cold, which wasn't unusual for summer in Colorado. By afternoon they'd see temps in the low seventies. Rex pulled his Stetson down low on his head and rounded his shoulders forward as he headed into the barn.

The other horses itched to be set free the moment he walked by their stalls, but Rex's focus on Sunday mornings was solely on Hope.

"How are you, girl?" he asked in a deep, soft voice. He saddled Hope with care, running his hand over her thick coat. Her red coat had faded, now boasting white patches along her jaw and shoulders.

Hope nuzzled her nose into his massive chest with a gentle *neigh*. Most of his T-shirts had worn spots at his solar plexus from that familiar nudge. Rex had helped his father on the ranch ever since he was a boy, and after graduating from college, he'd returned to the ranch full-time. Now he ran the show—well, as much as anyone could run anything under Hal Braden's strong will.

"Taking our normal ride, okay, Hope?" He looked into her enormous brown eyes, and not for the first time, he swore he saw his mother's beautiful face smiling back at him, the face he remembered from before her illness had stolen the color from her skin and the sparkle from her eyes. Rex put his hands on Hope's strong jaw and kissed her on the soft pad of skin between her nostrils. Then he removed his hat and rested his forehead against the same tender spot, closing his eyes just long enough to sear that image into his mind.

They trotted down the well-worn trail in the dense woods that bordered his family's five-hundred-acre ranch. Rex had grown up playing in those woods with his five siblings. He knew every dip in the landscape and could ride every trail blindfolded. They rode out to the point where the trail abruptly came to an end at the adjacent property. The line between the Braden ranch and the unoccupied property might be invisible to some. The grass melded together, and the trees looked identical on either side. To Rex, the division was clear. On the Braden side, the land had life and breath, while on the unoccupied side, the land seemed to exude a longing for more.

Hope instinctively knew to turn around at that point, as

they'd done so many times before. Today Rex pulled her reins gently, bringing her to a halt. He took a deep breath as the sun began to rise, his chest tightening at the silent three hundred acres of prime ranch land that would remain empty forever. Forty-five years earlier, his father and Earl Johnson, their neighbor and his father's childhood friend, had jointly purchased that acreage between the two properties with the hopes of one day turning it over for a profit. After five years of arguing over everything from who would pay to subdivide the property to who they'd sell it to, both Hal and Earl took the hardest stand they could, each refusing to ever sell. The feud still had not resolved. The Hatfields' and McCoys' harsh and loyal stance to protect their family honor was mild compared to the loyalty that ran within the Braden veins. The Bradens had been raised to be loyal to their family above all else. Rex felt a pang of guilt as he looked over the property, and not for the first time, he wished he could make it his own.

He gave a gentle kick of his heels and tugged the rein in his right hand, Hope trotted off the path and along the property line toward the creek. Rex's jaw clenched and his biceps bulged as they descended the steep hill toward the ravine. The water was as still as glass when they finally reached the rocky shoreline. Rex looked up at the sky as the gray gave way to powdery blues and pinks. In all the years since he'd claimed those predawn hours as his own, he'd never seen a soul while he was out riding, and he liked it that way.

They headed south along the water toward Devil's Bend. The ravine curved at a shockingly sharp angle around the hillside and the water pooled, deepening before the rocky lip just before the creek dropped a dangerous twenty feet into a bed of rocks. He slowed when he heard a splash and scanned the water for the telltale signs of a beaver, but there wasn't a dam in sight.

Rex took the bend and brusquely drew Hope to a halt. Jade Johnson stood at the water's edge in a pair of cutoff jean shorts, that ended just above the dip where her hamstrings began. He'd seen her only once in the past several years, and that was weeks ago, when she'd ridden her stallion down the road and stopped at the top of their driveway. Rex raked his eyes down her body and swallowed hard. Her cream-colored T-shirt hugged every inch of her delicious curves, a beautiful contrast to her black-as-night hair, which tumbled almost to her waist. Rex noticed that her hair was the exact same color as her stallion, which was standing nearby with one leg bent at the knee.

Jade hadn't seen him yet. He knew he should back Hope up and leave before she had the chance. But she was so goddamned beautiful that he was mesmerized, his body reacting in ways that had him cursing under his breath. Jade Johnson was Earl Johnson's feisty daughter. She was off-limits—always had been and always would be. But that didn't stop his pulse from racing, or the crotch of his jeans from tightening against his growing desire. Fifteen years he'd forced himself not to think about her, and now, as her shoulders lifted and fell with each breath, he couldn't stop himself from wondering what it might feel like to tangle his fingers in her thick mane of hair, or how her breasts would feel pressed against his bare chest. He felt the tantalizing stir of the forbidden wrestling with his deep-seated loyalty to his father—and he was powerless to stop himself from being the prick of a man that usually resulted from the conflicting emotions.

JADE JOHNSON KNEW she shouldn't have ridden Flame down the ravine, but she'd woken up from a restless, steamy dream before the sun came up, and she needed a release for the sexual urges she'd been repressing for way too long. *Goddamned Weston, Colorado.* How the hell was a thirty-one-year-old woman supposed to have any sort of relationship with a man in a town when everybody knew one another's business? She'd thought she had life all figured out; after she graduated from veterinary school in Oklahoma, she'd completed her certifications for veterinarian acupuncture while also studying equine shiatsu, and then she'd taken on full-time hours at the large animal practice where she'd worked a limited schedule while completing school. She'd dated the owner's son, Kane Law, and when she opened her own practice a year later, she thought she and Kane would move toward having a future together. How could she have known that her success would be a threat to him—or that he'd become so possessive that she'd have to end the relationship? Coming back home had been her only option after he refused to stop harassing her, and now that she'd been back for a few months, she was thinking that maybe returning to the small town had been a mistake. She'd gotten her Colorado license easily enough, but instead of building a real practice again, she'd been working on more of an as-needed basis, traveling to neighboring farms to help with their animals without any long-term commitment, while she figured out where she wanted to put down roots and try again.

She heaved a heavy rock into the water with a grunt, pissed off that she'd taken this chance with Flame by coming down the steep hill. She knew better, but Flame was a sturdy Arabian stallion, and at fifteen hands high, he had the most powerful hindquarters she'd ever seen. Flame's reaction time to commands and his ability to spin, turn, or sprint forward was quicker than any horse she'd ever mounted. His short back, strong bones, and incredibly muscled loins made him appear indestructible. When Flame stumbled, Jade's heart had nearly skipped a beat. He'd quickly regained his footing, but the rhythm of his gait had changed, and when she'd dismounted, he was favoring his right front leg. Now she was stuck with no way to get him home without hurting him further.

Damn it. She bent over and hoisted another heavy rock into her arms to heave more of her frustration into the water. Her hair fell like a curtain over her face, and she used one dusty hand to push it back over her shoulder, then picked up the rock and—*shit.* She dropped the rock and narrowed her eyes at the sight of Rex Braden sitting atop that mare of his.

The nerve of him, staring at me like I'm a piece of meat. Even if he was every girl's dream of a cowboy come true in his tight-fitting jeans, which curved oh so lusciously over his thighs, defining a significant bulge behind the zipper. She ran her eyes up his too-tight dark shirt and silently cursed at herself for involuntarily licking her lips in response. She tried to tear her eyes from his tanned face, peppered with stubble so sexy that she wanted to reach out and touch his chiseled jaw, but her eyes would not obey.

"What're you looking at?" she spat at the son of the man who had caused her father years of turmoil. When she'd first come back to town, she'd hoped maybe things had changed. She'd ridden by the Braden's ranch while she was out with Flame one afternoon. Rex and his family were out front, commiserating over an accident that had just happened in their driveway, resulting in two mangled cars. She'd tried to see if they needed help, to break the ice of the feud that had gone on since before she was born, but while his brother Hugh had at least spoken to her, Rex had just narrowed those smoldering dark eyes of his and clenched that ever-jumping jaw. She'd be damned if she'd accept that treatment from anyone, especially Rex Braden. Despite her best efforts to forget his handsome face, for years he'd been the only man she'd conjured up in the darkest hours of the nights, when loneliness settled in and her body craved human touch. It was always his face that pulled her over the edge as she came apart beneath the sheets.

"Not you, that's for sure," he answered with a lift of his chin.

Jade stood up tall in her new Rogue boots and settled her hands on her hips. "Sure looks like you're staring at me."

Rex cracked a crooked smile as he nodded toward the water. "Redecorating the ravine?"

"No!" She walked over to Flame and ran her hand down his flank. *Why him? Of all the men who could ride up, why does it have to be the one guy who makes my heart flutter like a school-girl's?*

"Taking a break, that's all." She couldn't take her eyes off of his bulging biceps. Even as a teenager, he'd had the nervous habit of clenching his jaw and arms at the same time—and, Jade realized, the effect it had on her had not diminished one iota.

"Lame stallion?" he asked in a raspy, deep voice.

Everything he said sounded sensual. "No." *What happened to my vocabulary?* She'd been three years behind Rex in school, and in all the years she'd known him, he probably hadn't said more than a handful of words to her. She narrowed her eyes, remembering how she'd pined over each one of his grumbling syllables, even though they were usually preceded by a dismissive grunt of some sort, which she had always attributed to the feud that preceded her birth.

"All righty then." He turned his horse and walked her back the way he'd come.

Jade stared at his wide back as it moved farther and farther away. *Damn it. What if no one else comes along?* She looked up at the sun making its slow crawl toward the sky, guessing it was only six thirty or seven. No one else was going to come by the ravine. She cursed herself for not carrying her cell phone. She wasn't one of those women who needed to be accessible twenty-four-seven. She carried it during the day, but this morning, she'd just wanted to ride without distraction. Now she was stuck, and he was her only hope. Getting Flame home was more important than any family feud or her own conflicting hateful and lustful thoughts for the conceited man who was about to disappear around the corner.

She shook her head and kicked the dirt, wishing she'd worn her riding boots. The toes of her new Rogues were getting scuffed and dirty. *Could today get any worse?*

"Hey!" she called after him. When he didn't stop, she thought he hadn't heard her. "I said, *Hey!*"

He came to a slow stop, but didn't turn around. "You talking to me? I thought you were talking to that lame horse of yours." He cast a glance over his shoulder.

Jerk. "His name is Flame, and he's the best damned horse around, so watch yourself."

His horse began its lazy stroll once again.

"Wait!" *Goddamn it!* She gritted her teeth against the desire to call him an ass and shot a look at Flame. He was still favoring his leg, which softened her resolve.

"Wait, please."

His horse came to another stop.

"I need to get him home, and I can't very well do it myself." She kicked the dirt again as he turned his horse and walked her back. He stared down at Jade with piercing dark eyes, his jaw still clenched.

"Can you help me get him out of here?" Up close, his muscles were even larger, more defined, than she'd thought. His neck was thicker too. Everything about him exuded masculinity. She crossed her arms to settle her nerves as he waited a beat too long to answer. "Listen, if you can't—"

"Don't get your panties in a bunch," he said, calm and even.

"You don't have to be rude."

"I don't have to help at all," he said, mimicking her by crossing his arms.

"Fine. You're right. Sorry. Can you please help me get him out of here? He can't make it up that hill."

"Just how do you suppose I do that?" He glanced at the steep drop of the land just twenty feet ahead of them, then back up the ravine at the rocky shoreline. "You shouldn't have brought him down here. Why are you riding a stallion, anyway? They're temperamental as hell. What were you thinking? A girl like you can't handle that horse on this type of terrain."

"A girl like me? I'll have you know that I'm a vet, and I've worked around horses my whole life." She felt her cheeks redden and crossed her arms, jutting her hip out in the defiant stance she'd taken throughout her teenage years.

"So I hear." He lowered his chin and lifted his gaze, looking at her from beneath the shadow of his Stetson. "From the looks of it, all that vet schooling didn't do you much good, now, did it?"

Ugh! He was maddening. Jade pursed her lips and stalked away in a huff. "Forget it. I can do this by myself."

"Sure you can," he mused.

She felt his eyes on her back as she took Flame's reins and tried to lead him up the steep incline. The enormous horse took only three steps before stopping cold. She grunted and groaned, pleading with the horse to move, but Flame was hurt, and he'd gone stubborn on her. Her face heated to a flush.

"You keep doing what you're doing. I'll be back in an hour to get you and that lame horse of yours."

An hour, great. She was aching to tell him to hurry, but she knew how long it took to hook up the horse trailer, and she had no idea how he'd get it all the way down by the ravine. She watched him ride away, feeling stupid, embarrassed, angry, and insanely attracted to the ornery jerk of a man.

Chapter Two

"WHERE'RE YOU HEADED?" Treat, Rex's oldest brother, hollered as Rex hooked up the horse trailer.

Treat owned upscale resorts all over the world, and until he met and fell in love with Max Armstrong, a woman he'd met at their cousin Blake's wedding—he'd traveled eighty percent of the time, negotiating deals and conquering competition. Rex had watched Treat change and adapt his life to match his newfound love. Within a few short weeks, he'd hired corporate underlings to take over much of his traveling, and he'd decided to put down roots in Weston and help Rex and their father on the ranch.

Rex was glad for the help, and Treat was a good man. They were long past the angst he'd felt about Treat taking off after college to start his resort empire, leaving Rex to hold down the fort at home. And even though they'd confided in each other many times over the years, Rex held his tongue when it came to admitting exactly whom he was helping that chilly morning. He wasn't proud to be helping a Johnson—even a beautiful, feisty one like Jade—but how could he leave her stranded? Hell, who was he kidding? His body was still humming from their brief encounter. There was no way he'd turn away—and there was no way he'd give his family a reason to doubt his honor.

"Just helping a buddy out. I'll be back in an hour or so," Rex answered, climbing into the smallest pickup truck they owned. He figured it would take him twenty minutes to get to the road that led into the ravine and another twenty minutes to maneuver down the shoreline—if the truck and trailer could even make it. *Maybe I should call her own damned family to get her.* He couldn't shake the feeling that he was on the verge of something dangerous, and he couldn't turn away, either. Rex Braden didn't leave damsels in distress. No matter who they were.

"Want me to come along?" Treat asked.

"No!" He didn't mean to sound so emphatic. "Sorry, it's early. Just get started on the morning rounds. Can you give Hope some water, too? I exercised her this morning."

"Sure, got it covered."

THE GRASSY STRIP along the shore was too narrow to take the truck all the way down to Devil's Bend, but he got pretty damned close. He wrestled with the lie he'd told Treat. Lying wasn't something he enjoyed, but if his father found out he helped a Johnson, all hell was liable to break loose. Rex had made the mistake of mentioning Jade's brother, Steve, after he pummeled Steve in high school for making a smart-ass comment about Rex's younger sister, Savannah. He'd never forget his father's eyes turning almost black and the gravelly, angry sound of his voice when he told him that the Johnson name was never to be spoken in their home—*And when I say never, I mean never.*

He reached Devil's Bend and slowed his pace before moving around the final curve. Jade spurred a hunger in him that he'd never felt for another woman. It was a risky game he was playing, allowing himself to be in the cab of the truck with Jade. He'd survived his attraction to her for all these years by steering clear of her—and now that he was about to come as close as he'd ever been with the woman he'd secretly pined for, he wondered if he'd be able to behave.

Jade's voice carried around the bend. "You're such a beautiful boy. You know I'd do anything for you, even get a ride with that obnoxious hunk of a man."

Rex's muscles tensed. *Obnoxious?* Okay, yeah, he could be obnoxious. It was the *hunk* part that gripped him in all the right places.

"What kind of a man treats a woman like that? Huh, Flame? An arrogant, self-centered one, that's what kind—and he probably has a tiny little thing in his pants, too—spurring on all that anger behind those rippling muscles."

What the hell was he doing here? *Tiny little thing? I'll show you a tiny little thing!* He considered leaving her there, but that would just give credence to her gibberish.

He took a deep breath and stomped around the corner. "Let's go," he said.

Jade flashed a victorious smile, telling him she'd known he was there all along.

She looked past him. "Where's your trailer?"

The way the sun reflected off of her blue eyes, making them appear almost translucent, stole all of his attention. Why did she have to be so damned pretty? Why couldn't she be a horrendously ugly woman instead of a skinny little flick of a woman with a wide mouth that he couldn't help but want to kiss? Standing beside his six-foot-three frame, she was at least a foot shorter than him, even with those fancy boots on.

She narrowed her eyes, and he fought the urge to lean down and take her mouth in his, to taste those lips, feel her tongue, and fill his hands with her firm breasts.

"Hello?" she said with an annoyed wave of her hand. "Could you stop ogling me long enough to help me with my horse?"

Shit. What was wrong with him? He shook off the momentary fantasy and grabbed the horse's reins. All that sexual frustration came out as a grunt and a harsh, "Let's go," as he marched off with her horse, as if Flame had been following him all his life, leaving her to scurry after him.

"How far is it?" she asked.

He stared at the ground before him, feeling the poor horse limping behind him. What the hell was she thinking? She couldn't weigh more than a buck five. She shouldn't be out here alone. Anything could happen to her.

"How'd you get the trailer down here? Was it difficult to come down the hill?"

He was so busy trying to calm his raging hard-on that his answer came out as a snap. "Jesus, just walk." *I* am *an ass.*

She stomped ahead of him then, and he didn't have to worry about being annoyed by her questions anymore, because as they loaded the horse in the trailer and settled into the small cab, she didn't say one word.

He didn't mean to be so unfriendly, but damn it, how was he supposed to react? She was so damned hot, and so damned annoying. Most women swooned over Rex, and this one...this one was downright pesty. And her sweet perfume was infiltrating not only his senses, but he could feel its delicious scent settling into his clothes. He rolled down his window as they pulled out of the narrow, winding dirt road that led away from the ravine. He navigated around giant potholes and took the ride as slow as he possibly could to protect the horse.

He stole a glance at her as she stared out the passenger window like a sullen child. Her slender nose tilted up at the tip, her cheekbones were high, like his mother's had been, and her neck was long and graceful.

The left wheel caught on a pothole and her body flew toward him as he brought the truck to a quick stop. She caught herself with her right hand on the dashboard and her left hand clutching his forearm. For a moment their eyes locked, and he swore he saw the same want in her eyes that he felt stirring within him. How good would it feel to lean over and place his mouth over her sensuous lips?

In the next breath, she was tearing herself away from him, breathing fire, her eyes dark as night, as she scrambled out of the cab. She tugged the edges of her shorts down and stomped to the back of the trailer, where she swung the doors open.

"If you hurt him, I'll kill you!"

What the hell was I thinking? Rex walked calmly to the rear, where the horse was safe as could be.

Jade closed the trailer doors and wagged her finger inches from Rex's face. "Don't you hurt that horse or else, you hear me? Who taught you to drive anyway?"

He smiled. How could he not? She looked adorable spouting off threats like she could carry them out. He had to stop thinking of her in terms of cute and sexy. She was a Johnson, end of story. He headed back toward the truck.

"Smiling? You're laughing at me?" She stalked back to the truck.

He climbed in beside her, and she stewed the rest of the way. He finally pulled up beside the trees at the top of her property and stopped the truck. Without a word, afraid of what might come out of his mouth, Rex stepped from the truck and headed for the trailer.

"Aren't you bringing him down to the barn?" she asked, hurrying out of truck.

He lowered the ramp and backed the horse out.

"Nope," he said.

"What? What kind of gentleman are you?" She yanked Flame's reins from his hands.

"The kind that knows better than to walk on Johnson property." He tipped his hat and smiled. "You're welcome." He wanted nothing more than to drive down that driveway with her in the cab of the truck, if for no other reason than to be next to her for a little longer, but he'd taken enough of a risk bringing her this far. He wouldn't dare give Earl Johnson any reason to start breathing down his father's back. He needed to get away from the Johnson property, and he needed another damned icy cold shower.

Chapter Three

JADE STOOD IN the road, watching Rex's truck disappear around the corner. Everything she thought she'd known about Rex Braden when they were younger seemed to still be true. He was a grumpy, cocky, beautiful man. *Damn him.* She had to admit, though, the fact that he'd actually spoken to her—and helped her get her horse out of the ravine—was far more than she'd ever thought possible between a Johnson and a Braden.

She walked Flame down the long driveway and into the barn. The familiar smell of manure and hay wrapped around her like a warm hug. The smell was too pungent for most people, but to Jade it represented everything she'd ever known and loved. It represented home. The sounds of the other horses brought a smile to her face, as she'd soon be setting them free in the pasture. She stroked Rudy's jaw as she passed his stall. Rudy was one of her favorite horses. He was a bright red sorrel with white stockings and a blaze, and he was not only magnificent to look at, but his spunky personality reminded Jade of herself. She wasn't exactly a rebel, but she wasn't a conformist either, often leaving her family and friends, and even herself, to wonder what she might do next.

She was relieved to find that Flame was no longer favoring his leg. She turned on soothing music and took a few deep breaths to calm herself down before moving to Flame's side. She closed her eyes for just a moment to focus her mind on Flame instead of Rex. She concentrated on his breathing and found the rhythm of his breath and his heartbeat. She ran her hands along Flame's back and sides, soothing his body with a series of slow, gentle strokes. She felt her body relaxing as the music and the feel of the horse soothed her as much as she did him. Jade had always believed that touch could heal, and although she put medicine first, she believed in a more holistic, compassionate approach to animal health care, and she included touch, which she also studied, in most of her healing protocols.

She wondered what Rex would be like if someone took the time to touch him in a soothing way. He reminded her of an injured animal. At first glance, they were cute and you just wanted to touch them, but get too close and they would bare their teeth. Jade knew the secret, though. Once she moved past those teeth and soothed their injuries, they were just as gentle as she first imagined they might be.

Yeah, right.

She really wasn't sure what to make of Rex. One minute he was mean as a snake and the next he was going out of his way to help her. She'd thought there was a flash of something between them when she'd been practically knocked into his lap. She had the overwhelming urge to kiss him, but then she looked into those dark Braden eyes and she saw a flash of something dangerous there—the heat of which she might not be able to resist—and she bolted. Besides, he ran so hot and cold that he'd probably reel her in only to turn her away, and she was *not* going to be the girl Rex turned down. That would be all she needed. Especially in their small town.

She ran her hand down Flame's healthy legs, gently squeezing each muscle beneath her hands before moving to the injured limb. She moved carefully along the areas behind his knee, no longer quite as worried about a ligament or tendon injury. He might have just had a bad step. She ran her fingers along the back of his knee and was relieved that there didn't appear to be any swelling or tenderness to the touch.

After icing his leg, she went back into her father's house to check her work schedule for the day. She wanted to make sure she had time to ice Flame's leg a few more times.

"Hey there, darlin'," her father called from his office.

She grabbed her calendar from the table by the door and walked into his modest office.

"Hi, Daddy." She kissed him on the cheek. Earl Johnson was a big man, weighing in at almost three hundred pounds. Even with his six-foot stature, there was no way around that belly of his. Her father had retired from his job as an agricultural engineer just a few years earlier. All her life, he'd managed their ranch in addition to his career. It seemed as though he worked from the moment he returned home from his job until long after she had gone to bed. And even with all that hard work, she couldn't remember a time when he wasn't heavy. He was a man who worked hard and loved to eat, and the combination caused Jade to worry about his health.

"Your brother called," her father said. "He's coming over next weekend. Your mother was thinking about lunch Sunday afternoon."

"Sure," she said, writing it in her calendar. Jade was a visual woman. She'd tried to use the electronic calendar on her phone, but it drove her crazy. She still relied on paper calendars and she assumed she always would.

"You heading out to the Marlows' ranch today?" he asked.

"Yeah, I was planning on checking on their mare before going to see my other clients." She flopped onto the upholstered chair beside his desk as she flipped through her calendar.

"You okay, sweetie?"

She nodded. "Yeah, I took Flame out, and he took a bad step. He seems fine, but I was stupid to do it."

"I wondered where you'd gone so early."

She read concern in her father's blue eyes, which had recently begun to look more gray than blue. Rex's words played in her mind. *The kind that knows better than to walk on Johnson property.* Maybe she'd just feel him out a little and see if the feud still ran as close to the surface as she remembered.

"I saw Rex Braden when I was out riding this morning."

Her dad lifted his eyes from the spreadsheet on his desk and in a calm, even voice said, "You did, did you?" He pressed his lips into a firm line, and a deep vee formed between his thick brows.

Chills ran up Jade's back. She recognized that shadowy look in his eye. She'd been reading her father's moods since she was a little girl. She felt the cadence of his breathing, measured his body language, and tested the waves of his stare, just as she did with the animals she cared for. At that moment, she saw a storm brewing behind those eyes and realized that the bad feelings toward the Bradens hadn't lessened one bit. Her father wasn't an aggressive man. One look was usually enough to get her or Steve to walk away from whatever he might find offensive.

"I'd better go get started before the day gets away from me." She rose to her feet.

As she passed his desk, her father reached for her hand with his warm, fleshy fingers. "Darlin', now, you know better than to do anything to embarrass this family, right?"

There was that stare again.

"Dad, I'm over thirty years old. Have I ever embarrassed you?" She flashed her best daddy's-little-girl grin to hide her clenching stomach.

"No, I don't guess you have. Just you stay away from those Bradens." He dropped his eyes back to the desk with a dismissive nod.

Jade sighed. *Hal Braden was your best friend for years. Isn't it time to bury the hatchet?* She walked out of his office knowing she'd never have the courage to say any of those things. Small towns bred small-town values: family loyalties and hard work. Who was she to break that bond? No matter how much she might want to.

Chapter Four

BY THE TIME Rex and Treat got through the morning chores on the ranch, Rex needed another shower—a cold one. He couldn't stop thinking about Jade and how she looked in those tight jeans shorts that barely covered the curve of her ass and the way her lean legs disappeared into those fancy leather boots. She was nothing like the women Rex usually dated. He gravitated toward tall blondes and preferred more demure, feminine women who wouldn't mouth off at every little thing. Finding those women had always been easy for him. There were enough nearby towns that he could slip in and out when he was in need of a quick release, and he'd maintained those drop-in relationships with women who didn't seem to want any more than he was willing to give—a quick bang a few times each month, without phone calls or further attachments. He had yet to meet a woman who stirred the protective urges that he had for his sister, and when he did, then maybe…just maybe, he'd want something more. Lately, watching Treat with his fiancée, Max, had stirred a desire in him for something more. But what they had was so pure and natural that Rex wondered if it would ever be in the cards for him. He wondered if he was even capable of such love.

He was brushing Hope and thinking about Jade's blue eyes when he felt his father's large hand on his shoulder. He had a momentary worry that his father somehow knew he'd helped Jade, but when he turned and saw his father's eyes, he recognized the familiar longing. He was thinking about their mother. Hope did that to them all. She'd been their mother's horse, after all.

"Son. How's she doing?" The men in the family got their height from their father, who stood eye to eye with Treat at six-foot-six, and their coloring as well, while Savannah took after their mother, with thick auburn hair and green eyes.

"She's good. I rode her this morning. She did well." Rex finished grooming her and brought her back into her stall. "Hannah's coming by later to practice showing Hope for the horse show next Friday." Hannah Price's father had bought several horses from Hal Braden over the years, and the fourteen-year-old's enthusiasm toward horses—especially Hope—had lit up his father's eyes. When Hannah asked if she could show Hope in the youth halter class, they'd all but jumped for joy. She'd been practicing for weeks, and Rex knew she'd do a damned good job.

"Good. I'll help her out. You got that meeting tonight?"

Shit. He'd forgotten about the volunteer meeting for the Weston Horse Show, which was taking place the following Friday and Saturday. He'd been volunteering for the last few years, but after the morning he'd had, it was the last thing on his mind. Still, he'd committed, and Rex took his commitments seriously.

"Yup, I'll be there," Rex said with a nod.

"Good, and don't you let them make you do any of that hokey crap they've been trying to do for years."

Rex laughed. "No hokey crap. Got it, Dad." As he went to check on the other horses, he listened to his father talking to Hope.

Rex and his brothers had been raised in a very loving, demonstrative family, and although hugs, pats on the back, and *I love yous* were common, whether they were in public or in the privacy of their own home, Rex had noticed through the years that he hadn't ever felt the same commitment, or deep emotional tug, toward any of the various women he'd dated. He'd begun to wonder if he ever would. The thought brought him back to Jade. He definitely had the urge to touch her, but with his testosterone raging at the sight of her, he wouldn't exactly call that anything more than a primal urge. Yet still, it made him wonder...

"How's Brownie doing?" Hal had grown up helping breed Dutch Warmblood show jumpers, and he'd carried the tradition onto his own ranch. Brownie was a generic name that Rex used for the bay foals. This particular foal was almost eight months old and had already shed the pale hairs on his legs to off black up to his hocks. He was a beauty, and as much as Rex enjoyed seeing a new family enthusiastically take on a new family member, he always felt a pang of sadness to let them go.

"Brownie's strong and handsome," his father said as he petted Hope. "You're doing great, old girl. Adriana would be proud."

His father swore on the ground he walked on that their

mother, Adriana, still spoke to him even after all these years. Rex didn't know what to make of his father's declarations, but he knew that months earlier, when Hal had suffered a bout of stress cardiomyopathy, otherwise known as Broken Heart Syndrome, Hal had been having a full-on, heated conversation about Treat and Max—and he'd been alone in the barn at the time. He'd gotten so worked up that he had all of the symptoms of a heart attack, scaring the daylights out of the entire family. Hal was as strong as an ox, and in the months since, he'd fully recovered. Rex couldn't imagine a life without his father around, and as he watched him now, he was glad that it was only a broken heart he'd suffered, and not something much worse.

JADE HAD NEVER been nervous in meetings, and practicing veterinary medicine, she'd come into contact with just about every personality under the sun. But when Rex Braden walked into the horse show meeting in Harvey and Ester Gesalt's yard, wearing black Ariat boots and tight-fitting Levi's, her pulse sped up and every nerve in her body began to do a fiery little dance. She found herself looking away, as if the black button-down shirt he was wearing was blinding like the sun.

This is ridiculous.

He's just a man, and a mean one at that.

Jade had badgered her best friend, Riley Banks, all afternoon for information on Rex. She couldn't get him out of her head.

Riley was the eyes and ears of Weston. If there was dirt to be slung, she had her shovel ready before anyone else was even awake. Surprisingly, she'd learned only two things about Rex: He hadn't dated anyone from Weston since high school, and he was always working. How could a man live for thirty-four years in one town—except for when he'd attended college—and have only two things on the must-know-about-him list? Two! Everyone had secrets and skeletons. God knew she did. She wondered what his were.

She surveyed him as he moved through the small gathering of community members that would be volunteering at the horse show, shaking the hands with the men and nodding at the women. She made a mental list of her own: He wasn't wearing his Stetson, and his thick dark hair brushed his collar. It was longer than was in style, which told her that he didn't really care what anyone else thought about him. That didn't surprise her, given the way he'd treated her earlier that afternoon. As he shook the hands of a few of the other volunteers, she noticed—and added to her mental list—that he had a nice, slightly crooked smile.

"Will!" He patted Will Prather on the back.

She added *sexiest voice around* to her list with a reluctant groan, and *more muscles per square inch of his body than any man she'd ever met.*

He laughed at something Will said and took a step in her direction.

Jade held her breath as their eyes locked, stopping him in his tracks. His smile faded, replaced with a scowl. He turned his back to her and lifted his chin.

She added *asshole* to her list and decided it was time to stop her mental musings, because along with that last declaration, she felt a twang of hurt at how he'd looked at her.

"Well, let's get down to business. We need to decide who will be volunteering for which event, concessions, etc." Harvey Gesalt and his wife, Ester, owned the Weston Riding Ring, and they'd hosted the annual horse show for the last seven years. Harvey and Ester were one of those couples that looked alarmingly alike; both stood about five-foot-three inches tall and had short gray hair and leathery skin. They were in their seventies, and inasmuch as they looked alike, they were also very different. In all the ways Harvey was hard—inflexible, demanding—his wife was malleable and amenable.

Jade tried to concentrate on what Harvey was saying, but with Rex just feet away, she could hardly think at all. She wished she'd had a chance to change before the meeting, but she'd been so busy with clients' animals and then she'd wanted to massage Flame's leg. As it was, she'd barely made it to the meeting on time.

A couple walked behind her, and she had to move to allow them to pass. Rex turned as the couple noisily thanked her for moving, and he shook his head, giving her a disapproving look for causing a disruption. When he remained standing at an angle instead of turning back toward Harvey, she silently tried to will him to turn around.

Turn around. Please, look away.

The air around her warmed, and she began to fidget like a child who had been in church too long—and damn if it wasn't because of Rex. She tried not to look at his biceps straining beneath his sleeves, and she tried to ignore the way his hair fell in thick, lustrous waves, but every pore emitted sexuality, and having not been with a man in months, Jade was having a hard time ignoring his potent masculinity.

Focus! Damn, she'd missed the information about the volunteers, which was the reason she was there.

"The concert is scheduled for eight o'clock Friday night, and the band is coming in from Allure. They were highly recommended," Ester said.

A concert might be fun. She wondered if Rex could dance. *Ugh, what am I doing? I'll go to the concert with Riley and dance this lust away.*

"We'll put the sign-up sheets on the table next to the refreshments, and we'll finalize the list and assignments at the next meeting."

Jade headed for the sign-up table. The sooner she signed up, the sooner she could leave.

"Dr. Johnson, how are you?" Caroline Mills owned an eight-year-old gelding, Jasper, who had become disobedient when ridden. When Jade examined him, she found he had a severe muscle spasm throughout his back and hamstring. After just two sessions of acupuncture and hands-on massage, he was back to his old self again.

"Caroline, please, it's Jade, remember?" Jade disliked the formality of being called "Doctor." Every time she heard the term, she thought of Dr. Baker, the old man who had been the town vet forever. "How's Jasper doing?" She glanced at the sign-up table and noticed a line had formed.

"He's doing great. You really do have magic hands."

Jade searched the line for Rex. He was nowhere to be found. Now was her chance to sign up and get out.

"Thank you. I hate to be rude, but I'd better get in line," she said, hurrying over to the table. *How long does it take to sign your name?* Jade tapped her foot, wishing the line would move quicker. At least she'd avoided a run-in with Rex. She let out a relieved sigh just as he came to stand behind her in line. She made the mistake of turning around, and his dark eyes jetted away from her.

He crossed his arms in a defensive pose, and Jade turned back around, trying to ignore the familiar woody, leathery scent of him, which reminded her of the barn. Her stomach tightened. She was hyperaware of his body just inches behind her.

Why was she so goddamned nervous around him, and why was he so damned rude, looking away from her like that? When the line finally moved, she scribbled her name on the sign-up sheet without even looking at what she was signing up for. She could figure that out later. She thrust the pen in his direction with a harsh scowl. *Two can play at this game.*

"How's Flame?" His eyes were serious.

Surprised that he cared, she answered, "He had a hard time making it down the driveway, no thanks to you." *Why am I being so snotty?*

REX WATCHED JADE stomp away, and he let out the breath he hadn't realized he'd been holding. When she'd bent over the table to sign her name, her shorts had ridden up just enough to expose the tender skin where her thighs ended and her rear end began, and he'd just about lost it. He'd been with plenty of beautiful women, but there was something about Jade that made his heart soar. He'd first noticed it when she was a carefree teenager, vibrant and eager in everything she did, with a ready smile. Even then she had a body that wouldn't quit, and now she was harder, louder, and her body had matured in ways that set his blood on fire. That strange combination touched him in all the right places.

Why'd she have to come back to town? He'd done so well not thinking about her when she was away at school. And now, every time he saw her, his body reacted with a visceral, carnal need. As she stomped away, he wondered why the one woman who lit his veins on fire had to be the daughter of his father's only enemy.

Chapter Five

JADE WOKE UP early on Monday morning and went down to check on Flame. She'd given him an acupuncture treatment after coming home from the meeting with the hopes of alleviating any remaining discomfort. She took him out of the stall and walked him for a few minutes, watching his gait, and was relieved to see him back to his normal self. She didn't want to take any chances. Rex was right. Flame could be temperamental, and he was a big boy. *Rex is a temperamental big boy, too.* If he had even a slight injury, he could reinjure it with one gallop. She decided to give him a rubdown and ice him throughout the day again, just in case.

While she was icing Flame's leg, she thought of Rex and again wondered if he might soften with the right care. She let her mind drift further and wondered if he would have offered to help if he'd run into her father or her brother down at the ravine. Had he helped her simply because it was her? Even though she knew she shouldn't, Jade wanted to know even more about him. She was an intuitive woman. She saw the way he looked at her, and she wondered if maybe he was thinking about her, too. She knew she was pushing the envelope with her next thought, and she knew she was rationalizing, thinking that she might be on his mind, too, to put her plan into motion, but she didn't care. Something told her that she should extend an olive branch and see if he grabbed hold.

She was headed toward the house when she saw her parents walking toward their car.

"Mom, Dad!" She jogged over. "Where are you going?"

Her mother looked pretty in her fitted blue dress. Jade had her father's eyes, but she had her mother's dark hair and slim figure.

"Just taking a quick trip to the bank. We'll be back later. How busy is your schedule today?" Jane Johnson smiled at her daughter.

"I've only got a few clients, so not bad. I'm going to ice Flame again later, too. He seems fine, but I want to be sure before I let him run."

"That's good, honey. You haven't heard from Kane at all, have you?"

Jade knew her mother worried about Kane, and she knew how often she bit her tongue rather than bring him up. Jade had been honest and had told them both about how he'd stalked her after she'd ended their relationship. For the first few weeks after she returned home, her father had been painfully protective every time she left the house. She hadn't heard word one from Kane, and until now, her parents had backed off about him.

"No, Mom. He's not going to come all the way out here looking for me," she reassured her. When she'd first moved, Kane had called her several times and had texted often. She'd finally blocked his number, and that seemed to put an end to it.

Her mother blew her a kiss before getting into the car.

Jade headed into the house and began mixing the ingredients for her mother's famous brownies. She was comfortable in her parents' kitchen, but she longed for her own once again. She was itching to get her own place, but she still wasn't sure that Weston was where she wanted to put down roots.

Jade hadn't done anything fun in weeks, and she needed a little inspiration to lift her spirits. She'd been too busy making enough money to cover her school loans, and recently, worrying about Flame's leg. Even if Rex wasn't an appropriate inspiration—*you know better than to do anything to embarrass this family*—as she licked the batter off of her finger, her mind traveled back to that moment in the truck. Being that close to Rex had stirred up all sorts of tingling in those secret places that she'd been trying to forget for the past few months. What would Rex's mouth taste like? Would he kiss aggressively, or move his tongue over hers slowly and lovingly? Would he taste like he smelled—manly and pungent—or would he taste so sweet she wouldn't be able to get enough of him?

The oven beeped, pulling her from her reverie. She had to stop thinking of him that way. She'd obviously gone far too long without being intimate with a man. *I really need to get laid.* Maybe she'd go out with Riley to someplace where no one knew her. Yes, that's exactly what she needed to do. She needed to get out or she *was* going to end up embarrassing herself for sure. But first she was going to take the brownies to Rex.

She put the brownies in the preheated oven and texted Riley.

Free 2night?

Ke$ha came on the radio, and she moved her hips to the beat of the music. *Dancing. That's what I need.*

Her phone vibrated with Riley's text. *Absofuckinglutely.*

She could always count on Riley. They'd been besties their whole lives, and even though they'd gone to separate colleges and Jade had stayed in Oklahoma after school, she and Riley had always remained close. She texted back. *Dancing?*

Less than thirty seconds later she had her answer. *Def! Allure? New dance club. Fingers. 8?*

Fingers? What kind of name was that for a dance club? It sounded dirty to Jade. She texted back, *Perfect.* She hadn't gone dancing in years, and now she couldn't wait.

THE WHITE SUV pulled into the driveway as Rex was coming in from the fields. At first he didn't recognize the truck as it crept down the driveway, but as it came closer to the house, he recognized Jade in the driver's seat.

"Oh, shit," he said aloud. *Just what I need.* Treat was inside handling his resort business, and thankfully, his father had gone into town. He stalked toward her car, trying to ignore the way each nerve rose to the surface of his skin.

When she stepped from her car in a short white skirt that hugged her slim hips and a dark blue tank top that accentuated her breasts, the world stood still. Rex's legs stopped moving, and he couldn't get his brain to think past her unimaginable beauty. She turned with a wide smile, and her hair fell into her face.

Years of pent-up desire rushed through him in flashes of images: his hands beneath her hair, his lips on her neck, his—

"Hi, Rex!" she yelled with a wave.

He shook the dirty thoughts away and closed the distance between them. "Jade." He tried not to sound angry, but even he heard a tinge of panic in his voice as she stole a glance toward the house.

"Well, hello to you, too. I brought you something," she said cheerfully.

She reached into her car, all those enchanting curves so close he could touch them as she bent over and reached farther. A groan slipped from his lips, and he tried to cover it with a feigned cough.

She came out of the car holding a plate full of brownies and kicked the door shut, hiking her skirt up just a little farther. "You okay?" she asked with an arched brow.

"Fine." *Cough, cough. Shit. I can't even look at her without getting a hard-on.*

"I brought you brownies."

His body was still in gawking mode.

"To thank you? For yesterday?" She smiled, holding up the plate of brownies.

She's off-limits. "Brownies? No need. Really. Anyone would have helped you."

She licked her lips, and he stifled another groan. *Time for another trip out of town.* He had to get her to leave before he said or did something he'd regret, or rather, he should regret.

"I don't think they would have." She pushed the plate toward him. "I know I can't stick around, with our families feuding and all, but no matter what their issues are, I didn't want to seem inconsiderate. Here." She shoved the plate toward him again, and this time, he took it.

"Thank you. That's mighty kind of you, but really, you should be going." He opened her car door for her and hoped she'd just jump in and leave.

"Look, I know our families don't get along, but do we have to be so mean to each other?"

"I'm a Braden; you're a Johnson. We shouldn't even be talking." *And I shouldn't be fantasizing about taking you right here against your car.*

Her smile faded to a disappointed frown. She narrowed her eyes. "Are you really as cold as you appear, Rex Braden?"

He couldn't slow his racing pulse. *I'll show you just how hot I can be.* He took a step forward, his hands fisting and opening repeatedly just to keep them from touching her. He'd dreamed about that body of hers, that luscious mouth, those legs wrapped around his waist, and since seeing her at the ravine, he'd taken three cold showers. He barely made it from breakfast to lunch without his body getting so overheated he was sure Treat could smell the testosterone coming off him in waves.

"I think you'd better go," he said, eyeing the open car door.

She spun on her heels, but before closing her door, she said, "And here I thought there was something more to you than an arrogant, self-centered Braden. Enjoy the brownies."

He watched her pull out of the driveway and cursed under his breath. Why the hell was he even in this position? What was he thinking? Things were fine before he helped her. He should have turned and ridden off the minute he'd seen who it was down at the ravine. He should have never given any Johnson the time of day, much less the beautiful one that made his heart sing.

"Who was that?" Treat called from the front door.

Rex looked down at the plate of brownies and had a complete brain freeze. Treat met him on the front porch and took the plate from his hands.

"Brownies, yum." He took one off the top and bit into it. "Aw, these are incredible. Who made them?"

Rex went to the sink and ran the water until it was freezing. Then he splashed it on his face. Treat leaned against the counter next to him and laughed.

"What's her name?"

They'd confided in each other about women their whole lives. Rex knew he couldn't pull the wool over Treat's eyes, and besides, he'd watched Treat change over the last few months, and he knew that if any of his siblings would be sympathetic, it would be him. Treat had gone from building a resort empire to building a life, his own family. Once he'd committed to Max, he'd become completely focused on her needs, putting her feelings first, spending time with her, loving her whether she was happy or sad. When they were together, they were always touching, nuzzling against each other, and sharing secret laughs. Rex couldn't help but feel a little jealous.

He looked at his oldest brother now, and he wanted to share his feelings and his concerns.

"You can't tell Dad," Rex said as he dried his face with a towel.

"What are we, twelve?" Treat teased. He ran a hand through

his thick dark hair. Treat had taken to forgoing shaving for a day or two each week, and today he sported a thick five-o'clock shadow, giving him a rugged look. At six-foot-six, he reminded Rex of the Marlboro man from the old commercials. "First of all, why would I tell Dad anything about your sex life, and second of all, why would Dad care?"

Rex sighed and ran his hand through his hair. "About yay high." He held his hand up to his neck. "Long dark hair, gorgeous. Just came back to town a few months ago."

He watched the lifting of Treat's eyebrows and the coy smile that crept along his lips as understanding dawned on him.

"No." Treat shook his head. "No way."

Rex shrugged. "It's not like I'm chasing her."

"Jade Johnson, Rex? What are you thinking?"

"That's just it. I'm *not* thinking. Other than every time I see her I can't stop fantasizing about what it would be like to…"

Treat was still shaking his head. He laughed a hearty, deep laugh.

"What's so funny?" Rex asked.

"You're so fucked." Treat's phone vibrated and, still laughing, he read the text and responded.

"Don't you feel like you have a leash around your neck carrying that damn thing around all the time?"

"Are you kidding? I love to hear from Max." His phone vibrated and he read the text, then said to Rex, "The best I can do is help you to get your mind off of her. I'm meeting Max tonight for a few drinks. Come along."

Chapter Six

"GIRL, YOU ARE smoking hot," Riley said. "I have the perfect dress for you next time we go out. I whipped up this gorgeous white backless number, and it'll fit you perfectly." Riley had a degree in fashion design, but after college, she hadn't been able to break into the industry and had also returned to her hometown.

"Running from a stalker definitely agrees with you," Riley said as she drove toward Fingers.

It was just like Riley to make a joke out of her life-altering situation. "He wasn't a stalker. Besides, it's more like not having sex for months on end agrees with me," Jade said with a smirk. She'd thrown on her sexiest black minidress in an effort to lure a man for a quickie. She wasn't proud of herself, and she'd be mortified if her father ever found out, but damn it, sometimes you just needed to scratch that itch. After the way Rex raked his eyes over her and then acted like an ass, she deserved a little ego boost.

"Months? Like, plural? Really? Why didn't I know that?" Riley hadn't aged a bit since college. She was a curvy woman, and she wore the curves well. She'd never given in to perms or waves, and her straight, shoulder-length brown hair remained the same, with the recent addition of longish bangs, which gave her a playful appearance no matter how she was dressed. Tonight, with her skinny jeans and black blouse with a plunging neckline, she definitely looked playful.

"You knew. Who have I been with since moving here?" Jade asked.

Riley pursed her lips and swished them from side to side. "Hmm." She held up an index finger, then lowered it. "I think you might be right."

"I know I'm right." She laughed.

Riley pulled into the parking lot of Fingers, and Jade's nerves twinged. It'd been a long time since she'd gone out looking to bed a man. *Have I ever?*

"Are you sure I look okay?" she asked.

"Hell yes, woman. Better than okay. What's with you? You aren't usually nervous about how you look. You know you're hot," Riley said.

Jade blew out a breath. "I can't tell anymore. I've kind of been given conflicting messages lately."

"From who? Want me to take them down?" She grabbed her purse, and before Jade could reply, she said, "Come on. Let's get in there and have some fun."

A neon light read, LADIES NIGHT, MONDAY NIGHTS, 6–10P.M.

Jade tossed a sneer at Riley. "You could have told me."

"Would you have come if I had?"

Jade weighed her answer. "Maybe. I mean, my whole goal tonight is to get lucky, so…"

Riley was a head taller than Jade. She threw her arm around Jade's shoulder and rested her cheek on her head. "I've got your back, sister. I'm the designated driver, so we'll liquor you up. I'll do a sober check of any guy you want—I won't let you get into a car with anyone drunk, and I'll personally review their driver's license and take down name and address in case your body goes missing tomorrow. And if you don't get lucky, I'll tuck you in tonight."

"You're the best, Ri."

"Yeah, I know."

REX SUCKED DOWN his beer, and for the first time in what felt like forever, his body relaxed. He loved music, and his foot bounced to the beat on the hardwood floor. The beat of the music lured the females onto the dance floor, giving him plenty of entertainment.

"So, Rex, Max and I are considering building a house nearby," Treat said.

Rex enjoyed spending time with Max and Treat. When he'd first met Max, he wasn't sure she'd be enough for his oldest brother. She was very casual, donning a ponytail and jeans on most days, but once he'd gotten to know her, he realized how smart and warm she really was. Shortly after they'd met, she'd begun to wear more feminine, sexier outfits, and Rex could see the appreciation in Treat's eyes—the way his eyes drank her in, in the same way Rex knew his eyes drank in Jade. He knew he shouldn't even look at Jade that way, but no matter how hard he tried not to, his body and eyes had a mind of their own.

"About time," Rex teased. Treat could afford to buy half of Allure if he wanted to, so it surprised Rex that he'd remained at their father's house for so long. Treat had been working out the final details with his new staff and redefining his business infrastructure. *One thing at a time*, he'd told Rex two months ago.

"Not that you're waiting for me to leave with bated breath or anything," Treat said with a tilt of his glass.

"Nah, it's cool. I'm happy for you. Where?"

Treat pulled Max against him and kissed the side of her head. "Wherever Maxy wants."

"I think we should stay closer to your Dad. You guys have so many family functions, and with Treat helping on the ranch and running his business, it makes sense that he should spend less time in the car. Besides, Weston is less than half an hour from Allure, so it's not a big deal for me, and Chaz will let me work from home when I want to." Max had worked for Chaz Crew, the owner of the Indie Film Festival, headquartered in Allure, for the past ten years, and she had no intention of leaving, no matter how much money Treat had.

"I'm all for it. The closer the better. I like having you guys around." Rex took another swig of his drink, scanning the dance floor. Fingers had opened just a few weeks earlier, and although Rex had been there only once before, he had heard that Monday nights pulled the best-looking women from all of the nearest communities. Not that he would go home with anyone while he was with Treat and Max, but a little eye candy never hurt. He scanned the dance floor, trying to find someone who caught his eye enough to take his mind off of Jade, but no matter how pretty the women were, no matter how tight their clothing was or how curvaceous their bodies were, none of them was as appealing as Jade, and it was starting to piss him off. He had to get that woman out of his head.

The song changed to a slow tune, and Max took Treat's hand. "Dance with me," she said with a flirty grin.

Treat climbed from his booth. "Duty calls," he said with a smile.

Max rested her head on Treat's chest, and Treat's hands slipped around her waist. The couples next to them shifted, and there, across the dance floor, sitting at a table with Riley Banks, wearing a tight black dress that barely covered her thighs, was Jade. She had two empty glasses before her, and her cheeks had a rosy glow. The muscles in his arms tensed. He set his beer down, not realizing he'd slammed it until droplets flew over the rim and splattered across the table.

What the hell is she doing here?

A tall, blond-haired guy approached Jade, and Rex sat up straighter, narrowing his eyes, assessing him in one quick glance: too friendly looking, all smiles and—look at him, touching her arm, her shoulder, *sitting down at the table?*

Rex took a slug of his beer, his eyes locked on the trio. Jade was smiling, but her eyes darted around the room. Rex knew women, and any woman whose eyes darted wasn't interested. *Get outta there, buddy.*

"Rex, you look like you're ready to kill someone," Treat said as he sat down. Max squeezed in beside him.

The guy rose to his feet and reached for Jade's hand. She followed him to the dance floor, then pressed her hands flat against his chest and rested her face between them, moving her body way too close to his.

Rex fisted his hands beneath the table.

"Rex," Treat said as he touched his arm, "go cut in."

"With who?" Max asked.

Treat nodded toward Jade.

"Hey, that's the girl on the horse, the one who rode up when I smashed your car." She kissed Treat, then said, "The best day of my life. The day you proposed." She twisted the engagement ring on her finger.

"Yup," Rex said. "That's the one."

"Rex, she's so pretty, and the way she looked at you that day, I'd say she really liked you. You should ask her to dance, but maybe after they finish," Max urged.

"Nope," he answered.

"Why not? You only live once," she said.

"Our families have been feuding forever," Treat explained. "Well, our fathers have, and you know how Rex is about family loyalty."

Max took a sip of her drink. "Well, as far as I'm concerned, all's fair in love and war. I vote he makes a move."

For the next hour, Rex watched Jade and the blond guy, just waiting for the guy to make a wrong move. He didn't mean to count Jade's drinks, but he was. She'd had four, and that was a shitload of alcohol for someone her size. She had no business drinking that much.

"We have to go," Max said. "Rex, I'm really glad you came

with us, but I have to work early tomorrow."

Treat purposely blocked Rex's view of Jade, and in a firm voice, he said, "Rex, let it go. You missed your chance tonight. There's always tomorrow."

Rex gave Treat a harsh glare. "Was there always tomorrow for you and Max?" He shook his head at his admission, then tried to cover his tracks. "I'm just going to make sure she doesn't get herself into any trouble."

"You okay to drive?" Treat asked.

"Fine. I've only had two beers. I think I can handle it."

"See you when the sun comes up," Treat said as he and Max left.

By the time Treat moved out of Rex's way, Riley was gone and Jade was alone with the guy. *What kind of friend would leave her alone?* Rex reminded himself that she wasn't his to take care of, but as she stumbled to the dance floor again, her dress hiked up her thigh and the guy walking behind her, his eyes trained on her ass, the fact that she wasn't his didn't mean squat. He moved to the edge of his seat, ready to step in.

Chapter Seven

THE ROOM WAS spinning, in a good way. Jade hadn't thought about Rex in at least twenty minutes, and blondie— what was his name? Tom? Tray? Tim? Tim, that was it— seemed really nice. Riley took down his information before she left and he said he'd take Jade home, but she wasn't ready to go. Now that she was on the dance floor again, she wanted to dance.

Jade wrapped her arms around Tim's neck and swayed to the music. His hands felt so nice on her lower back. God, she'd missed being touched. He inched his hand down, and something in Jade sobered. She was going home with this guy. That's not what she did. But oh, his hand felt warm. If she closed her eyes, she could pretend he was Rex just to get through the night—to get past her desire for that sexy, frustrating man. Just one night to lessen her urges.

"Let's get out of here," he whispered in her ear.

She nodded, but her legs stood still as she focused on his face. He wasn't that good-looking, but he was nice. Too nice. He was kind of a wimp. *I'm going home with a wimp when what I really want is to go back to Weston and figure out how to get Rex to notice me. Rex. One-hundred-percent man. Asshole. Why do I even want him?* She remembered the way he'd turned her away earlier in the day, with all that anger bubbling beneath his skin. What was that all about? Thinking of his skin brought her back to his body, his muscles, the way he smelled when, so masculine and...hot.

Tim took her hand and led her toward the door. Her legs were moving, but she didn't want to go. Her brain yelled, *No! Stop!* But her lips weren't moving. She was too drunk and too conflicted to speak.

In the parking lot, he wrapped his arms around her and pulled her against him. His body was so lean. Too lean.

"I'm going to kiss you now," he said, putting his thin lips over hers.

Jade pushed him away, but he had too tight of a grasp on her arms. She was trapped between wimpy guy and the car—and he was far too strong to be pegged as wimpy. She pushed at his chest, the smell of his breath making her gag. Against his lips she eked, "Stop!"

He came up for air, and Jade gasped a deep breath. She turned to flee, but before she could get away, he pulled her to him again. His eyes darkened and his hands clenched her biceps so hard it brought tears to her eyes.

"You know you want it, you tease."

"No!" she finally yelled just before he slammed her back against his car and kissed her again.

She closed her eyes against the sight of him, tears streaming down her cheeks. She flailed, trying to get away, and suddenly his arms released her. Her lips were no longer pressed against his. She snapped open her eyes.

"The lady said no." Rex held Tim up by his collar, several inches off the ground. His teeth clenched, his bulbous muscles straining against Tim's weight.

"Okay, okay. She wanted it. She was asking for it," Tim said.

Rex lifted him higher with one arm and slammed him against his truck.

Jade was too stunned to move. What was he doing there? Why was he helping her again? He was going to kill that guy. Rex cocked his right arm and her brain kicked awake.

"No, Rex! He's not worth it," she screamed in a shrill voice through her tears.

Rex looked between Jade and the guy, then with one snap of his wrist, pulled the guy to his face. Like an angry dog baring its teeth, he seethed, "If I ever catch you treating a lady like that again, I will rip you to shreds." He tossed the guy to the ground and grabbed Jade roughly by the arm.

"Get in the truck."

She took one look at Tim writhing on the ground and scrambled into the truck.

Rex started the car, and without a word, drove down the road and then turned into a CVS parking lot, stopping beneath a streetlight. When he turned to face her, anger hovered behind the blatant concern in his eyes.

Jade's body trembled and shook, and she couldn't stop the flow of tears that wet her cheeks. She flushed with embarrassment. What would have happened if Rex hadn't been there?

Rex gently took her face in his hands. They were so big, so

strong, lethal when wrapped around that man's collar, and now his touch was tender and soft.

"You okay?" he asked.

She sniffled, nodded.

"Did he hurt you?" His eyes ran down her arms.

Jade instinctively rubbed where Tim had grabbed her arm, and it hurt to the touch. Rex ran his fingers lightly down her arms. His body visibly tensed with the intimate touch.

"Why did you do that?" she asked. "Why did you grab him like that?"

Rex furrowed his brow. "He was hurting you."

"But I could have handled it." She knew she couldn't have, but the idea of being a damsel in distress again—twice in two days—was too much. She wasn't weak, and she didn't need saving—even if Rex Braden made the perfect, handsome knight in shining armor.

"You couldn't and you didn't," he said.

He smelled like warmth and alcohol. His eyes narrowed, and she felt a tug down low. Suddenly, she was leaning forward. Oh God, she was going to kiss him. No, she couldn't do that. He'd all but thrown her in her car earlier in the day and sent her away. She had to get away before she did something stupid. She flung open the truck door.

"I don't need saving!" She stumbled from the truck and stood in the dark, clutching her purse. She swiped at her tears as sobs rose from her chest. How the heck could she forget him if he kept showing up and saving her? *What the hell am I doing?*

She heard his door slam, and he stalked toward her, slow and determined. His legs were slightly bowed, his arms arced out from his sides from the sheer volume of his biceps. Jade pressed her lips closed tight.

"I'm not leaving you here," he said in a deep, sexy voice. He might as well have said, *I want to take your clothes off and lick you all over.*

He took another step closer, and she watched the muscles in his chest, straining against his shirt, rising and falling with each breath.

"Please get in the truck, Jade," he said.

I don't trust myself. She shook her head.

Rex let out a loud breath and ran his hand through his thick hair. Jade ached to do the same, to slip her fingers beneath his hair and ease the tension at the base of his skull, to tame the inflamed muscles on his neck.

"Jade, Bradens don't leave women in dangerous situations. Get in." His tone was firm, his eyes pleading.

She shook her head again.

"I'm not going to ask again."

There was the anger. Jade crossed her arms. If she set foot in that truck, she would not be able to keep herself from reaching over and doing God knows what that she'd regret in the morning when she was sober. Her father's words rang too clearly to ignore: *You know better than to do anything to embarrass this family.*

"I can call Riley to come get me," she said.

"I'm right here. She's twenty minutes away and probably asleep by now."

"So what? She'd come." She sounded like a petulant child when what she really wanted to say was, *Don't call Riley. I want to go with you.* Her father's warning held her back.

He stepped even closer. His exhalations became her inhalations as he lowered his face so close to hers she could see the pupils of his eyes deepening. Jade's heartbeat thundered in her ears, blocking out the noise of the traffic. Her cheeks became warm, and she closed her eyes, thinking he might kiss her. Suddenly she was draped over his shoulder, his muscles digging into her stomach.

"What are you doing?" She pounded his back, her small fists barely making a dent as he opened the truck door with one hand and tossed her onto the seat with a firm command.

"Don't move."

Chapter Eight

JADE FLUNG HER body toward the door, trying to escape. Rex was too big, too strong—an immovable wall. He grabbed both of her wrists in one hand and held them over her head. In an effort to push him away with her feet, she fell back on the bench of the truck, taking him with her. Her hands were still held captive in his palm, his other hand pressed into the bench beside her head. Her body lay beneath him, and boy, did he feel good. His hard shaft against her leg sent shocks through her core.

Face-to-face, breath-to-breath, they didn't say a word.

Kiss me. Just fucking kiss me already. She could barely breathe under the weight of him, but she didn't care. Her body ached for him, and she had no control of her hips as they pressed into his groin or of her chest as she arched toward him. She had to know how his lips felt on hers even if for only one kiss. Her heart might burst from her chest if he didn't kiss her soon.

"I told you not to move," he finally said. His words were forced, harsh.

Jade couldn't answer. All she could do was remember to breathe in and breathe out as he released her wrists, swung her legs into the truck, and flung the truck door closed. She lay there in the awkward position, her arms high above her head, her legs on the floor, the vee between her legs pulsing, wanting, and then his door was open and he was settling into the driver's seat. Jade pulled herself to an upright position as he started the car. Her pulse still raced, her body still ached, and he wouldn't even look at her.

When they turned off the highway into Weston, her urges and her anger simmered to a boil.

"You had no right to kidnap me. I was just fine. Maybe I wanted to be with that guy. Maybe it felt good that he wanted to be with me. You don't know what I was—"

Rex looked at her from the corner of his eye. He drove down the three-mile stretch of rural road that led her to her father's property. Trees lined the pavement and arched over the road like an umbrella, creating a long, dark tunnel.

"Look at you. What kind of a man throws a woman into a truck like a hostage? What kind of a man doesn't talk to her?" Jade didn't feel the truck slowing beneath her as she flung accusation after accusation at the man who had just saved her from a guy who wanted nothing more than to screw her. "Look at you, sitting there all smug and proud of yourself for rescuing me. What the hell makes you think I wanted to be rescued?"

REX COULDN'T SPEAK. He didn't trust himself to say one single word to her, not when she was all riled up, with her breasts heaving up and down, calling out to him. When she was beneath him, it took all of his willpower not to answer the plea of her pressing hips. She smelled so sweet, and damn it if he didn't have to stifle a groan when she pressed her breasts into his chest.

Every accusation she thrust about his manhood spurred him on. Desire had been mounting all night as he'd watched her press her body against that guy on the dance floor the guy's hand sliding down to her ass. If she said one more word about him being a man, he was afraid he wouldn't be able to restrain himself. A man could take only so much before he gave in to the urges that adrenaline and testosterone pumped through him.

"What kind of a man hauls a woman over his shoulder like a sack of feed? I swear, Rex Braden, no wonder my father hates your family."

Rex swerved to the side of the road and slammed the truck into Park. Jade flew across the seat, falling into his arms. He could taste the sweet alcohol on her breath. Every nerve caught fire with the weight of her hips against him. He tried to deaden his simmering rage, and as he pulled her closer and looked into those seductive sea-blue eyes, he recognized that simmering heat for what it was and lowered his mouth to hers. Her body went rigid, then relaxed beneath his touch as he deepened the kiss. Every lick of her tongue gave rise beneath the zipper of his jeans. Holy shit, she tasted good. He explored her mouth with his tongue, learning every curve, the arch of her palette, then drew away with her lower lip between his teeth. She licked the tender spot, and he had to have her again, had to savor her. His mouth was on hers and he never wanted to come up for air. He placed his hand beneath her silky hair and pulled her mouth tighter against him. She moaned as he dropped his hand to her waist. She was so small in his grasp, so feminine and sweet. He'd waited to feel her lips on his for nearly fifteen years, and they were everything he'd dreamed and more.

She wrapped her arms around his neck and pulled her legs beneath her, leaning forward on her knees as she kissed him deeper.

He parted from her long enough to look down at her dress hiked up to the crest of her thighs, her knees opened to him, and her eyes—those deep valleys of blue—tantalized his already raging desire.

"Jesus, you're delicious. I've wanted to taste you for years."

"Taste me," she said, and reached for his mouth again. She took his hand and drew it to her thigh.

Rex's chest swelled with need as he ran his hand beneath the edge of her dress and felt her damp heat through the thin veil of her panties. She moved in closer, urging him on, her hips pushing against his fingers until they were damp, too. Something in the back of Rex's mind told him to stop. His father would never forgive him if he found out that Rex had dishonored him this way. But as he slipped a finger under the edge of her panties and felt those wet, sensitive folds of skin, he knew he had entered territory from which he could not retreat.

"Rex," she said breathlessly, trailing kisses down his neck to the ridge of his shoulder, where she sucked until he thought he might come.

He slipped his fingers inside her, and she gasped a breath before taking his mouth against hers in a deep, greedy kiss. He teased her with his thumb as his fingers stroked her sweet, velvety insides. He buried the lingering thoughts of his father and wrapped his arm around Jade's waist. In one swift move, she was beneath him, his fingers still teasing, probing, furtively seeking the spot that would send her over the edge. She fumbled with his shirt, and he tugged it over his head, tossed it on the floor.

She leaned up and took his nipple in her mouth. He groaned as she sucked and teased him with her tongue. He couldn't breathe; he had to have more of her. He pushed her down with his free hand and pulled her dress up to her neck. God, she was beautiful, lying there in her black panties and lacy bra. She grasped the back of his head and pulled him to her breast. He licked her through the fabric until she arched into him with a needy moan, then unhooked the front clasp and exposed two beautifully perfect mounds. She trembled beneath the slow drag of his tongue around her taut nipple.

Her skin shimmered against the darkness as he dragged his tongue down the center of her belly, slowing to take little suckles of her skin. He felt her tighten around his fingers, and he probed faster, harder, until she grabbed his wrist and bucked against his hand, her orgasm pulsing around him, drawing out sexy little moans as she climbed higher and higher. She called out his name as she reached her peak. Tiny aftershocks clenched around his fingers, still buried within her, until she lay spent, panting, one arm across her forehead, the other still grasping his wrist.

"God, you're beautiful," Rex said, as he drew his fingers from between her legs and sucked them slowly between his lips.

Chapter Nine

I'M DYING. I just know it. Jade lay on her back beneath Rex, unable to think past the orgasm she'd just had with nothing more than his fingers. *Jesus, what could he do with the monster trapped in his jeans?* She could barely breathe. Her legs were numb, and her skin was so sensitive she thought she might have another orgasm with the lightest of touches.

Rex drew his fingers from his lips with a hungry look in his eyes, and Jade's body responded with a gentle tug from her center. *So cowboy is a dirty boy.* A thrum of excitement ran through her as he rolled his eyes down her body, her knees splayed wide, her panties still on.

"Jade," he said in an unsteady voice.

His voice alone had her craving more of him.

"We can't do this," he said as he moved away.

Jade stopped breathing. If she wasn't dying before, she surely was now. What the hell was he talking about?

"Rex?"

He leaned over her and snagged his shirt from the floor, slipped it over his head.

Jade sat up and touched his arm. "What's going on? Did I

misunderstand something here?" *When you had your fingers inside me? Or maybe when you were sucking the taste of me off of them?*

"It was a mistake," he said, staring straight ahead at the darkened street.

"A mistake?" she snapped. "This? This was a mistake? I was a mistake? Is that what you really mean?" She tugged her dress down. "Look at me," she said, barely keeping the neediness and anger from her voice.

Rex dropped his eyes.

"Rex Braden, what is wrong with you? Are you trying to make me feel like a cheap whore? Was that your plan all along? Take me so no one else would, then toss me aside like I was a conquest?"

Rex met her angry eyes with a sorrowful gaze. "Jade, if you were a conquest, then I didn't do a very good job of conquering you, did I?"

She felt the sadness in his voice like a slap to her angry face. "Why, then? Is it me? You don't like who I am?" She looked out the window, stifling tears. "That makes no sense," she said with a feigned laugh. "If that were the case, you wouldn't have even helped me in the first place."

He pulled her to him, brushing her hair from her cheek. "It's not you. It's our families. This could never work. No matter how much we might want it to, it's not like the Hatfields and McCoys of Weston are going to throw their arms up in the air after a forty-year battle and be done with it. It's a fantasy. You're forbidden fruit."

Our families. You know better than to do anything to embarrass this family, right?

"That is ridiculous. We're adults, for God's sake. Why does it even matter what happened so long ago?" She pushed away from him and stewed. "Why can't we just be like any other couple? Make out? Date? Tell them and make them deal with it? Be a man, stand up, and stake your claim."

"We don't even know what *this* is," he said testily. "And if you question my manhood one more time, Jade Johnson, I swear to you, I'll..." He scrubbed his hand down his face and eased the tension from his tone. "Look, you've only been back a few weeks; my family is going through changes. This whole thing might be nothing more than a reaction to circumstance."

She spun in his direction and narrowed her eyes. "A reaction to circumstance? Is that what this was?"

He shrugged.

"Is that all you've got? A shrug? Really, Rex? You just told me that you've wanted me for years. I don't call that a reaction to circumstance."

His silence was like a spear through her heart. She wasn't going to sit there and try to convince him that whatever it was between them was worth exploring. She liked him—a lot—and every time she looked at him, she craved his touch. Having tasted him, and having felt him inside of her, she'd crave even more of him now. But she'd misjudged him. If she wasn't worth standing up for, even in the discovery stage of whatever this was, then fuck him.

She swung open the door, grabbed her purse, and jumped from the truck. "Thanks for the ride," she said right before she slammed the truck door and stomped off toward the driveway.

REX PUNCHED THE steering wheel with a grunt. *Damn it. Damn it. Damn it.* This was so fucked up. He finally felt something for a woman—really felt something—and he'd fucked it up. When he'd seen her with that guy, it had triggered a massive protective urge that until then he'd thought belonged only to his family. When he kissed her, when that sweet tongue was stealing his brain cells lick by delicious lick, everything became fragmented. He wanted to touch her, taste her, and *consume* her, protect her, love her, and heal her in equal measure. And as he watched her stomp down to the barn, with only the moonlight leading her way, all those feelings radiated within him like little pinpricks. The divine feeling of being with her coalesced with the guilt of having been with her and left him watching the one person he wanted spiraling away out of reach.

Chapter Ten

STUPID DIDN'T EVEN come close to describing how Jade felt when she woke up the next morning. She'd gone into the barn the night before, flicked on the light, and sat outside Flame's stall. Her body was still reeling from the feel of Rex's rough, strong hands touching her, inside of her, exciting her. She'd shivered with the memory, then gave in to the tears that pulled at her heart. Before she'd gone to bed, she showered, trying to scrub the thoughts of him away, washing herself under the cold water until her skin went numb.

Now, hours after he'd touched her and she'd tried to scrub his touch away, she could still feel the way her body hummed to life with the first thrust of his tongue in her mouth. When his fingers entered her, he'd brought her to new heights. No man had aroused her to orgasm with just his hands before. That had to mean something.

She looked in the mirror as she dried her hair. "Right?" she asked her reflection. At almost thirty-two years old, she knew how these things worked. The chances of her and Rex ever getting together again were slim to none, and maybe that was for the best. She really didn't want to hurt her father. She knew the damage it would cause if he ever found out. She'd chalk last night up to a mistake. *The heat of the moment.* Now, if she could only convince her heart to do the same.

She iced and massaged Flame's leg and was pleased to see that he was still walking normally. She was fairly certain that he was perfectly fine and what he'd experienced was a quick nag of pain rather than a sustained injury, but she'd still take it slow with him for one more day. She knew he was climbing out of his skin to be set free. *Like me.*

Inside the house, she was reviewing her schedule for the remainder of the week when her mother appeared in the kitchen.

"I thought you were sewing Daddy's new curtains for his office today." Jade's mother was the best seamstress around, and her father was continually asking for new curtains, blankets, even shirts, *to keep her creative juices flowing.*

"I am. I just wanted to visit with my daughter."

Her mother sat beside her on the couch in her capri pants and flowery blouse. "Jade," she said in a voice that made Jade stop what she was doing and look into her mother's brown eyes. "What's your plan?"

"My plan, Mom?"

Her mother put her hand on her leg. "Honey, you know I love you, but you've been here nearly eight months. I just want to know what you're thinking."

Jade smiled. "Ah, I get it. You want me to get out. You and Daddy are used to having the house to yourselves, and now I'm in the way?" She wasn't hurt by the thought; she was just a little surprised by it.

"No, no. It's not that. I mean, I guess it is a little. Children are supposed to grow up and define their own lives. Granted, you had a bad experience with Kane, but you can't let that hold you back from starting anew." She folded her hands in her lap and looked at Jade expectantly.

"I am. I have a number of clients, and I'm trying to figure out where I want to be with all of this. I mean, do I want to stay here in Colorado, or move somewhere else altogether?" *Which at the moment seems like a really good idea. Maybe then I could completely forget Rex and his captivating moods.*

Her mother nodded, but Jade could tell she had something else to add.

"Mom, what is it? Did I do something? Do you want me to pay rent? What's really bothering you?"

Jane pursed her lips and furrowed her brow, glancing at Jade and then back to her lap.

"Mom, whatever it is, just spit it out, please." Her chest tightened just watching the anguish on her mother's face.

"Let's take a walk." Jane nodded toward Earl's office.

"Sure." Jade followed her mother out the door, noticing determination in her gait and a quickness in her pace. The knot that had tightened in her chest twisted and pulled. She could remember the handful of times her mother had taken her out of the house for a discussion, and none of them were to relay positive news.

Once they'd cleared the yard and were deep into the property by the cattle field, her mother's shoulders relaxed, and she slowed her pace.

"Mom, what's wrong? You're starting to scare me a little."

"Honey, please don't let your father know I said anything. Normally, I wouldn't talk about family business, but you're an adult, and with what's going on, I think you need to be aware—"

Jade touched her mother's arm to get her attention. When her mother took a breath, Jade said, "Mom, you're rambling. I won't tell Daddy. Is he sick? Are you sick?"

"No, it's nothing like that." Her mother looked at her then, giving a little shake of her head and letting out a sorrowful sigh. "We might have to sell the ranch." She choked on the last word, holding back tears. Her hand covered her chest.

"Sell it? Why? I thought the business was doing well." Sell their home? The ranch was the only home she'd ever known. She and her brother had grown up there, and her father had owned the property for forty years. *The feud.* She wondered if not selling the property that they owned with the Bradens had had a severe impact on their finances. The Bradens had plenty of money, but she wasn't so sure that that was true of her family.

"Your father has worked very hard to take care of all of us. He's a good man and he runs an honest business. It would kill him to know that I told you about this before he did."

"Okay, I won't say anything. You have my word." *Sell the ranch?*

"He thought the business would bounce back, and it hasn't happened. The bank has been very gracious and for three years has fronted us the money to continue, but now..." Her eyes ran over the fields, the cattle, the house.

"Mom, if the property that Dad bought with the Bradens was sold and he received half of the profit, would that enable him to keep the ranch?" She searched her mother's eyes as she contemplated the question.

"With what land is going for now, there's a good chance it might, but your father is a prideful man. That property is dead to him."

But not to me.

"WHAT THE HELL are you doing?" Rex hollered at Treat, who was loading the truck with fencing materials.

"Whatever animal got the fence in the winter has been back. There's a twenty-foot section torn out in the lower pasture." Treat threw another roll of wire into the truck. "Are you all right? You seem on edge."

"Fine." Rex was far from fine. He'd stewed all night over the way things had ended with Jade, and what made it even more difficult was that every thought he had carried with it her scent, her taste, the image of her writhing with pleasure as she moaned beneath his touch. He'd spent the night angry and aroused, and it was a deadly combination. Anger surged through his limbs, and no matter how he tried to quell the mounting confusion, it kept ending the same way—as one bursting ball of rage.

"Wanna come give me a hand?" Treat asked.

Treat didn't shy away from the grueling physical labor, and he was able to use his honed negotiating skills to save them thousands over the course of just a few months. The man was a stealth businessman. Stealth or not, he was in Rex's line of fire.

"Leave it. I'll take care of it later," Rex snapped.

"No, I've got it."

Rex wanted a fight. He was aching to release his pent-up frustrations. "I said, leave it," Rex challenged.

Treat set the last of the wire in the truck and leaned against the tailgate. "What crawled up your ass and died?"

Rex took a step forward and fisted his hands. He ground his teeth so hard he was sure they'd crack, but he didn't care.

"Take a breather, Rex."

Treat took a step toward the front of the truck, and Rex strong-armed him, stopping him in his tracks.

"What the hell? We're too old for this shit, Rex. You have an issue, deal with it." Treat pushed past him and climbed into the truck.

Rex grabbed him by the collar and pulled him out.

"What the fuck?" Treat challenged him, chest to chest. "You really want to do this over a fence? Fine." He threw down his gloves and fisted his own enormous hands. "Go ahead. Take a swing. I haven't had a good brawl in twenty years."

Seeing his brother ready to fight just to appease him pissed him off even more. He slammed the truck door shut and spat, "Fuck! Fuck, fuck, fuck."

"That's more like it," Treat said with a pat on Rex's back. "Spit it out, so it doesn't coil up and fill you with venom."

Treat leaned against the truck while Rex paced, sweating in the afternoon heat.

"Wanna talk about it?" Treat asked.

Rex stopped pacing and stared at his brother. "You can't possibly understand! You have the woman you want, and she obviously adores you. You never have obstacles that stand in your way that are bigger than you. You're the *golden* child."

Treat laughed. "Is that what you think? The golden child? I sure as hell wish I felt that way. It would be a hell of a lot better than going through all the shit Max and I went through for seven months. There are no golden children, Rex. It just looks like it when you're so deep in your own shit that you can't see the grass."

"Come on, Treat. You've always done what you wanted when you wanted. Women lined up to be with you."

"They lined up to be with all of us, and the guys lined up for Savannah. We're good-looking, successful people. You know you've never hurt for the company of a woman. They swoon around your muscles like you're Adonis himself."

"Right," Rex sneered. He leaned his hand on the truck and looked at Treat. "I've put my whole life into this ranch, for this family. Everything I've ever done is for this family." He ran his hand through his hair and paced again. "Do you know why I don't sleep with the women in our town?" Before Treat could answer, he said, "Because I don't want to embarrass Dad. Because I don't want him to feel like he can't hold his head up high because his son is a douche bag who sleeps with women and never looks back; that's why."

"Rex—" Treat shook his head.

"It's true, bro. I've got no ties to the women I sleep with. Ever."

"And?" Treat asked.

Rex leveled him with a harsh stare.

"None of us do—or in my case, did—Rex. Look at Hugh.

He's got a different woman on his arm every night, and he can't even remember their names. Dane's got women all over the world, and Josh, hell, we don't even know how many women he sleeps with—it could be one or it could be one hundred. He's been snapped in all the rags with some of the hottest actresses and models around. I doubt long-term commitment has ever entered his mind, considering he's never brought any of them home."

"Yeah? Well, even if I want ties, I can't have them."

Treat shook his head. "Jade. You're talking about Jade?"

Rex clenched his jaw. He wanted to tell Treat what had gone on the night before, but he was ashamed at how far he let it go before pulling the plug—and he was pissed that he'd been the one to stop them from going any further. They'd been so intimate, and he wanted so much more, but not like that. Not in a truck. Jade wasn't some girl from another town. She wasn't *some girl* at all. He wouldn't have sex with her and then walk away, and he couldn't be with her without hurting his father. The whole situation sucked.

"I should have put two and two together," Treat said with a supportive smile. "You're a good man, and you're loyal. So stop giving me that *I'm not worthy* shit and stop dancing around the crux of your issue. Either tell me what the hell is going on with her—or what you want to go on—or let me get back to work."

Rex didn't know what he wanted. He only knew what he needed, and what he needed came in a mouthy little package and lived a few miles down the road.

Chapter Eleven

"IT'S BEEN TWO days and it feels like a year." Jade took a bite out of her pepperoni pizza. She brushed the crumbs from her jean shorts and sighed. "No, you know what it feels like, Ri? It feels like when we were in high school and we had crushes on the Daniels twins, remember? Remember how we'd fantasize about phone calls that would never come? It's exactly the same thing."

Jade and Riley sat outside beneath an umbrella in the middle of Weston Town Park, sharing four slices of pizza. It was a beautiful Thursday afternoon, and the park was Riley's attempt at pulling Jade from what Riley had coined as her friend's *man depression*. Jade had too many worries lately. Between Rex and her father's decision about the ranch, she felt a bit weighed down. She pushed away the thoughts about her family's ranch and turned her thoughts to Riley instead.

Riley looked silly with her hair pulled up into two ponytails, which Jade knew she'd done just to make her laugh—and it had worked. Now Riley shook her finger at her. "How can you even compare the two? First of all, I don't remember either of the twins ever saying you were *delicious* or that they'd waited years to *taste* you."

Jade groaned. "I need to stop telling you things."

"In your dreams. You're about as good at keeping a secret as a push-up bra. And, by the way, next time we go out to get you laid, please tell me you don't want the guy *before* I leave. I feel horrible for leaving."

"I told you to go. You didn't do anything wrong. It's just, when he touched me, I..." She shuddered and scrunched her face. "He reminded me of an overgrown boy, not a man, and then he'd turned into a whole different person altogether—mean and aggressive, and not in a good way."

"Oh, and we do prefer men, don't we?" Riley finished her pizza and jumped off the chair, smoothing down her skirt.

"Why don't you ever wear the clothes you design?" Jade asked.

"Around here? Right." Riley laughed. "Where are you working this afternoon?"

"I've got a client across town, then a massage for a gelding over off of State Street," Jade answered. "More important, what should I do about my cowboy?"

"Your orally fixated cowboy?" Riley said with a wink.

"Shh," Jade said as an elderly couple walked past. "I never said he was orally fixated."

"No, but given the..." She sucked her two fingers, causing Jade to cringe. "I'd say there's a good chance you've got some good loving waiting for you."

"You're such a pig." She shoved Riley as they headed toward their cars. "I need to know what to do. It's not like I can call him, or stop by."

"Not unless you want a dead man on your hands. Your father would whip out a shotgun to save his precious little girl from a wicked Braden boy."

"Thanks."

Riley put her arm around Jade. "What are friends for? Okay, so let's see, you're volunteering at the horse show. That's one place you'll see him."

"True, but we'll both be busy."

Riley stopped walking. "Tell me what you want to happen. I mean, you knew what was going to go down when you let yourself start fantasizing about his ginormous trouser snake. You knew about your dad's hatred for them."

Jade shrugged. "I thought...I don't know. I guess I never thought we'd even get together, so I never really took it that far."

They walked down the footpath toward the feed store.

"Well, Ms. Vet, time to stir up some medicine for your achy-breaky heart or convince the big lug to run off and marry you and live happily ever after in some other town."

"You are absolutely no help at all," Jade snapped. *What was I thinking? There is no solution to this mess.*

"Oh, I think I am. Whose idea was it to come to the park?"

"Yours?" Jade arched a brow.

Riley put her finger on Jade's cheek and drew it toward the feed store. Jade's jaw dropped open as Rex climbed from his truck. He stretched his arms above his head as soon as his boots hit the pavement. She gasped a breath and ducked behind Riley.

"Riley! How did you know he'd be here?"

"I've listened to you whine like a starving baby for two days straight. It was either this or buy you a pacifier." She rolled her eyes. "Live here long enough and you know what time your neighbors go to the bathroom. He picks up something for Hope here every Thursday. Like clockwork." Riley pulled Jade out from behind her.

"Hope?"

"Yeah, geez, where did you grow up? The horse his father bought for his mother when she first got sick. I swear they treat that horse like it's really their mother."

"That's so sad." The ache in Jade's heart wasn't new. She'd known about Rex's mother dying when he was just a boy, but now, with her new feelings for him, the ache was deeper.

"I know. Now focus. Look at that fine specimen of a man." She leaned on Jade's shoulder and spoke into her ear. "Strong, wide back, ass made of stone, thick thighs, good for, well, you know."

Jade swallowed hard. She knew just how thick his thighs were and how thick the thing between his thighs was, too. She shook her head to clear away the heated memory. "So you brought me here to...ogle him?"

"Ogling is nice, isn't it? But no. I figured you could go down there and actually talk to him."

Jade shook her head and tried to back up, but Riley was standing behind her like a blockade. "No, not a good idea. The whole town knows about the feud, and it'll get back to my father somehow. Besides, I don't know if he'll even talk to me in public."

"That's not true. You said he talked to you at the volunteer meeting."

"Like I said, I've got to stop telling you things." Butterflies swirled in her stomach as she watched Rex walk into the feed store.

"Go talk to him. I have to go back to work anyway." Riley bent down and kissed Jade's cheek. As she hurried away, she held her pinky and thumb out and wiggled them by her face. "Call me!"

I could retreat, pretend I was never here. I don't have to do what Riley tells me to do, although she's always been right in the past. She told me to leave Kane before I ever opened my practice. Jade was contemplating leaving when the feed store door swung open and Rex walked out carrying a feed bag over his shoulder and a brown bag in his arms. He held the door open for a woman and her daughter, and when he glanced up the hill, Jade turned her back, hoping he hadn't seen her.

When she turned back around, Rex was heading up the hill toward her. She clutched her stomach as he closed the gap between them, the bag from the store in his arms. *Who gave the butterflies speed?*

"Jade." His face was a blank slate, his eyes just as silent.

"Hi," she said, feeling her cheeks flush and privately wincing from the heat.

With his silence, Jade felt like a bubble had formed around them and nothing else existed. She wanted to reach out and touch him, anywhere, everywhere, just to know he was real. She wondered if he wanted the same thing.

The silence was deafening. Maybe she misread him. *Oh God, how embarrassing.* She had to remember that he'd said being together was a mistake, and unless she wanted to drive a wedge the size of Nebraska between her and Rex, she'd better go along with it. Being able to talk to him was better than being forced to ignore each other forever. She reminded herself that it was only one night. One make-out session, one blissful orgasm. *Oh God, stop thinking about that. Friends. I can do this. Focus on being friends. Right. Friends who aren't allowed to really be friends at all.*

JADE STOOD ON the hill in her sexy boots with the sun illuminating her from behind like an angel. Rex took it as a sign. He'd been existing on cold showers and coffee for two days, wrestling with how to handle the situation with Jade. Maybe some things were meant to be, like his mother and father and Treat and Max. Maybe he was supposed to be with Jade, even if only secretly...for now.

She wasn't smiling when he approached. A lump formed in his throat over the way he'd ended things so abruptly when they were together. God, she looked cute in her tight scoop-neck T-shirt with THOROUGHBRED across her chest. His body remembered the feel of her beneath him. He shifted the bag to cover the evidence.

He wanted to talk to her about what happened between them, clear the air, but after saying her name, he felt a rush of adrenaline, an overwhelming urge to take her in his arms and apologize, throw caution to the wind and stand up for whatever might be. He could take the heat. He would do just about anything for her.

"You were right," Jade said. "What happened was a mistake, and it should never happen again."

The air expelled from his lungs, like he'd been punched in the gut. *A mistake?* A mistake. Isn't that what he'd told her, after all? Just being this close to her made his heart beat a little harder. He didn't need to sleep with her. He just wanted to be with her, to get to know her better. *A mistake?* He couldn't be with her anyway. It was a pipe dream, a fantasy. He had all the intimate time he'd ever get with the woman he'd pined for year after year, and if that was all he was going to get, then damn it, it was better than nothing, even if it wasn't near enough.

"I'm glad you understand." The lie tasted like acid, like it was burning a hole through him even as it came off his tongue.

"I do." She nodded. "Our fathers…they'd never be okay with"—she ran her finger in a line between them—"this."

He wanted to take her hand and pull her to him, just to feel her heart beat against his.

"Right." He looked away to hide the sadness that he knew was written all over his face. He'd never been able to hide his feelings well, and the emotions he was riding were coming in powerful, evident gusts.

"What'd you get at the feed store?" she asked.

He looked down at the bag. He'd forgotten he even had it in his arms. "Molasses cookies." His voice sounded like all the energy had been sucked from it, and he noticed Jade's eyes shoot up at his. He cleared his throat, then said, "I come by and get sweet feed and molasses cookies for my mom's horse."

She nodded, still holding his gaze. "Horses love both those things."

How could she be so calm and cool about this while his heart was being torn to shreds right in his chest?

"Is it an older horse?"

"Huh?"

"Your mom's horse. Is it an older horse?"

"Oh yeah. Hope's getting up there, slowing down a bit." He watched the way her eyes danced when they talked about the horse, and it almost made him wish he were a horse, too.

"Hope, that's a nice name. Is she eating enough? Have you noticed weight loss? Is she turning her head toward her flank a lot? Getting regular exercise?"

"I almost forgot you were a vet," he said in response to her pointed questions. "She slowed down a little this past year, but she's a strong, healthy horse. Hope's the horse I was riding that morning at the ravine." *The ravine.* That's when it all started. He smiled at the memory of her picking up that heavy rock and tossing it into the water. It seemed like they'd been on one hundred dates since then, though they hadn't been on any. "My father's entering her in the open event at the show."

"That can be really stressful for a horse who isn't doing well," Jade said.

"I know. He knows that, but he said our mom would have wanted it. He doesn't care if she wins or loses. He just..." How could he tell her that his father still talked to his dead mother? How could he not? "He said Mom would have wanted her to compete again." He shrugged.

She smiled. "I guess he would know. I mean, he knew your mom best, after all."

"True." The small talk was killing him.

"Still, have you tried any massage? It can alleviate depression and also help with energy."

"Depression?" She reminded him of his mother, the way she spoke of animals like humans. His pulse spiked, and he pushed away the desire to explore her thoughts further and see if she had more ideas that were similar to his mother's. "It's a horse, not a person."

She sighed. "Funny, I didn't take you as the kind of person who defined a line between which species had feelings and which ones didn't." She took a step backward.

"I didn't mean that." *Goddamn it. Now I've screwed up again.*

"I guess taking care of feelings isn't your strong point." The muscles in her thighs tensed, and she took another step backward. "I gotta go. Good luck with Hope."

Chapter Twelve

JADE LEFT A message on Riley's voicemail just as she pulled up to her client's barn. "It's me. I just wanted you to know that you have officially been knocked out of Queen Gossip of Weston status. Remember what Jennifer Aniston said about Brad Pitt missing a sensitivity chip? Well, guess what? Now hot cowboy can keep Brad company in that department. Gotta run. I still love ya, but you owe me."

Jade was still chewing on Rex's disregard for Hope's emotions when she stepped from her car. Before walking into the Schafers' barn, she took a minute to calm herself down. She couldn't very well help heal a horse's emotional or mental imbalance if she was tied in knots. She leaned against the side of the truck, took a few slow, deep breaths and blew them out slowly. She had to put Rex Braden out of her mind. Completely. That was the only way to move forward. Sex is sex. *Anyone can make you feel good. Not that good.*

"Jade?" Patti Schafer waved as she came down from the house.

"Hi."

"I heard that you're volunteering at the show. That should

be fun this year." Patti was Jade's height and round as a basketball. Her jeans rode up high above her waist, and the short-sleeve shirt she wore pulled across her ample bosom. Each button looked as though it might pop with her next deep breath.

"Yeah, I'm looking forward to it." *If you call not being able to breathe for six hours while I avoid Rex fun.*

"My niece Hannah is showing Hal Braden's horse in the open class. She's so excited. You know how little girls are about getting all dolled up."

Just the mention of a Braden sent her heart aflutter. This was not good. She needed to get her mind off of Rex Braden, not on him. *Or under him.*

"How's Berle doing?" A quick diversion of subjects would help. Patti had named her horse after Milton Berle, and Jade knew better than to question a pet's name. It was like questioning a child's name. Something she just didn't do.

"He's doing well. He hasn't had any more issues since you cleared up the colic, and I think the massages are helping. He's eating well, but still just a little…off." Patti had gone to school with Jade's mother, and she was one of the most caring animal owners Jade knew. As soon as Jade had moved back to Colorado, Patti had called and asked her to take over Berle's care. She had been using a veterinary practice outside of Weston that her family had used for generations, but when the vet she trusted retired, she hadn't felt like the new vet connected with her horses. Jade had wondered why she didn't ask Dr. Baker, the town veterinarian, to care for her horses, and her answer was just what she'd expected; he didn't do any hands-on work with the horses. He'd been practicing veterinary medicine for forty years and he believed massage was "hooey," though Dr. Baker and Jade got along just fine. She respected his practice, and he respected her efforts as well. Even if he didn't believe in her holistic approach, he never disrespected her abilities.

"Well, let's see if we can't fix him right up."

The barn was quiet and cool. Berle stood in the center aisle, secured to the stall by his lead. He was a sweet-natured, handsome, chestnut quarter horse gelding with a flaxen mane and tail. He lifted his nose as Jade approached. She stroked the side of his strong jaw.

"Hey, Berle. How's my boy today?" When Jade was around horses, everything else fell away. All she thought about as she looked into Berle's trusting eyes was making him feel better. Luckily, Patti was completely in tune with her animals, and she'd noticed a change in Berle's behavior right away. They were able to diagnose and treat the early stages of colic before it became too difficult to manage, and now Jade was providing post-colic comfort. Jade believed that no pain—in human or animal—could occur without affecting their mental and emotional state in some way. She knew Berle's being "off" could be caused by something as simple as needing a Chi adjustment. Jade was used to hearing snide comments, such as the one Rex made, about animals and their emotions, but that didn't make those comments any easier to swallow. Luckily, Patti had not only been receptive, but excited about the idea of helping her horse to heal.

"I hear you're feeling a little off." She stroked his side gently. "We're going to help you feel better today." She put her hands on him, fingers stretched wide, and felt the rhythm of his breathing. She was most comfortable when she knew the natural rhythm of the horse she was working on, and by taking a few minutes to connect with them, she and the horse were more relaxed.

She used the fingers on each hand as she stroked and pressed along his meridian. Although she would concentrate on the area around his stifle, the complex joint in the horse's hind leg, she massaged along the entire stomach meridian to encourage the elements of stomach and earth to balance. She began with the junction of the two prominent veins that ran just below his eye, which were dilated and pressing through the surface of the skin, indicating Berle's relaxed state. From there, she moved up his jaw and down his neck, taking her time to stroke him gently, feeling for gritty or spongy muscles or changes in temperature beneath her fingers. She moved gently to the underside, behind his left front leg, then used the palm of her hand as she moved across the meridian line of his ribs and along the lower outside of his belly.

She took a deep inhalation as she moved toward his stifle joint. The smell of fresh hay filled her senses, centering her once again. She could find point thirty-six on the stomach meridian in her sleep. Some people called it the "probiotic point" due to its immediate soothing effect when a horse had digestive issues. As she faced Berle's head, she closed her eyes and slid her palm on his stifle, cupped it, and her thumb fell naturally into a groove in the bone just below the head of his tibia.

After giving a massage treatment, Jade's mind and body often remained in a place of peacefulness. Her body became just as relaxed as the animal's, and though her muscles might be tired, she barely felt the discomfort. Instead, she focused on the ease of her breathing and the soothing calm that warmed her.

As she climbed into her car and headed toward home, she allowed her mind to drift to Rex. Once again, she wondered what he might be like if he was soothed by touch—not hormone-driven, sexual touch, but quelling, tranquil touch.

She slowed down as she passed the Braden ranch, wondering if losing his mother at such a young age meant that he was touched, held, and comforted less. She knew enough about the Bradens to know their father loved them all and would do anything for them. Anyone in Weston knew that. But had they been adequately touched? Had their father rubbed their backs when they were ill or lain with them and brushed their hair away from their foreheads when they were sad?

The sun dipped from the sky, and in the late-afternoon haze, the ranch had a serene feel. The fields of grass blew in the breeze, and she couldn't help but slow almost to a crawl when Rex came into view, riding Hope. He was looking into the distance, his Stetson moving up and down against the gray-blue sky as they trotted along. Her heart whispered a longing, and when Hope turned toward the road, it took her a minute or two before she realized that she was staring. She drove away thinking about Rex's muscles beneath her hands as she massaged the harsh exterior away, revealing whatever vulnerabilities lay beneath.

The minute she pulled into her driveway, all thoughts of Rex fell away, replaced with the reminder of her family possibly losing their farm. She felt a dip in the pit of her stomach. She owed too much in school loans to help them financially, but maybe there was another way. If she could mend that fence between Hal Braden and her father...just maybe...

Chapter Thirteen

EARLY SUNDAY MORNING, after another cold shower and another fitful night's sleep, Rex mounted Hope for her predawn exercise. Even with his thick flannel shirt and his leather Stetson trapping in the heat on his pate, he still felt a chill as Hope walked out of the barn and into the yard. He let her lead the way today and assumed she'd head toward the back trail, but instead Hope rounded the barn toward the trail that headed east. His father's gruff voice caught him by surprise. He knew his father wasn't on the phone—he didn't carry a cell phone, and Rex couldn't remember the last time he'd been up that early.

He found his father, also clad in a flannel shirt, hat, and jeans, sitting on the dewy grass by a water barrel behind the barn. His head was bowed, his arms stretched over his knees, and his left hand was grasping his right fist, releasing, then grabbing it again. Rex drew his brows together.

"Dad?"

Hal turned his head, and Rex dismounted at the sight of strain on his father's face. Deep lines crossed his leathery skin.

"Dad, what is it? Is it your heart?"

While Savannah and some of his other siblings had written off his father's supposed conversations with his mother, Rex lived night and day at his father's ranch, and he wasn't so sure. Having heard his father talking to seemingly no one too many times to count, some of those times ending with him teary eyed, Rex wasn't as quick to disbelieve. The look on his father's face had Rex reliving the painful few days he'd spent in the hospital and the troubled look he'd had in the hours before.

"No, it isn't my heart," Hal snapped.

Rex looked around the empty acreage. "Who are you talking to?"

"Who do you think I'm talking to?"

"Mom." He didn't mean to sound like he was simply relenting to a stupid question, but he wasn't quite sure what to make of the situation.

"Of course it's Adriana. Who else would it be? She's giving me fits, all pissed off about something." He pushed to his feet and grumbled, "Damn woman."

Rex smiled. Even when his father was complaining about her, the love in his eyes still blazed. It occurred to him then that he had much the same feelings about Jade. Her mouthiness drove him batty, but in a way that also drove a stake right through his heart.

"Want me to skip Hope's ride? Remember what happened last time you got all worked up." Rex had more respect for his father than any other man alive. He'd taught Rex to be a man, to stand up for his family, and the value of loyalty and honor, the principles Rex held in the highest regard. There was no denying, though, that his father had a softer side. He saw it every time he interacted with Savannah, every time one of his children had trouble and needed help. As he stood beside the man who meant the world to him, he wished he could confide in him about Jade. If she had been any other woman, from any other family, his father would have wrapped her in his arms and welcomed her without even knowing a thing about her. If one of his children fell in love, he loved right alongside them. He'd proven that with Max the first day she pulled into their driveway. His father had taken her under his wing and swept her into the family fold—and Treat hadn't even been home.

He contemplated telling him now. *Dad, I gotta talk to you about someone. It's Jade, Dad, Jade Johnson.* He imagined his father's likely response. *Son, you know better than to bring that no-good family's name onto our property.* On the heels of Jade's desire to just be friends, there was no point in getting him even more riled up.

"I'm fine, Rex. Hope needs you. Take the old girl out. I'm not staying out here anyway. I'm going back to bed." He turned to look into Hope's empty stall and shook his head. "That mother of yours is something else."

Rex watched his father saunter away. At times like these, he wanted to believe his father was still in contact with his mother. In fact, he felt a stab of jealousy at the idea.

THE WIDE TRAIL to the east of the ranch wound deep into the woods, parallel to the road. The woods provided a buffer from the pavement, but during the afternoon and evening, the bustle of trucks and horse trailers carried in the wind. In the predawn hours of Rex's Sunday ride, the air carried only the sounds of scurrying on the forest floor and the rustling of leaves in the gentle wind. He was glad for the silence, though the farther Hope drew him away from the ranch, the nearer they were to the Johnson ranch, which caused his heart to beat a little faster. Rex worked hard not to translate that racing pulse into a spurring of gait. He wanted to prolong his Sunday-morning ride, not shorten it. He controlled the adrenaline rush by gripping the leather reins a little tighter and clenching his jaw against the thoughts that were causing his stomach to tighten.

Hope plodded along. She was comfortable on all of the trails around the ranch. Hell, she'd been riding them for more than twenty years; she should be comfortable on them. But today it was Rex who was uncomfortable as they neared the breach of the trail where it feathered out into a wide-open field bordering the Johnson property. He pulled on the right rein to guide Hope toward the road. She remained steadfast in her pace and direction, heading straight for the Johnson driveway.

Rex tugged harder, gave her a tap with his booted heel, and still she worked against him. The harder he urged, the more she pulled her head in the other direction. *Stubborn old girl.* Given that Hope had never been a temperamental horse and that behavioral changes in horses often reflected distress, Rex paid extra attention to her. He leaned forward and ran his hands down her neck.

"It's okay, Hope. You're doing fine. I'll follow your lead just as long as you don't move down their property and get Mr. Johnson all riled up."

Hope *neigh*ed, moving her head up and down in an exaggerated fashion.

"Alrighty. You lead. I'll ride," Rex said with a smile. Hope had a hold on his heart like Savannah and his brothers did. Everything about Hope reminded him of his mother, from her sweet demeanor to her graceful beauty. And now, he realized, her stubbornness, too.

The grass gave way to gravel as they reached the edge of the Johnson driveway, and Rex held his breath as they crossed. Their modest brick rambler was built in the center of their property. It was much smaller than the Braden's sprawling home and built closer to the road. The house was dark, and Rex wondered if Jade was still asleep and if she dreamed of him as often as he did of her.

When they reached the end of the driveway and Hope's foot met the grass once again, she stopped. The sun was beginning its ascent, and Rex knew that any rancher worth his weight would soon be switching on their lights and preparing for the day.

"Come on, sweetheart," he urged, giving her a little tap with his heel while stroking her mane. Hope didn't budge. "Let's go. Come on, baby." He snapped the reins lightly, but Hope didn't even flinch.

Rex stole a glance at the house just as someone walked across the stretch of grass between the house and the barn.

"Damn it, Hope. Now we have to move. Come on, sweet girl," he urged again. His patience frayed a little more with each passing second as he watched the figure. He squinted into the rising sunlight, noticing the smooth, lithesome movements that he would recognize anywhere. Jade turned toward the pasture and stretched her arms toward the sun and then out to the sides before lowering them. He caught his breath at her radiance;

alone in the early-morning hours, against the backdrop of blossoming trees and sprawling pastures, she was a harmonious vision of beauty. Rex watched her with a passionate heart, aching to sit beside her. He rubbed his right palm with the fingers of his left hand; the feel of her silken hair lingered. His mind didn't run with the thought in the direction of fistfuls of her hair or that glorious body against his. Instead it moved in an equally fervent, though more pervasive, fantasy of sharing coffee, talking, getting to know each other on a more personal—more intimate—level than solely sexual. As that unfamiliar yearning took hold in his gut and she continued into the barn, Rex realized that Hope had begun a slow walk across the grass and into the adjacent woods. She veered down a meager trail, taking each step with care, stopping when she needed to adjust her angle but remaining true to her path, wherever it was that she was heading.

Rex didn't move to correct the guiding horse. She'd led him to discover something about himself that he had never experienced before—and it occurred to him then, as Hope positioned her body parallel to the barn doors, under the cover of the trees, that perhaps he'd been looking for Jade all his life. Maybe each woman he bedded, he'd been unknowingly comparing to the Jade he'd known as a girl and then as a young woman. Silently, secretly pushing away thoughts about the woman he continually drove away in an effort to remain loyal to his father. Perhaps, he thought, as he watched her beautiful silhouette in the shadowy glow of the barn, her hands splayed on the enormous stallion's side, her head bowed, just maybe, pushing those thoughts away had been a mistake.

Chapter Fourteen

STALLIONS WERE TEMPERAMENTAL, moody, and far too strong for most people to ride. Jade was not most people. She'd loved Flame from the moment her father had brought him home a handful of years before. He'd had such a sweet disposition and a stellar pedigree that it seemed wrong to keep the boy isolated, and she'd insisted on his socialization. She was glad she had. Flame was a happy, well-adjusted stallion who had a remarkable ability to stay on the calm side of his raging hormones.

The other horses whinnied as Jade knelt on the stiff hay and checked Flame's leg. She stroked his ribs and ran her hand slowly down his strong muscles and along his sleek bones. The strength of horses had always captivated Jade. They'd towered over her as a child, all muscle and vigor, and when they ran through the fields with their manes flying out behind them, they took her breath away. From mucking the stalls to grooming their matted, sometimes muddy, manes, the gentle giants had always beguiled her.

Jade gave Flame a kiss on his jaw and put him back in his stall. It had been a week since she first encountered Rex down at

the ravine, and when she'd woken up before dawn this morning, she'd lain in bed thinking about him and wondering if he
was out riding Hope. She'd stared at her ceiling until she
remembered every detail of his face, from the sliver of a line that
ran from the left side of his mouth to a dimple beside his chin
that appeared only when he smiled in a certain way, to the way
he narrowed his eyes right before he kissed her. For a flash of a
breath just before their lips met, they'd open wider, then close
upon the warmth of their coming together. She'd slid her hand
beneath her underwear as she remembered the stroke of his
tongue on her breasts, the strength of his hands across her ribs,
and the touch of his fingers on her most sensitive skin. Aroused,
she'd allowed her fingers to travel lower, to that place he'd been,
imagining her touch as his. She'd closed her eyes, retrieving the
sound of his hungry voice. *I've wanted to taste you for years.*
Pulling forth his scent until it was all she could smell. Her
arousal peaked, and she moved her hips beneath her touch until
she struck the same chord he had, and her insides pulsated
around her finger, Rex's name on her lips.

Flame nudged her with his nose, pulling her from her fantasy. *I have to stop doing that.* She couldn't keep thinking about
him. He had done nothing to dissuade her from the just-friends
suggestion. She'd thought, for a second, that she'd seen hurt or
disappointment in his eyes, but in the next moment it was gone,
and then he'd made that stupid remark about horses and
depression. She'd just have to force herself to stop thinking
about him altogether. Whatever sparks had flown between them
had to be extinguished.

As she headed toward the tack room, she tucked her hands

into the pockets of her jeans and shivered with the brisk morning chill. She pulled one of the barn doors closed, and when she reached for the others, she heard a rustling in the woods. She followed the sound with her eyes and saw a silhouette. She started, her hand flying to her chest. The figure behind the leaves of the trees came into focus. *Rex.*

"Jesus, you scared the shit out of me," she said as she moved toward him. "What are you doing? Spying on me?"

Hope came through the woods to the edge of the grass, then stopped. Rex held her reins loosely in his right hand. With his left, he removed his Stetson and pressed it to his chest.

"It wasn't my intention to spy on you, but I think that's what ended up happening," he admitted.

She smiled and bit her lower lip, trying to quell the excited girl in her who was jumping up and down and squealing, *He likes me! He likes me!*

"Well, at least you're not trying to blame Hope."

Rex leaned forward and patted Hope's neck. "How could I blame her for knowing just where I needed to be?"

"Rex Braden, you confuse the hell out of me." She took a few steps closer to him and petted Hope's cheek.

"I confuse the hell out of me, too," he said with a shake of his head and a smile.

Her heart swelled when that adorable dimple made a momentary appearance.

"So, is this a *friendly* visit?" *Or can I jump up there and make out with you?*

He narrowed his eyes as they took a slow stroll down her body. She quivered under his evocative gaze.

He put his hat back on that sexy head of his. Now that Jade knew what it felt like to have his mouth on hers, her hands tangled in his hair, it was just about all she could think of as he nodded. *Please tell me you want more, too.*

"Friends, just as you said," he answered.

Friends? Friends! Her blood simmered. "Friends don't ogle friends like that." She spun on her heel and went into the barn, slamming the enormous door behind her.

Chapter Fifteen

JADE STOMPED AND cursed through the day. She didn't know if she was angrier at herself for saying they should just be friends in the first place, or at Rex, that ignorant, conceited, beefcake of a man, for agreeing with her. She'd allowed herself to instantly forget her offer and acceptance of their friend status in the space of one five-second leer. What was wrong with her? She was swept up in the hope of something more with a man who didn't know how to give it. She was done hoping, and trying, and wanting anything more from Rex Braden.

She slammed the plates on the dining room table and was setting the glasses out when her father came into the room.

"What's got your sugar in a state, darlin'?" he asked as he kissed her cheek.

"Nothing. I'm just having a rotten day." *Month, year...life.*

"One of your customer's animals doing poorly?" He took a bite out of the corn bread her mother had made earlier that morning for Steve's visit. Corn bread was his favorite, and Jade guessed that with the news they were about to unload on him, her mother was doing all she could to try to butter him up. He worked as a park ranger in Preston, Colorado, just outside of

Allure. Steve was two years older than Jade, and although they got along well and she really enjoyed his company, with his schedule, they didn't get together as often as she would have liked.

She touched her father's arm. "Dad, that's for Steve. You know Mom will give you the evil eye for digging in before he gets here."

He grinned, licking the crumbs from his lips. "Your mother can give me anything she wants. I lived here well before Steven came along." He laughed at his joke, sitting down at the head of the table. "Tell me about your rotten day, darlin'."

She flopped into a chair and blew out a breath. *I love to be touched by a Braden boy. I love to hear his voice, and I even love to argue with him.* "Oh, you know, same stuff, different day. I've gotta make some decisions, and I just can't seem to get my head in the game enough to focus."

"Tell me what you're thinking. Maybe I can help."

Her father could be an excellent listener when he wanted to, and the way he rested his forearms on the table and set his wide jaw, causing his jowls to jiggle, made her want to curl up in his lap like she had as a little girl, just to hear him say, *Everything will be just fine, darlin'. You just let Daddy take care of this one.* Only now she knew, not only could her father not take care of this one, but he was the reason she couldn't take care of it herself.

"Daddy, I'm a grown woman living in her parents' house. I haven't reopened a practice, and I really don't know if I want to do that, officially—I mean, with an office and all—or if I want to continue doing what I'm doing. I don't know where I want to live—"

Her father held up his hand. "Hold up there, Jade. What do you mean where you want to live? You're not considering going back to Oklahoma, are you? Because as your father, I will stand between you and that decision no matter how old you are. That man is behind you. Leave it that way."

She smiled at his protective nature. "I know. I'm not considering Oklahoma, but there are a million cities out there, a million states. I just don't know if Weston is the right place to put down roots. It's so…small." *I'm lonely, and if I stay here I'll only ever want to be with Rex. And I can't. And I hate it. And I want to go back to bed and not come out until I'm old and gray and so senile I can't remember him.*

Her father leaned back and crossed his hands over his protruding belly, nodding his head. "That all makes sense. But, Jade, you're an intelligent, well-educated woman. You know that in bigger cities it will be harder to carve a niche out for yourself without contacts and referrals. Why, the community here might be small, but they welcomed you back with open arms. You could have a bigger practice than you ever hoped for."

Thinking of open arms, her mind danced around Rex again. *And luscious lips.* "You're right, and I'm very thankful. But, Dad." She shook her head. How could she tell her father what she was really feeling?

"There's the most beautiful girl in Weston."

Jade sprang to her feet. "Steve!" She wrapped her arms around her handsome brother. "God, I've missed you." She tousled his dark hair. "Are you going for the shaggy look? Look how long your hair is."

"Yeah, well, when you live in the woods, you tend to forgo the barbershop." He cracked a wide smile, revealing his slightly crooked, pearly whites.

She hadn't realized how much she missed his positive energy.

"I like it. It suits you, gives you a..." She spread her fingers wide and washed circles in the air with them. "An artsy, or rather, a hot mountain-man, look. Meet any sweet woodsy chicks lately?"

"Pfft. Women and their nails and hair." He laughed. "As soon as they hear what I do for a living, they're usually off to find the next rancher or business owner." Steve would never earn much as a park ranger, but he enjoyed wildlife too much to ever do anything else. The idea of being cooped up in an office, or even on his father's ranch, would have been too stifling for him. He was most at home in the wilderness.

"Someone will come around." Jade began to wonder why so many Weston men remained single into their thirties. *Then again*, she thought, *I'm no spring chicken either.*

"Did I hear Steven?" Her mother's smile lit up the room as she embraced him. "Let me look at you." She put her hands on his shoulders with an appreciative nod. "As handsome as ever. Are you eating enough? Do you need anything for your cabin? I made a big lunch, so you can take home leftovers."

"Ma, I'm fine, really," he said. Steve kissed her cheek and joined Jade and their father at the table. "So, Pop, tell me why it was so urgent that I come down this weekend?"

Jade's mother cast a glance at her. "Shall we eat first?" she asked.

Jade helped her mother bring the food to the table. She'd prepared a full meal to accompany the corn bread: roast beef, mashed potatoes, salad, and a bowl of cut-up fruit. All of Steve's favorites.

They filled their plates, but Jade was suddenly too nervous to eat. She'd been thinking about the financial issues that her mother had mentioned, but somehow, sitting down and talking to her father about them would make them real. She scooped a bit of fruit onto her plate and reached for the corn bread.

Steve smacked her hand. "Release the deliciousness."

She stuck out her tongue at him and took the biggest piece.

"Pop, you sounded pretty stressed on the phone. You want to share the news, whatever it is, so we can deal with it and enjoy our time together?"

Steve got his directness from his father and, Jade suspected, his ability to handle the ups and downs of life without being thrown into heart-stopping furies, while she and her mother tended to deal with matters of the heart by borrowing trouble and worrying themselves silly before they even knew what they were dealing with.

Her father sat up straight in his chair. "Yes, Steven, I think that's a good idea."

Jade tried not to turn her attention to her mother's fidgeting beside her. When Earl Johnson spoke as the patriarch of the family, it was best to give him her full attention, or deal with him quizzing her on exactly what he'd said later.

"Your mother and I have been doing a lot of thinking lately about the ranch and about us, where we're headed, that sort of thing," he began.

"Heading?" Steve looked at his mother, then his father again. "Are you going somewhere?"

"That's what we're deciding. You have your own place and your own life, as you should, and Jade here, well, she's about to embark on the next chapter of her life. When she does, it'll be just your mother and me here again." He looked at her mother, and Jade could feel a thick wave of support stretching between them. "Running a ranch is a lot of work, and we're thinking about downsizing."

After being taken into her mother's confidence, Jade put two and two together and realized that her father was just cushioning the fall. Of course he wouldn't admit to his children that the ranch was going to be taken away because of a financial hardship. Downsizing was a far more acceptable way for a prideful man to leave the home he'd lived in for more than three quarters of his life.

"Downsizing? Pop, are you moving out of Weston, or downsizing and remaining in town? You're not exactly retirement home age, so I'm not sure how this makes any sense."

"Neither your mother or I will ever go in a retirement home. We'd sooner live in your cabin. Got it?"

"Yes, sir," Steve said with a smile.

"We're thinking about subdividing the property. We have far too much for me to really take care of anymore, even with the staff we carry. I think it's about time we slowed down, spent a little more time together."

Her mother blushed.

"I think it would be good for you and Mom to have some time together when you're not also taking care of the ranch. It really does eat up your time, Dad, but is there anything else feeding into this decision?" Jade hoped he'd tell them the truth so they could talk about the subdividing of the other property, but she'd already decided that even if he didn't come clean, this was the perfect time to bring it up.

"No, darlin', there isn't. I'm getting older, and I worry about your mother being alone, taking care of all this land if something were to happen to me."

Something in his voice rang true to Jade, and instead of questioning her father's explanation, she began to question what her mother had told her. Perhaps her mother had it wrong. The honesty in his voice told her that her father was downsizing to protect her mother later in life, just as he'd said.

She stuffed a piece of cornbread in her mouth to try to stop herself from asking about the other property, but she couldn't deny that she had her father's directness in her blood. "What about the other property?" she asked.

He drew his brows together and set his eyes on Jade. "The *other* property?"

She focused on a slice of peach on her plate, poking it with her fork. "Yeah, that property between us and the Braden ranch?"

His eyes bore a lightning-hot streak to her heart. His breathing picked up its pace, and she heard every anxious exhalation.

"What about that property, Jade?" he asked with a stone-cold tone.

How about you sell it and keep the ranch, if this is really a financial decision? "Well, I don't know, but it would seem like if you were going to subdivide property, that might be a good piece to hack off and sell, since no one is using it."

His stare didn't falter. Jade continued in a shakier voice. "I just thought...why let it sit unused? I mean, it's been forty years, right?" She smiled, hoping to soften his resolve. "That's gotta be worth a pretty penny, so..."

Jade understood his unwavering brooding. He was a prideful man who wasn't used to being questioned by his children. She lowered her eyes, wishing she had the guts to say what she really wanted to say. *If you sell that property, maybe Rex and I could date like normal people and figure out if this relationship is worth fighting for.*

"As I was saying," her father began again.

"Wait, Dad. Jade's got a point." Steve's eyes lit up. "You're sitting on a valuable piece of property over there. It could set up you and Mom for retirement. Maybe it's time to reopen that stream of communication." If Steve felt any hesitation about the topic, he didn't give an ounce of indication.

Then again, he wasn't falling for a Braden.

"That might be so, Steven, but we're not touching that property. We're talking to the bank about subdividing the lower two hundred acres, and once we have that done, we'll see where we stand." Her father picked up his fork as if he was done with the conversation.

"So what happens to that land after you and Mom die?" Steve asked.

"Steven!" Jade snapped. She couldn't believe he brought up their parents dying—and in the same breath as the land.

His father didn't even make an effort to mask his anger. "Steven Joseph Johnson, if you are just waiting for us to die so that you can have that property—"

"Chill, Pop. I don't want that land. I was thinking more about conservation property. It's a way to protect the natural habitat for animals, and it's a tax write-off. If you and Mr. Braden don't want to argue about it or do anything with it, it's the perfect solution to let bygones be bygones."

Yes! Please! Please jump at this!

"No matter what happens with that property, bygones will never be bygones," he said with a final chomp on a piece of meat. "Jane, this is the best roast beef I had in ages. Thank you for making such a nice lunch."

There was her answer—clear as day—black and white. Along with the realization came another splinter to her already broken heart.

Chapter Sixteen

MONDAY AFTERNOON BROUGHT scorching heat. Bare-chested, Rex stood with Hope at the side of the barn. He'd just finished shampooing her tail in preparation for the show. His chest muscles jumped as he rinsed the remaining lather from her tail, and he was in the process of conditioning when his father stormed into the barn with a scowl on his face.

"Something happen in town?" Rex asked.

"You could say that," Hal grumbled.

Rex lathered up the conditioner. When his father didn't continue, he asked, "Anything I need to worry about?"

His father came to Hope's side and ran his hand along her shoulder. "How's our girl?"

"Perfect."

"Good."

"You going to tell me, or avoid the topic altogether? I can go either way." Rex arched a brow and smiled.

"Eh, it's the Johnsons. Looks like they're downsizing."

Rex stopped working on Hope's tail. Ranchers didn't just downsize. Selling off pieces of a ranch wasn't done without first taking extreme measures to keep it intact. While the Bradens had been blessed with family money that came down for generations, the Johnsons hadn't. If Earl Johnson was chopping up his property, it meant he'd come upon hard economic times. It also left a world of possibilities for where they'd end up.

"Hard times?" *Where will that leave Jade?*

"Looks like it." His father crossed his arms and leaned against the barn wall. He rubbed the stubble on his chin. His biceps jumped in a familiar nervous pattern. Sadness percolated beneath his father's tanned skin, emanating from his dark eyes, the creases in his forehead, and the third sigh to leave his lips in less than five minutes.

"Wanna talk about it?" Rex asked, in the same have-it-your-way fashion his father might have used to address him. He'd be happy to listen, or to give his father his privacy.

His father looked up, his mouth clenched in a tight line. He nodded a slow, silent nod.

Rex went back to work on Hope's tail while waiting for his father to answer. He didn't believe Hope would place at the show, but he'd damn well make sure his father had every reason to be proud of her.

"There was a time that Earl Johnson was my best friend," his father said.

Rex nodded, knowing that telling his father he'd already known that wouldn't help one bit and would likely stop him from sharing more.

"For years, he was my go-to guy, you know? We had plans, all sorts of plans, when we bought the properties. We were going to sell that land and make a fortune. He'd run cattle. I'd sell breed horses. Our kids would marry, and we'd be linked for life."

Rex raised his head. *Our kids would marry, and we'd be linked for life* had his attention. He moved to Hope's face and petted her jaw. She nuzzled him between his ribs. *How could you have known, old girl?* He kissed the crest of her head.

His father had said Earl's name only a handful of times, and it was always followed by a grunt and a snarl. Hearing his father say his name without that hostility surprised him. The fact that they'd been best friends wasn't news; it was widely known in Weston. They'd grown up together, dated alongside each other, caused a ruckus together as teens. It had all fallen apart in the years following their joint purchase of the land between their properties.

"I just hate to think of him falling upon hard times," his father said.

Rex saw himself in his father: the gruff exterior, the harsh words said without regret, and the pliable heart that could be twisted and turned and fooled; but inside that heart was a memory, and certain loves that went in never came back out. Rex hadn't realized those connections could reach farther than his family until his own heart had taken a roller coaster ride with him as the unwilling passenger. The hills and valleys of the last few days made his heart's ability to reach beyond his family palpable.

"You thinking about that land?" Rex asked as he rounded Hope with the hose and began rinsing her tail.

"Not for that bastard," his father said as he pushed from the wall and stalked off.

He smiled at the familiar arrogance, but his mind was already running down a different path. He had been loathing the idea of attending the volunteer meeting for the horse show that evening after what happened at Jade's barn that morning. He'd agreed to what she wanted—friendship. The way she stalked off left him floundering and angry all over again.

Now that anger subsided, replaced with concern. Was she sad about the ranch? Angry? He wanted to see her, to know she was okay. He wanted to talk to her and ease any sadness she had. Maybe she'd known they were going to downsize. Losing a ranch, even part of a ranch, was devastating. He'd hate to think about his father giving up a single acre. Rex was paid handsomely for his work on the ranch. He had simple needs, and he'd pocketed nearly every penny of his income for just that reason. If ever there came a time—which in his heart he knew there never would—that his father needed anything, he wanted to be able to step in. He wondered if Jade had known of her father's plans before she'd returned to Weston.

If his father was softening toward Earl Johnson, what might that mean for *them*—if there even was a *them* to consider anymore.

Chapter Seventeen

JADE THOUGHT ABOUT her parents all afternoon. By the time she was done giving Berle his afternoon massage and had gone home to shower, she'd convinced herself that her father had to be downsizing by choice and that their finances were just fine, which made her wonder why he wouldn't just sell it all off and move into town. Then again, with the value of land and how much they loved their home, she was sure that he would rather allow her mother to remain in the home she adored and had raised her children in. Her father had a big enough heart to have lied to her mother about the reason for downsizing, too. Her mother would never allow him to do something so drastic just for her. She wished she could be certain about her father's motivations.

She was dreading the volunteer meeting, and had even considered canceling her involvement, but she couldn't do that to the Gesalts. She was still stewing over her run-in with Rex, and she knew her stupid heart would still do somersaults when she saw him at the meeting. She couldn't eat dinner and finally gave up on doing anything that needed her brain to function. She took a cold shower to wash off the sweat she'd earned and to calm her nerves.

She'd hoped there would at least be a small drop in the unseasonably warm temperature before the evening, but she hadn't been so lucky. Jade dressed in her lightest sundress. The spaghetti straps tied at her shoulders, which was a little juvenile, but she didn't care. She'd have gone naked to keep cool if she wasn't afraid of being caught in the Weston grapevine before the night's end. She pulled her hair up into a high ponytail and forwent her leather boots for a pair of white sandals.

As she neared the Gesalts', her stomach was doing flips. She'd find out what her appointed volunteer position was going to be, and then she'd hightail it out of there and go down to Rights Creek for a swim. When she and Riley were teenagers, they'd go down to the creek at night and skinny-dip. The creek had been one of their favorite haunts. Just thinking about how free she felt back then brought a smile to her lips. Rights Creek was about a mile past her house. She'd park at the end of the long dirt road and walk through the trail. She felt refreshed just thinking about it.

The gray sedan behind her had been following her since she'd turned onto the main road. She glanced in her rearview mirror and thought of Kane, remembering the way he'd shown up at her house uninvited and how he'd been everywhere she was for the few weeks after their breakup. She was glad he hadn't become a real stalker and followed her back to Colorado. She turned into the Gesalts' driveway, and the gray sedan kept going. Even though she'd clearly seen that the driver was not Kane and was in fact an old man, she breathed a little easier, then chastised herself for being paranoid. All the stress must be getting to her.

There was very little in life that Jade was afraid of, but as she pulled her car up beside a red Ford F250, she noticed Rex's truck parked by the barn. A fleeting panic skittered through her. How was she supposed to act around him? He wanted a friendship, which she'd been stupid enough to say she wanted. *How can I act like a friend when I want so much more?*

She took a deep breath and weaved through the crowd toward the table. She focused on what she needed to do to survive the evening without being swallowed by lust or embarrassment. *Get in, get my assignment,* and *get out. In, out, swim. In, out, swim.*

There was no line at the volunteer table, and she scanned the sign-up sheets for designations. She trailed her finger down to her name and ran it across to the positions. Gate attendant. Great. She could handle that. She scanned the list for Rex's name and looked beside it. *Gate attendant. Shit.*

Her heart thundered against her ribs as she spun around to leave and bumped right into Rex's rock-hard chest, momentarily stunned into silence.

"I'm sorry. Did I hurt you?" he said, placing his hands gently on her shoulders.

Jade's mouth went dry. She swallowed hard and looked into his concerned eyes. In any other situation, a man holding a woman the way he was—standing so close she could feel his heartbeat between them—would indicate a natural, intimate discussion, perhaps, or a kiss. Jade would have given her right arm to be in either of those situations instead of gaping at the man she craved and could not have while he looked her up and down and asked if he'd hurt her.

"I'm fine," she managed.

Hold me again. Please. I'll trip; just catch me.

JADE'S ARMS WERE silky smooth beneath his hands. He hadn't meant to be in her way, and now, as he looked into those deep pools of blue and smelled her scent, so fresh and feminine, he didn't want to let her go. But with her hair pulled away from her face, giving him a clear, beautiful view of her delicate neck, the immediate response within his Levi's drove him to release her and forced his mind to work again.

"You're in a rush." *Nice line. Idiot.*

"Um, yeah. I…"

"Jade." He locked eyes with her, momentarily losing track of what he was going to say.

She licked her lips, and he had to shove his hands in his pockets just to hide his arousal. Those damn innocent eyes and that sensual tongue sent a dangerous rush of desire through him. She wasn't his to want.

"Friends." *Goddamn it.* The reminder left his lips before he had a chance to think.

Jade shook her head. "Friends? You're really something. Don't worry. There's no need for you to drive it into my brain. I've got it."

She stormed away, and this time, instead of standing there like a blundering idiot, he was right behind her.

"Jade, wait." He caught up to her at her car and reached for her arm. She shook him off. "You're infuriating! All I want to do is talk to you."

"I know," she spat, and opened her car door.

"What kind of response is that? I don't know why you're so irritated with me."

She shoved the key into the ignition. He had to make a quick decision. He grabbed the keys from her, and she struggled with him to keep hold.

"What are you doing? Let go." She pulled with all her might.

Rex realized how ridiculous things were getting and he let go of the keys. Jade fell across her seat.

"I'm sorry." He smiled, stifling a laugh. The whole situation was stupid. He was a thirty-four-year-old man chasing down a woman and wrestling for keys. Jesus, he'd lost his mind.

An unfamiliar sedan pulled up beside his truck at the entrance to the parking area and parked beside him. He drew his eyes back to Jade in her sweet little dress, feverishly starting her car.

"What are you so afraid of?" he asked.

"You're always laughing at me, and we're always wrestling in...trucks." She shook her head, and she, too, was soon laughing. "We are pathetic."

"A little," he said. No one had come out of the sedan, and he wondered what the driver was doing on the other side of his truck.

"Did you want something?" she asked in a friendlier voice.

Do I ever. "Just wanted to talk, that's all. But I can see you're in a hurry, so don't let me keep you." He watched her mulling over her answer. She looked at him, then at the steering wheel, then at him again. She rolled her lower lip into her mouth and licked it as it unrolled.

She was killing him, action by sensuous, mind-blowing action. One stroke of her tongue at a time.

She relaxed into the driver's seat.

"I'm sorry I was watching you the other morning," he said. It was the one thing he'd really wanted to tell her. He'd never spied on a woman before, and when she'd first noticed him in the woods, sitting on Hope, captivated by her silhouette, he'd felt all sorts of wrong and even more sorts of right all at the same time. But in that crazy mix, he realized that she'd probably thought he was a little like a Peeping Tom.

She looked up at him through her thick, dark lashes. "I didn't mind."

And just like that, she flipped back to the tempting seductress who'd told him to taste her. Every nerve in his body challenged him to kiss her, touch her, do something to indicate his desire, but if he'd realized one thing, it was that he was not the best interpreter of her moods, so instead, he smiled.

A man came around the bed of his truck, and when Rex looked up, the man curiously retreated. Something was off about the look in the man's eyes, and Rex wondered if he was messing with his truck.

"What the hell?" he said.

"What's wrong?" She looked back at his truck.

"Nothing. Some guy's by my truck."

"Did you want to talk? I guess I can stay for a few minutes."

Rex saw the guy pop his head around his cab, then disappear again. He was torn between finding out what the hell that guy was up to and trying to salvage things with Jade.

"Look, you're obviously sidetracked. Why don't we catch up another time?" Jade slammed the door and started her car.

"Jade!" he said, but she was already pulling out of her parking space. She sped off, and the sedan that had been next to Rex's truck backed up and looked as though it was going to follow Jade. Rex's pulse soared, and he took off running toward the sedan, legs pumping, biceps pulsing. *Jade.* Just as he reached the rear bumper, the man he'd seen peering around the bed of his truck stepped from the car.

"Hi," the gray-haired man said. "I'm looking for the Carroll house? I've circled the area twice, but I can't see the addresses on the mailboxes. It's so darn dark."

Lost? He'd completely misconstrued the man's intent—and there was no denying what he felt. The urge to protect Jade was ten times what he felt for any member of his family. He had to find her.

"Pull out of the driveway and make a left. Third house down on the right." He spoke quickly, pulling his keys from his pocket and heading toward his truck with one thing on his mind: finding Jade. He pulled onto the road behind the old man, who was driving way too slowly. Two minutes later, the old man pulled into a driveway and Rex put the pedal to the floor in search of Jade's car. She couldn't have gone far.

He sped toward Jade's house. Knowing he'd overreacted about the guy by his truck pissed him off even more. He'd had a chance to talk to her and he'd blown it again. He was at her house a few minutes later, and her car wasn't there. He continued down the road, cursing at the situation. Life was a hell of a lot easier when he wasn't driven by his heart, but that option no longer existed.

He pulled onto a dirt road to turn around and caught sight of Jade's car parked between two large trees. *What the hell?* When he pulled in, his headlights shone on the trees beside her car, illuminating carvings covering most of the trunk. Rex smiled as he realized where he was. He parked his truck and headed down the dirt path.

He hadn't been to Rights Creek since he was a kid. He'd always preferred the ravine to the creek, although he knew plenty of kids who hung out there when they were teenagers. Guided by the moonlight filtering through the trees, he followed the narrow path to the wide creek. He heard a splash before he saw movement in the water.

Beneath the iridescent moonlight, Jade swam lazily through the water. She glided with strong, fluid strokes, and when she reached the middle, she dove headfirst like an elegant swan beneath the surface. Her naked body slithered quickly behind, her bare bottom arcing up in the air before plunging deep with one last kick of her legs until she had disappeared completely. Rex was mesmerized as she breached the surface again. Her breasts bobbed over and under the water as she wiped the water from her face.

He couldn't be caught again watching her like a psycho, and yet he couldn't turn away as she swam to the water's edge and pulled herself from the water. She'd taken her hair out of its tether and now it stuck to her creamy skin. Rex did the only thing he could do. He moved toward her like a thief in the night.

"Jade, it's me, Rex," he called softly, so as not to startle her.

She gasped, reached for her clothes, and quickly put them on.

"I didn't come to spy on you. I promise. I thought this guy was going to follow you out of the Gesalts' and...Oh hell, Jade..." *How the hell can I explain this?* "I guess I did follow you, but I didn't know you were skinny-dipping."

She sat down on a fallen tree with her back to him.

"May I join you?" *Please God, cut me some slack here.*

"It's a free world."

Not really. Not where you and I are concerned. He sat beside her, and suddenly he wasn't sure what had felt so urgent. He couldn't put two coherent thoughts together. Her nipples peaked the thin fabric, and without her hair tumbling in waves, there were no distractions from her electric-blue eyes.

Chapter Eighteen

JADE SHIVERED AS he approached, both from the coolness of being wet and the excitement of being with Rex. He was so cute when he was embarrassed. She hadn't encountered him in this tentative mood before, and she found it titillating. The fallen tree on which they sat had deteriorated in several places, leaving only a small area that was viable enough to sit on. He sat so close to her that she grew warm almost instantly.

"So you followed a guy you thought was going to follow me?" She smiled at the thought. If he hadn't actually followed someone, it was a romantic story, and if he had, it was a possessive *and* romantic gesture. Either way, she couldn't ignore the meaning behind his actions; her attraction was reciprocated, at least on some level.

"There was a guy, but he wasn't following you," he said with a smile.

"Mm-hmm," she teased.

"A gray sedan. He was lost."

"I saw that car. When I was on my way there, it was behind me. I had a feeling it was following me, but then it didn't pull into their driveway when I did."

"He was just lost." He turned to face her. "Jade," he said softly. "I want to talk to you. I'll be the first to admit that I haven't got much experience with meaningful relationships."

"Meaningful relationships?" *Is he saying what I think he's saying?*

"Okay, relationships with women. Period." He sighed.

He reached to find the right words, which she found endearing. She bit her lower lip and listened. It would be so easy to put words into his mouth and then silence them with a succulent kiss, but that could wait. More than wanting that kiss, she wanted to hear what was so important that he'd followed her down a dark road at night, risking anyone finding them—kids who might talk about them in town, or a neighbor who might have seen him follow her. She knew the chances of either were remote, but surely he must have thought of them, too.

"I…you…I said *friends* because I thought that was what you wanted, and being your friend was better than being someone who never spoke to you at all. I want to get to know you—all of you. I'm not a kid anymore. I don't play games, and I'm not interested in chasing women or any of that."

Her pulse was racing, making it hard to concentrate on what she wanted to say. "I thought *you* wanted to be friends. With everything that's wrong between our parents, I thought that was what you needed."

He looked down, and Jade's heart skipped a beat. *That is what he needs.* She saw regret in his eyes when he lifted his face to hers.

"I don't have anything figured out right now as far as they're concerned, but I knew when I saw you in the barn that you are the person I never knew I was looking for. You ignite something in me that has never been touched by anyone else. Not even close."

"It's called anger." Listening to his honest confession stimulated something deep within her, and she reached for his hand. "I want the same confusing thing you do. I think maybe I always have."

He took her face in his hands and brought her lips to his in a sweet, gentle kiss. It wasn't enough. Jade pressed her mouth harder, probing his tongue with hers. Her entire body rippled with goose bumps as his whiskers scratched against her upper lip and his right hand cupped the back of her neck, greedily kissing, stealing her breath as his and then pulling away sharply, leaving her breathless.

"I want to know you, Jade. Not just in the physical way. I want to get to know you. I want to date you. I want to know what makes you happy and what makes you sad. I want to know all the stories from when you were a little girl, and I want to know the dreams that keep you up at night. I want to learn about you in all the ways that matter."

Don't cry. Don't cry. Don't cry.

"I've never wanted any of that before, with anyone."

He searched her eyes, and she wondered if he could see that she'd waited her whole life to be cherished, and she could hardly believe that the man who wanted to know her was the man she'd spent so many years dreaming about. And also the man whose family her father abhorred. She covered her mouth with her fingertips, thinking of her father. She had to get rid of those thoughts. Now. There was no way that she was going to even try to resist what she felt for Rex. She felt his strength weaken with his confession and saw vulnerability in his dark eyes, sparking a desire in her to help him regain his strength and calm his nerves, like she did for her horses. She slid her fingers beneath his hair and drew him to her, capturing his lips with hers. She probed and licked and kissed until any lingering thoughts were gone and all that existed were the two of them, their breathing, in tune with each other.

She climbed onto his lap and wrapped both arms around him, feeling his hard shaft beneath her. She kissed him harder, pressing her body against his. When she finally came up for air, the smile on his lips reached all the way to his eyes.

Her lips tingled from the pressure, and she licked them lightly, enjoying the sensation of the pain and the healing wetness at once.

"You kill me when you do that," he said in a ragged voice. He ran his index finger along her lips, and she took that finger into her mouth and swirled her tongue around it, closing her eyes and moving in slow, pulsing beats. He groaned, then gasped in a sharp breath.

"You're making it hard for me to stay on track here. I'm only human."

She drew his finger from her mouth and put her lips beside his ear. "Then don't stay on track," she whispered. She had never wanted a man the way she wanted him, or felt as right about being with someone regardless of how wrong her father might think it was. She trusted her heart, and as much as she longed to hear his intimate confessions, they could wait. She wanted to claim the moment as theirs, claim him as hers, and give herself over to him. Everything else could wait.

She slid from his lap and untied the right strap of her dress.

The fabric fell softly across her breast. She drew him to his feet. His hands trembled as much as hers as she laced her fingers into his. The only sounds were their warm breaths, the beating of their hearts, and the sweet movement of the water. Jade put her hands on his chest, like she'd done with Flame so many times before. She felt like she'd spent her life calming horses in preparation for this one night. Rex Braden was her stallion. She rested her forehead between her hands and closed her eyes. The smell of the wet earth, mixing with Rex's unique leathery, woody scent, brought a smile to her lips. The sound of water bubbling over rocks at the ends of the creek soothed their private world. She slowed her breathing to match his pace and willed her heart to beat to the same rhythm.

He placed his hands on the small of her back. The light pressure sped up her pulse. She opened her eyes and looked into his.

"Let me do this," she said.

He lowered his lips to hers, a feather across her needy mouth, as she pulled free and reached for the button on his jeans. She put her thumbs in the sides of his jeans and drew them down, lowering her body as she pushed them to his ankles. She'd forgotten about his damned boots, and he laughed as he knelt down, nearly toppling over as he lifted his feet and she removed his boots, freeing him from his jeans.

He reached for her, and Jade stepped away, shaking her head.

"Let me," she repeated. Jade had never been ashamed of her sexuality. It empowered her, and as much as she loved letting a man steer their sexual interludes, with Rex she wanted to—had to—do what she felt he needed most. *Her touch.*

JADE STOOD BEFORE him with one shoulder bare, looking like a pixie in the moonlight. She untied the strap on her other shoulder and her dress dropped to the ground. His body awoke with eagerness at the sight of Jade naked before him. He reached for her, and she tethered him again with her words.

"Let me."

He was a man, through and through. Testosterone ran through him thick and ready. He drank in the essence of her— shoulder to hip, the curve of her belly just above her dark curls. The temptation to touch her was too strong. He reached out again, needing to feel those exquisite curves.

She stood on her tiptoes and whispered, "Let me," again.

She ran her fingers down his sides lightly at first. Then she clamped her hands around his hips, applying pressure with her palms. Her hands were small against his body as she traced the lines of his abs across his stomach and back up to his chest. He closed his eyes, feeling the pressure of his boxer briefs trapping him beneath the soft fabric.

Jade's fingers pressed against the hair on his chest, creating a rough sensation against his skin. She moved in closer, her breath on his skin, and she kissed as she touched. Rex's nerves tightened, while his muscles relaxed. The strange dichotomy of sensations had him craving more of her.

He reached for her again, and she pushed his hands down to his sides. He'd never allowed a woman such control, and now he knew why. No one else would know just how to touch him the way Jade was. Her caress was slow and thoughtful. He could feel love coming through her fingertips in soft pulses.

Her nipples brushed softly against his chest. Her hands twisted lightly against his skin, her fingers pointing down as she walked them toward his boxers, applying gentle pressure with her palms.

"Jade," he whispered.

She kissed the space between his ribs where Hope nuzzled him so often, and her hands slid beneath the waist of his briefs, rubbing, caressing the tender area beneath his erection.

"Touch me," he said.

"Shh," she whispered.

His body trembled beneath her teasing. She slid his briefs to the ground and ran her hands first down his left leg, with pulsing grips along his muscles until she reached his foot, which she lifted gently, freeing him from the thin veil of cotton. He was on the verge of coming apart and she hadn't laid one finger on his most sensitive areas. He clenched his teeth, restraining the surge of heat that fought for release as she slid her body against his and moved behind him, reversing the sensation as she worked her way back up his legs.

Rex opened his eyes, and the sight of her hands, now reaching around him from behind and grasping his hips with a firm, possessive grip, pulsing the tension from the muscles, tamed the primitive need to take her, replacing it with a hypnotic hunger for more—more touch, more teasing, more Jade.

She massaged his back, his sides, trailed kisses up his spine and slid her hands beneath his arms, massaging his pecs as he might her breasts. It was shocking and almost indescribable the way it emasculated, then instantly aroused him. Her touch transitioned from firm to tender with each breath, and by the time she returned to his front, he thought he might come with a graze against her skin.

She pressed her body against his and he had to have her. He took her in his arms and kissed her with the promise of more. He could smell her arousal as she gyrated against him, anchoring him in a thrumming heat.

She pushed away with a shake of her head and a wiggle of her finger. "Let me," she whispered.

He groaned again as she grabbed his obliques and pressed— hard—with her palms, then lowered her head and licked along the center of his stomach.

"Jade, please. Let me," he begged, grasping her shoulders.

She ignored his plea and pushed his hands from her skin as she licked along the crease between his thighs and the tender skin beneath his erection. At the same time, she cupped his balls, moving her fingers just gently enough to send him up, up, up toward the crest of an orgasm. Just when he thought he couldn't restrain himself any longer, she slid her finger along the length of his shaft, then lowered her mouth around him. He moaned into the night at the moist heat that enveloped him as she drew her lips up and down the length of him, until the tip hit the back of her throat. Then she drew him out, and the shock of the air against the wet from her tongue sent a shiver rushing through him.

She took a step back, dragged her eyes along his body, lingering on the place her mouth had just been, and licked her lips.

He reached for his jeans.

"I'm not done," she said.

"Jade, I can't take it."

"Then why are you reaching for your clothes?"

"Condom," he said with urgency.

SHE FROWNED. HIS hand stopped midair. She wanted to feel him. All of him, not a latex sheath. She was on the pill, and sure, she knew all about sexually transmitted diseases, but didn't everyone get tested these days?

"Are you worried about who you've been with?" she asked honestly, cringing inside while she waited for the answer.

"No, but…"

She moved closer, touched her fingertips to his stomach.

"I've never had sex without a condom. Not once in my life. Not even as a teenager. I was always too afraid of getting someone pregnant," he admitted.

"You're thirty-something and never felt the wetness of a woman wrapped around you, pulsing against you?"

He groaned. "Not once."

Between his trembling and his intoxicated voice, she felt his potent need.

"I'm on the pill," she said, and took his nipple in her mouth, licking lightly in circles, feeling it pebble beneath her tongue.

"What about you?" he asked.

It hadn't even dawned on her that he'd ask.

"Two guys without condoms. Ten and eleven years ago. I've been tested multiple times since then." She held on to his waist, feeling him throb against her, and waited while he processed his need.

"You're on the pill and there've been only two men?"

"Boys in college, and yes. The pill was to protect my future. Condoms were for my health."

She kissed the tiny scar beneath his chin. She hadn't expected this much discussion, and she was about to reach for his pants and grab the condom when he looked into her eyes and asked, "Why me? Why now? I need to know."

"Because it's *you*. It's always been you."

He lifted her into his arms, and she wrapped her legs around his waist, her arms around his neck. His arms were so strong, his body so warm from the heat of the night, and as she slid down upon him, accepting him, taking in all of him, they both moaned with surrender to the ceaseless pleasure. He held her bottom and moved her in an even rhythm.

"Jade," he whispered. "Jesus, you feel like heaven."

She kissed him, and he moved one hand to the back of her head, pulling her harder, devouring her in an aggressive kiss.

Their bodies slid against each other's sweat with every stroke, every glorious thrust. She was slick with need as he moved her quicker.

He groaned with pleasure, his cheek against hers.

He tried to take her mouth to his, but she couldn't kiss, could barely breathe, as she arched against him. He took her breast in his mouth, sending tiny shocks through her center, the sensation mounting as she felt him swell and fill her completely. His legs tensed as he dropped both hands to her thighs and moved her faster, deeper, until she called out his name into the night and he was panting and grunting in the same continuous beat as they rode the crescendo of their heat, then slowed to a panting, obsessed kiss.

She had never felt so full, so alive.

They kissed as he carried her to the water's edge and walked them into the creek.

"I've never felt so close to anyone in my life." He kissed her tenderly.

Beneath the water, he slid out from between her legs and used his fingers to tease and taunt her again. She hung on to his neck, letting him touch her as much as he wanted, as much as he needed.

"I want you," he said in a husky voice.

"You have me," she answered between kisses.

He slid his fingers inside of her, feeling for the bundle of nerves that would send her over the edge again. "Come for me, only me. I want you as mine."

Her mouth wouldn't work. He knew just where to touch her to send her right over the edge again. Her head fell back as she gasped. "Oh God."

"For me, Jade. I'm a possessive bastard. I never knew I was, but the idea of you with anyone else kills me. I want you like I've never wanted anyone before."

She forced herself to right her body and take his cheeks in her hands. She'd never wanted anything as much as she wanted what he asked for.

"I'm yours. Through and through."

He used his thumb to tease her as he brought her again to the place where her sight failed and the breath was sucked right from her lungs. She grabbed at his bare shoulders and clenched her eyes, succumbing to another mind-numbing climax.

Chapter Nineteen

THEY LAY ON the grass beside the creek, staring up at the starry sky. Jade's head rested against his chest, her arm across his belly. He'd never wanted to spend time with a woman after having sex. His MO had been to fill his need, then escape before any talking could occur. With Jade, he never wanted to leave her side. He still couldn't believe he'd told her he was a possessive bastard, and as he lay there next to her, warmed by her body beside him, he knew it was true. The thought of her with anyone else would be too painful, and yet he still couldn't reconcile the thought of telling their families.

"Maybe this is all infatuation. Forbidden fruit and all that," Jade said.

"Maybe," he teased, though he knew it was anything but.

She poked him in the ribs. "You're supposed to promise your undying love to me and reassure me that this is real."

He closed his eyes, already feeling like they'd been together for years.

"What now?" she asked.

"This is pretty great," he said with a smile.

"Yeah, it is."

He felt her body go rigid against him, and he turned to face her. "I'm not one of those guys who knows how to say things that I know aren't true, and I'm not a kid, Jade. I'm thirty-four. I've lived enough years to know real from fantasy, and to want to live within both worlds can be dangerous. For everyone." He ran his finger along her cheek, then kissed her forehead.

"What are you saying?" she asked.

"I'm saying that what I said was true, all of it. I do want you as mine, and mine only, just as I want to be yours and yours only. I want to be part of your life." He leaned on his elbow and rested his hand on her belly. He felt her heartbeat quicken beneath his palm.

"But?" she asked in a thin voice.

"But we have to take other people's feelings into consideration. We owe our families that much while we figure this out. I don't believe in leaving bodies in the wake of anything, including lo—" He swallowed the word. He couldn't love her after only a few days of heady need, could he? "Including this."

She was quiet, and he leaned over her, then took her chin in her hand and said, "I'm not saying that we need to not see each other. I'm saying that we need to be tactful. We can't throw something like this in our families' faces, or flaunt it around town. There are too many people who could get hurt, and I won't—we can't—be the cause of that."

"So, you're thinking what? That we sneak out like kids after dark?"

He smiled. She was getting riled up, and she was radiant when she was feisty. "No, I'm saying that, for a while, we're discreet. I haven't had a chance to woo you, and I want to. I've never wanted to woo anyone before. I want to take you out to dinner and talk over candlelight. I want to see movies and make out in the back row. I want to walk around the Village and window-shop. God, Jade, don't you see? I want a life with you, and in order to have that life, we have to tread gently on other people's hearts."

"And what if we do those things and you decide you don't like the person you meet in me?"

He lifted her chin. "It's not going to happen, but if it does, then better that we find out before we cause our families undue trauma, don't you think?"

"I hate it when difficult things are the smartest things to do," Jade said in a sullen voice. "You're making perfect sense. I don't want to hurt my family any more than I want to hurt yours, but I can't quite piece together what you're getting at," she said.

"I guess you mean besides wanting to have night after night of passionate sex until you forget how bullheaded I am and your brain is helpless against my wily ways?"

"Yeah, what you said," she said with a smile.

He could look at her smile all day and never tire of it. She had three smiles that he'd clearly defined so far: the flirty, come-hither smile; the feigned, I-don't-want-to-but-I'll-listen-anyway smile; and the adventuresome, rebellious smile that lit up her face when she was rapturous with life. He couldn't wait to learn more about her.

"I guess what I'm thinking is that we meet outside of town for now and do all the things we want to do."

She shot upright. "Outside of town? Like, completely hide from the world?"

"Not the world, but yes, from our families and this little town with far too many ears to the ground and too many mouths feeding the grapevine." He knew she'd be upset, but he wasn't ready to relent on this. He hadn't worked his whole life to honor his family only to throw it all away when they could handle the situation tactfully without hurting anyone.

"So you just want to pretend we're not together?" Her smile wiped clean, replaced with a firm line, just as he'd expected.

"Jade, only to the town, not to the world. I know it seems juvenile, but our families deserve this, and we deserve a chance to build something together without the world crashing down on us."

She rose to her feet and crossed her arms. He rose beside her and wrapped his arms around her waist, pulling her close, so she was forced to look into his eyes.

"Listen to me, please. We're not kids. It's not like Daddy is going to say to you, *You can't date him anymore.* This is a full-on family feud. This is us being caught in the crossfire of the Hatfields and the McCoys. I want a fighting chance with you. When you said you just wanted to be friends, it about killed me. I've taken more cold showers in a week than I ever did as a teenager. When we know how we'll each react to situations, when we've built a solid base that we know can withstand the pressures of our parents, then we'll figure out how to handle it *together*. And hopefully, we'll move forward as a couple, stronger than we ever imagined. I want us to work. Please give us a fighting chance. Work with me, Jade. Please."

The tension deflated from her shoulders and arms. He felt her relax into him.

"How can I say no to *that*? How can a gruff cowboy know all the right things to say to soften a girl's heart?"

"I'm not softening a girl's heart. I'm wooing the woman I want to share my life with."

Chapter Twenty

JADE COULDN'T HELP but check the woods by the barn Tuesday morning. Her body still tingled with thoughts of the evening before. She felt complete for the first time in her life. She wasn't crazy about hiding from everyone she knew. She'd much rather shout her feelings from the rooftop. But Rex was right. Their situation was not an easy one, and though she felt like she and Rex were right together, despite their confusion at the beginning, she was also smart enough to believe, as he did, that it was essential that they were absolutely certain about each other before they caused what was sure to be an uproar like Weston had never seen before. The problem was, she was sure. She didn't need time. She'd loved him all her life. She'd just never realized it before last night.

She pushed the barn doors open, breathing in the dewy air and the tangy smell of manure under the morning sun. Her stomach took a little dip at the sight of the empty woods. Until last night, she hadn't realized that Rex didn't carry a cell phone. That would make things difficult, but he assured her they'd communicate without issue, and given how he'd surprised her the evening before—the depth of what he wanted, his tender words, the fact that he hadn't ridden bareback between the sheets before her, all things she'd never expected—she knew he'd find a way.

She brought the horses out into the pasture and watched them gallop into the morning. The freedom of a horse was one of the most beautiful sights she'd ever seen. The way their tails flew out behind them like lightning in their wakes took her breath away.

Today was the first day she'd allow Flame to run, and as nervous as she was, she was excited for him as he nodded his big head, nosing her shirt the second she appeared beside his stall. She stroked his jaw, and around his neck, found a note hanging from a red ribbon.

"No way," she said aloud.

She untied the bow and removed the note. She'd never seen Rex's handwriting before, and now, as she took in the words, each in full caps, with quick strokes that feathered at the end, she ran her fingers over them. Knowing Rex had taken his time not only to write it, but to show up at the barn and approach the largest of their horses, at the risk of being caught by her father, made her quiver all over.

SWEET JADE, PLEASE ACCOMPANY ME TONIGHT ON OUR FIRST DATE. I'LL BE WAITING RIGHT OFF OF EXIT 2, 8 P.M. IF YOU'RE NOT THERE, I'LL KNOW YOU WERE BUSY. I CANNOT WAIT TO SEE YOUR LOVELY FACE AGAIN. R

Jade let out a *whoop!* and shook her arms and hips in a little happy dance.

"Life is beginning to look up, Flame."

"What was that little dance I saw you doing?" her father

asked.

Jade froze, nervously tucking the note into the back pocket of her shorts.

"Oh, you startled me. I'm…excited because Flame's leg is all healed. I'm taking him out to the lower pasture now." *I can't breathe. I'm going on a date. A date! With Rex!*

Her father walked over and pulled the remaining ribbon from Flame's neck. He stared at it and lifted his eyebrows at Jade.

She snagged the ribbon from his hand. "I was practicing putting ribbons in his mane. I must have missed that piece." She pretended to work her fingers through the rest of his mane. "I think that's the last of it. Thanks!"

She guided Flame from his stall, hurrying out of the barn to avoid any further questions.

"Darlin'?"

She froze. "Yes?" She turned to face him, and her father crossed his arms over his belly.

"I'm glad to see you're in better spirits today. I was worried about you."

Guilt sliced a jagged edge in Jade's heart. "Me too, Dad." *But I hate that I can't tell you that it's Rex who has raised my spirits.*

"You're not too torn up about subdividing the ranch? I thought that of you and Steven, you might be more upset."

She blew out a breath to calm her nerves and answered honestly. "I would do just about anything to save this ranch. Everything I know, I learned right here, with you and Mom. Mom taught me to make dandelion wreaths in the upper fields and to grow every vegetable under the sun in her little garden.

You taught me how to nurture animals, how to ride, and, Dad, you taught me how to think beyond the differences between animal and humans right here in this barn. But if you want to subdivide—I mean, if it's really what you want—then you have a right to do that. But if it's driven by something else, I'll do anything I can to help you keep the property."

Her father smiled a warm, comforting smile. The tension that she'd seen in his cheeks was gone, replaced with a softness and warmth. "You're a good girl, Jade."

No, I'm not. I'm a liar and a naughty, naughty lover. "Thanks, Dad." The fact that he made no distinction in why he was giving up part of the ranch did not go unnoticed by Jade.

"Oh, Dad, I'll be home really late tonight. I'm going with Riley to Preston to visit some girlfriends." The bold-faced lie made her feel as though she'd just placed her head on a chopping block.

"Okay, darlin'. Just be safe."

And the chopper just dropped a little lower.

As soon as she was in the field, she called Riley.

"Deets, sister. And I want all of them. Did you see him at the meeting?"

Jade smiled at Riley's enthusiasm. "What are you, the dating police?"

"Yes, and if you don't tell me something good happened, I'll have to put you in the slammer. Besides, it'll alleviate the guilt I have about leaving you at Fingers."

"Ugh, right. You do owe me. I saw him. I more than saw him," Jade teased.

"Yeah? And is Sexy Rexy *all that?*"

"*All that* and more. I've never felt like this before. He...I don't know what it is. We were bashing heads so much, but I wonder now if all that head bashing was because we're not supposed to be together."

"Who says?" Riley's voice was filled with protective harshness.

"No, I mean because of the family issues, not that we're not destined to be together. Anyway, we went to Rights Creek and..." Jade paused. The intimate details of her night with Rex seemed too personal to share, even with Riley, with whom she'd shared her darkest secrets. "And it was just a really nice night."

"I'm happy for you, even though I can tell you're hiding something. I can only assume it's some dirty secret that is too spicy to say over the phone. So, what now?"

"Now you're covering for me, so don't be seen by my family tonight."

"Ooh, we're going covert? Dodging Daddy? You sneaky girl, you."

Jade laughed. She loved the way Riley pushed and teased at all the right times. "Yes, but he thinks I'm with you seeing girlfriends in Preston and out late."

"When in reality?"

"I'm going on a date with Rex." A date. She loved the sound of it, and began to anticipate what it implied: holding doors, holding hands, remaining clothed, being in public together. "We're going outside of Weston, so please back me up."

"Like a pickup truck," Riley teased. "I feel like I'm seventeen all over again. You're really good for my ego."

"Yeah." She smiled. "Well, I have a feeling I'm falling a

little, so if this doesn't work out, I might show up on your doorstep, brokenhearted and needy at three a.m."

"I'll have the vodka ready just in case. Oh, don't forget. I've got that hot little white backless number. Come by and get it. I can't wait to see you in it. Good luck, girlfriend, and remember, I have raked Weston clean, and there is no dirt on that man. None. Zip. You might have found the only man alive who can look like Superman and not remove his cape at every chance he gets."

Don't I know it.

REX HAD GROOMED the horses and put them out to pasture, then he'd taken care of the bills and placed orders for the next month, and finally, he was able to spend time with Hope. He didn't know why, but taking care of Hope eased the longing he had for Jade. He was grooming her when his father came down to the barn. Hope would never again have the sheen of younger horses, but to Rex, she was still a beautiful horse.

"Where's Treat today?" his father asked.

"He went into town to pick up some things for his office."

His father nodded, patted Hope.

"You know Hope's got plenty of years left on her, Dad. She could live another eight years or so." Every time his father looked at Hope lately, a sadness appeared in his eyes, and Rex felt as though his father was feeling in some ways that he was losing their mother all over again. She'd loved Hope so much that each of them was touched by that feeling of losing her all over again to some extent.

"I know it. I'm just thinking of other things," his father said.

"Earl Johnson?"

His father gave him a hard stare. Rex had wondered why he didn't just pay for whatever had caused the issues so many years ago. They had enough money to buy the land outright six times over, much less pay for subdividing and legal ·fees, and they didn't need the income from the property. He'd spent the entire night thinking about that damned piece of property and Jade's family. His father was a generous man. He gave willingly to several charities. He'd be the first to offer to help in most any situation, and yet, where Earl was concerned, it was like that side of him didn't exist.

Rex kept his eyes on Hope and his hands busy with the brush while he spoke. "Why didn't we ever just buy out the Johnsons, Dad? I've never really understood why you let things get so bad." The minute the words left his lips, he regretted his word choice. *Why you*…like it was all his father's fault.

"I'm a man of principle, son. And on principle, you stick to your word. I stuck to mine. He didn't stick to his. That's pretty damned easy to understand."

"But you said yourself that he was your friend. So what if he couldn't hold up his end of the bargain." His voice rose despite his efforts to restrain his emotions. He was fighting for Jade, but his father wouldn't see that—and he might not even care, given that she was a Johnson. "We have more money than God. Was it really worth throwing away a friendship based on principle?"

His father stood tall next to him, dropping his shoulders, expanding his chest to its full breadth, and looking down at Rex with angry, dark eyes.

"Son, there are some things that cannot be brushed aside." With that, his father stalked off.

Rex knew it wasn't going to be an easy situation to rectify, but now it appeared that *impossible* might not be a strong enough word to describe what he and Jade were facing.

Hal stopped short and turned to face Rex again. His face was pinched tight. Illuminated by the afternoon sun, he looked larger than life, and with the power he'd always held over them, which Rex was only just now realizing, he thought he might just be. He mumbled something under his breath that Rex could not make out, then finally spat, "Your mother's worried about you."

"Dad." This was the last thing he wanted to deal with right now. Delusion or not, every time Hal mentioned his mother to him, he relived the sadness of her loss all over again.

"Hear me out. I'm not on the same page as her this time, so I'm not going to tell you what she wants you to hear, and Lord knows she'll probably strike me down for not doing as she's asked, but a man's gotta stand by his decisions." He lifted his strong arm and pointed at Rex, lowering his head and deepening his stare. "You be careful where you tread, son."

Chapter Twenty-One

THE BRISK NIGHT couldn't have arrived soon enough for Rex. Between his father's comment and thoughts of Jade, he'd felt hamstrung all afternoon. He stood beside his truck, just off of the exit ramp, feeling a little scandalous. He'd gone over the options in his mind time and time again, and this was the only way for him and Jade to have a fighting chance. What he felt for Jade was so much bigger than *like*. She consumed his thoughts every second of the day. He wondered what she was doing, how she was, when he'd see her again. Minutes dragged by like hours and hours like days.

Treat and Max's relationship mirrored the pieces and flashes of the love he remembered seeing between his parents, and he never thought he was capable of feeling whatever those emotions were that made Treat want to rearrange his life just to be with Max, or that made his father keep his mother's voice alive for twenty-six years. And then came Jade.

Seven minutes felt like seven hours, and as it neared eight o'clock, he worried she might have changed her mind. Then, just as that worry was taking hold in the pit of his stomach, headlights from the exit shone across the side of his truck, and

Jade pulled in beside him. His cheeks stretched with a smile, and his heart bloomed in his chest. He opened her door, reminding himself that this was a proper date and not to attack her the moment he saw her.

Jade smiled, and her eyes danced with enthusiasm. "Hi," she said in a breathy voice.

He took her hand as she stepped from the car. Her scent and the feel of her hand in his was enough to send pulses of desire through his veins. She stood on her tiptoes and kissed him on the lips.

Aw, shit. Her tender lips, the gentle flick of her tongue, were like a dare. He wasn't an ice king, after all. He deepened the kiss, and she responded with a sweet moan, pressing her body against his. It was like torture to pull apart, but he forced himself to do just that.

"Good to see you, too," she said, slipping her finger in his belt loop and kissing him lightly on the lips again.

"Girl, you're playing a dangerous game." He heard the edge in his voice, like all his nerves were wrapped around the neediness in him.

She arched a brow. "Where to, my secret lover?"

God, could she be any sexier? He put his hand on the small of her back as they went to his truck, and his hand touched bare skin. He stole a furtive glance, then gritted his teeth against the swell of hunger that took him over when he saw all that bare flesh revealed by her backless dress. How in the hell would he keep from thinking about that all night?

BEING TRAPPED BESIDE Rex in the cab of his truck was nothing short of torturous. Her body was already reacting to the heat radiating from his body when they'd kissed. How was she going to make it through the evening?

"I hope you like music," he said.

"Love it." *Love it? That's all you've got?*

The mountain peaks disappeared into the night sky on the outskirts of Allure. Jade hadn't been there in months, and when he pulled into the parking lot of Bar None, a restaurant and bar known for being a little less touristy than others, she became a little more nervous. She'd been there years before with Riley, during a college break. They'd danced and sang karaoke and had a fun time, but it had been forever since she'd been on a real date.

Rex opened the door for her, and when they entered the dim restaurant, live music filtered through the air. They followed the hostess to a booth by the small stage, passing by a table of men gawking at Jade and making no effort to hide their eager eyes. Rex put his hand possessively around her.

This should be interesting.

After her experience with Kane, Jade knew that there was a possessive line that, if crossed, would send her running for the hills, and her eyes were open to it. *I'm a possessive bastard. I never knew I was, but the idea of you with anyone else kills me.* Rex had been honest with her, which was something to be appreciated, she supposed, but it occurred to her that she needed to know if she had another Kane on her hands. He had nearly punched that guy outside of the other bar, and while a protective nature was admirable, a stalker mind-set was anything but. As much as she hated herself for thinking about doing what she was about to do and probably ruining their first real date, she knew she didn't want to waste any of her life on someone who would end up driving her out of another town—no matter how many things she loved about him.

"Dance with me?" she asked.

The band was playing a song that was neither fast nor slow, which Jade knew would work to her advantage.

"I'm not much of a dancer, but sure," he said.

One bonus point for dancing.

On the dance floor, she felt very small next to him. His boots made him almost six and a half feet tall. She rested her head on his chest and closed her eyes. The buttons of his shirt jumped beneath her cheek with every beat of his heart. They moved in perfect unison. His fingertips grazed her bare back, and she almost decided to forgo her test to remain close. But it was something she needed to do. For a moment she wished Riley were there to tell her she was doing the right thing and give her the courage to do it. She conjured up her voice. *Better to know now than later. Just do a quick test, not an all-nighter.* She smiled and moved slowly from his grasp as the tempo kicked up a notch. Her hips swayed in an exaggerated fashion as she ran her hands seductively down his chest. She felt him stiffen beneath her touch, his eyes darting around the room and landing on the table of men, who were looking at her with wide eyes and lusty grins as they tossed quiet comments around like a basketball.

She almost abandoned her plan then and there as Rex's eyes narrowed. She worried about making a scene, but in the next beat, his body began to move just as stealthily as hers. He met her, move for seductive move, paying no attention to the men at the table, and before she knew it, all the women in the room were gawking at him. She quickly realized she'd been had. While she was scheming up her plan, he'd already been one step ahead of her.

By the time the song ended and they landed back at their booth, they were both laughing.

"That was so fun," she said. "I thought you weren't much of a dancer."

He shrugged. "I didn't say I couldn't dance, just that I wasn't much of a dancer. I've seen better."

His eyes never faltered from hers. Not one single glance at the table of men who were still ogling her, or at the women who were all but drooling over him. They ordered dinner and danced to another upbeat song.

Back at the table, they talked easily while they ate, and Jade had never felt so comfortable with a man. The first-date angst and her worry over his possessiveness was long gone.

"There's so much I want to know about you," he said.

"I'm afraid I'm not very exciting." His eyes were serious, and she realized that she wanted to know about him, too. "Have you ever not wanted to work on the ranch?" she asked.

"Never. Taking care of horses and working the ranch is all I've ever wanted to do. There's something very gratifying about breeding such beautiful, powerful creatures and knowing we can handpick the owners." He leaned back in the booth, and a dreamy look swept through his eyes. "My mother used to say that picking a horse's owner was as important as picking an adoptive parent for a child. When I was about six, she brought me down to the barn with her to groom one of the horses, and she said, 'Look into the eyes. Every person, and every horse, carries the souls of the ones before them. In those eyes, you'll see kindness or you'll see something else. When that other appears, don't try to look past it—just move on to the next buyer.'"

Jade had heard stories of her father breeding horses in the years before she and her brother were born, but she couldn't remember why he'd gotten out of that business and went to work for the agricultural engineering firm until he retired to run the ranch full-time.

"I think your mother and I would have gotten along very well," she said. "I feel the same way about animals and people." She remembered how he'd reacted when she'd talked about depression in horses, and it gave her pause.

"You actually remind me a lot of my mother—from what I can remember of her. Like right now, you look like you swallowed a bug, but you aren't even eating. Want to talk about it?"

Am I that transparent?

"My mother had this one uncomfortable look that I re-member, and she only pulled it out on very rare occasions, but when she did, you knew she was on the verge of confronting you about something you'd done—and in my case, I was usually guilty of ignoring my schoolwork in lieu of helping my father with the animals, or my brothers and I had broken something when we were wrestling."

He smiled, and Jade could see him enjoying the memories. She wished she would have known him as a friend when he was a boy. She had a feeling they would have gotten into all sorts of mischief, and she had to wonder, if they'd been friends, might they have developed into something more as teenagers?

"So, do you want to share what's behind that worried look?" he asked again.

Honesty has to come first. She swallowed the nerves that tried to steal her voice. "The other day by the feed store, I was asking you about Hope, and you made a comment."

He reached across the table and took her hand in his. "Jade, when you said that, the way you said it, the look in your eyes, it was all so reminiscent of my mom. Your eyes were so serious, and it sounded so natural for you to link animals with human feelings. I grew up with a dichotomy of beliefs between my mother and father, and after my mother died, all of my father's beliefs fell away. Suddenly he saw exactly what she had, and to this day, that has never changed. If anything, it deepened. Your beliefs, and the way you wore them on your sleeve for all to see, were so close to my mother's that it...it stunned me for a minute. And by the time I had regrouped, it was too late."

She searched his eyes for an element of deceit, a feigned reasoning, but what she saw was so much richer than anything she'd ever imagined: pure and simple honesty and regret. She knew she could trust him. No matter what they faced, he'd be honest and his actions would be pure. He had needed her touch as much as she needed to touch him. Her touch had more than its calming effect on him. What she learned was so much more than she'd imagined might be buried beneath that gruff exterior. Rex was a loving, passionate man whose honesty and love came in droves, cushioned with a tenderness that he saved for only those closest to him. She understood that now. Jade felt the moment sear into her memory, and she knew her heart had just crossed a defining moment in not only their relationship but also in her life.

Chapter Twenty-Two

REX WASN'T GOOD at keeping secrets, and he was even worse at lying to people's faces, but the closer he got to Jade, the more secrets and lies he saw in their future. She was so easy to be with, so right. Talking with her at dinner was every bit as natural as it was necessary. He'd never shared his thoughts about his mother and the lessons she'd taught him about animals and humans with anyone. Not even his siblings. With Jade, they didn't just fall from his lips; they jumped. He wanted her to be part of his past and part of his future, and he wished she could have known the soulful beauty of his mother.

Now, as they walked hand in hand through the Village in Allure, with the trees that lined the sidewalk sparkling with little lights—one of the romantic things Allure was known for—he knew he didn't want to continue hiding their relationship from their little Weston world. He also knew that it was ridiculous to think a solid foundation could be built on a handful of nights, so he tucked away the desire to share his joy with the people he loved until an appropriate amount of time had passed.

Jade pulled him up the stairs of an eclectic shop with a wooden sign above the door that read, JEWELS OF THE PAST.

He smiled, loving the feel of her excitement as it radiated through her hand. The little shop was chock-full of vintage clothing and jewelry, books, and other knickknacks. A woman in a long flowing dress called out to them from the back of the store. She had a mass of dark curls that tumbled down her back and a wide, pleasant smile. She lifted her hand in a wave, and the bangles that covered her wrist to elbow tinkled and clinked against one another.

"Welcome to a little piece of heaven," she said as she neared. "My, my, look at those eyes of yours," she said to Jade.

Jade blushed, and Rex's heart warmed.

The woman sidled up to them, looking at Rex for a beat longer than Jade. "What are you two lovers looking for today?"

"Whatever my girlfriend wants," he answered. God, he loved the way that sounded and the pride it evoked within him.

JADE SPUN AROUND. *Girlfriend? Girlfriend!* Gleaming like a fool, she laced her fingers into his.

"I'm not looking for anything in particular. We're just browsing," Jade said, smiling up at Rex. Her heart beat triple time, and the stupid smile on her lips refused to ease.

Rex laughed, and it was a sound that she hadn't heard often enough. His laugh was deep, loud, and joyous, like he'd finally let all those layers of tension go.

"Nonsense," the woman said. "Everyone is looking for something." She winked at Rex. "They just don't know it yet."

She crossed her right arm over her stomach and stroked her chin with her left hand, studying the two of them as they moved through the shop, touching items and pointing out the things they each loved.

Jade reached up and touched the wind chimes that hung from the ceiling, then snuggled in to Rex's side as their music rang out. He took her hand and dragged her to a glass cabinet full of jewelry, where he wrapped his arms around her waist from behind. She couldn't remember a time when she'd been happier.

"Look at the amber," he said to Jade, pointing at a necklace with a ragged-edged sliver of amber edged in silver.

"It's one of my favorites." Jade snuck a glance at the woman and whispered, "She's staring at you."

Rex looked, and his lips spread into a sexy grin. "What can I say? I'm a sexy monster," he teased.

She turned to him and touched his cheek. "Damn right you are."

"But I'm your sexy monster." He kissed the tip of her nose.

The woman's eyes grew wide, and she said, "Oh my goodness." She scurried toward them. Her finger shot up toward the ceiling as she passed. "I have just the thing. I'll be right back."

SHE HURRIED TOWARD the back of the shop and Jade giggled. She picked up a treasure box. "I had one of these when I was younger. I used to keep all of my most sacred treasures in it."

"You are my treasure." He pulled her close. "I wonder where she went," he said, looking toward the back of the shop. He was intrigued, not only by what the woman thought *just the thing* was, but also by the new feelings that had gripped him so strongly—the realization that Jade was *the one.* He felt like a switch had been flicked somewhere in his body, and the life he lived was no longer whole. It was no longer his to claim. Instead, as he thought about what he had to do the next day, his mind immediately included Jade, and he wanted to know what she was doing. He wanted to kiss her good morning and hold her as she fell asleep at night, and it had all happened in the space of the evening. The pieces were tumbling into place moment by precious moment, and he hadn't even seen it coming until just now. *When he knew.*

The woman burst through the curtain at the back of the store with her hand held high.

"Here it is!" she said. She stopped before them, carrying a little antique jewelry box. "Do you two lovers believe in fate?" she asked with a hopeful smile.

Jade and Rex exchanged a smile. "Yes," they said in unison.

"Me too. I knew a girl when I was in high school. I had lived in a little town outside of Weston then, and we were bused into the bigger schools, you see. Anyway, her name was Adriana, and she was the most beautiful little gal I'd ever seen. She gave me this, and she said that I would know who it was meant for. When I opened the store, I tucked it away with the rest of the little items I'd gathered over the years and forgot about it until now."

Rex couldn't breathe. This wasn't happening. The room began to spin, and his chest tightened. He released Jade's hand and latched on to a wooden bookcase that was off to his right.

"Oh goodness, are you okay?" the woman asked. She guided him to a velvet chair in the corner.

"Rex? What's wrong?" Jade asked.

Rex put his elbows on his knees and covered his face, trying to gain control of his breathing. Why the hell were tears welling in his eyes? Fuck! He wished he were anywhere but with Jade. She couldn't see him fall apart, and why the hell was he, anyway? What was wrong with him?

"I'll get him some water," the woman said as she rushed off.

Jade knelt before him. He felt her hands on his knees, heard the worry in her voice. "What is it? Do you need a doctor? What can I do?"

One of her hands moved to his back, and she rubbed gently up and down, soothing the raging panic that had engulfed him. He breathed in deeply and out slowly until he was sure he could handle whatever it was that was going on.

"Rex? Is it a panic attack?" she asked.

He shook his head, desperately wanting to speak but not trusting his voice. He clenched his fists and jaw repeatedly, until finally, his chest loosened and his breathing returned to near normal. He lowered his hands as the woman handed him a glass of water.

She locked her eyes with his. "This is how it happens," she said. Then she shook her head. "I'm just really out of practice. Had I known, I would have been more tactful."

"What are you talking about? What happens?" Jade asked.

Rex reached for her hand. He had a feeling that this time, he needed her strength.

The woman touched Rex's shoulder. "Dear, are you related to her?"

He nodded. "Her third son. I have four brothers and a sister." A lump lodged itself firmly in his throat, and the more he tried to swallow past it, the damper his eyes became.

She looked at Jade. "Sometimes I just get a sense of something, and I've learned to just sort of go with it. But this type of connection hasn't happened in so long that I didn't expect it, and I surely didn't completely connect it as a coherent thought until I saw him falter."

Jade rose to her feet. "I still don't understand."

The woman took her hand. "What I'm about to give you is from his mother, dear. It was meant for the two of you."

"But how?" Jade looked at Rex.

He pressed his thumb and forefinger against his eyes, wiping the tears from them. He blinked away the dampness. "I felt it. When we were walking outside, I knew. Something came over me, and there was no doubt in my mind what it was. Jade." He rose to his feet. "Remember when I told you that you were the woman I never knew I was looking for?" Before she could answer, he said, "It was true. When we were walking toward the store, I knew without a doubt that you were the one woman for me. I can't imagine going through each day without you." He took her hand in his, trying to bite back the rush of emotion. It was too soon to say the three words that he felt so strongly, but he looked into her eyes and he knew no amount of time would ever be enough. "I'm falling in love with you, Jade."

The woman smiled, and he watched Jade swallow…hard.

"It doesn't make sense. It's been only a few days, and it's crazy, especially given what's going on with our families. But I know it to be true, and I have no idea how to explain how I know, because it's as crazy as what just happened here."

Jade hadn't said a word, and he knew he'd blindsided her, but he wasn't going to lie to her, and not telling her how he truly felt was a lie. He had to trust his instincts.

Rex lifted his damp eyes to hers. "This is fast and really impetuous."

Jade laid her hand on his wrist, narrowing her eyes, looking at him so seriously that for a second he thought he might have acted too soon. In the next breath, she said, "And so right."

All the best moments of Rex's life crashed together in that moment, and they fell away, as if they'd never needed to exist, because that very second, when Jade became his, was the only best moment he would ever need.

He scooped her into his arms and kissed her with every bit of love he'd never felt before. Jade came away flushed and clung to him like she never wanted to let go.

He turned to the woman and held out his hand. "May I?"

She handed him the box, and touched his hand. "Adriana was a very special person."

"Thank you." He opened the box with shaking hands. Inside, there was a charm and two silver chains. He picked up the little charm and held it in his palm. The silver sparkled beneath the fluorescent lights.

"Do you know what that is?" the woman asked.

"It looks like two bodies intertwined," Jade said.

"It's the dance of two lovers," the woman and Rex said in unison.

She continued. "Everything in their lives was meant to keep them apart, and against all odds, they found their way to each other. When they did, they danced. The myth says that after dancing"—she took the charm from Rex's hand—"their souls became one, and from that moment on, they lived within each other, no matter if they were together or apart." She drew the charm apart and looped one silver chain through the charm of the naked woman and one through the charm of the man.

"That's the most beautiful thing I've ever heard," Jade said, just above a whisper.

Rex wrapped the chain with the man around Jade's neck and hooked it beneath her hair. Then Jade did the same for him. They stood that way for a long time, their eyes saying all the things that their voices were just not up to producing: *I love you. I've always loved you. I am yours.*

Chapter Twenty-Three

THEY WERE SILENT on the drive back toward Jade's car. A quiet contentment filled the space between them. Rex held her hand in his, and her other hand had held the charm against her chest since they'd left the store. Even if Jade hadn't believed that there was more to this world than met the eye, what just happened would have made her a believer. She waited for Rex to say something, not wanting to rush him. When they reached her car, he parked and turned toward her.

"I'm not ready to leave you yet," he said. "I swore I was going to behave on our first date, but, Jade, I need to be close to you. I want to be close to you. We don't have to do anything at all, but I want to hold you beside me."

Without any thought, she said, "I want that, too." Everything between them moved so quickly, but at the same time, it didn't scare her. It felt right; it felt real.

"You sure?" he asked.

"I've never been more sure of anything in my life."

He backed out and sped back to Allure, then pulled into the parking lot of the Allure Marriott. Every step toward the entrance made her heart beat faster. She had a fleeting thought about how she could manage to stay out all night without her father worrying. *God, I really have to move out of their house. Soon.*

"Your best suite, please?" Rex pulled out his wallet at the front desk.

"Sir? That would be our presidential suite, at the rate of twelve hundred and forty dollars a night," the slim young man with the pasty skin said in a disbelieving tone, one that clearly indicated that he expected Rex to change his mind.

"Perfect," Rex said.

"Twelve hundred and forty dollars a night? Rex, we don't need that." *Jesus, what is he doing?*

He touched her cheek, and she knew this was something he wanted to do, not to prove anything to her, but because he wanted to do it as a gift to them.

They came off the elevators on the top floor. At the end of the hall, a set of white double doors awaited them, complete with fresh roses in vases on either side.

"This is too much," Jade said.

"Nothing is too much." He ran the card through the electronic reader and the door clicked open.

Jade took a step toward the room, and in one swift move Rex swept her off her feet with one arm behind her knees and the other behind her neck. When she began to protest, he kissed her lips.

"Let me," he said with a teasing smile.

He carried her over the threshold, and she gasped at the sheer size of the room. The back wall was a sheet of glass, with views of Allure set against the backdrop of the mountains. Jade felt like she was floating above the beautiful little town.

Rex kissed her more deeply, then set her on her feet.

"Have you been here before?" she asked, then instantly wished she hadn't. "No, please, don't tell me. I want to believe this is just ours."

"It is just ours." He brushed her hair from her shoulders. "I've never taken another woman to a hotel. I've never ridden a roller coaster. I've never taken a bath with anyone else, and I've never woken up beside a woman without wanting to run. I look forward to so many firsts with you. Just you."

She swallowed the emotions that welled inside of her. "What about our families?" she asked.

"I'm not thinking past right here and now. I'll have you home before morning, and we'll still have to figure things out, but I want this. I want you. Even if it's only for a few hours. I want to remain in our private little world."

"Me too," was all she could manage. She wanted all those things just as badly, but she kept waiting for the other shoe to drop.

REX OPENED A bottle of wine that the front desk had sent up and turned down the lights. Seeing Jade on the oversized sofa, with her bare feet tucked beneath her, he'd never felt so much like he was in the exact right place at exactly the right time. There was a large-screen television mounted on the wall, and he laughed to himself. Talking with Jade was all he wanted. Beside the television was another set of double doors, which he assumed led to the bedroom.

He handed Jade a glass of wine and sat beside her. "I meant what I said. I don't need to fool around. I just want to spend time with you, and not in a car or a restaurant or a store. I wanted to relax with you beside me."

"This is wonderful," she said, but her voice was strained.

"What is it? Too much too fast?"

She smiled. "No. I need to let my parents know I'll be even later or they'll worry."

Her loyalty to her family struck a chord with him and made him love her even more. "Sure. Call them."

She smirked. "And tell them what? Um, hi, Dad. I'm at a hotel with Rex Braden, and I'll be back in the morning?"

He touched her leg, and his body instantly heated up. "Not exactly that. Where does he think you are tonight?"

"Out with Riley, in Preston visiting girlfriends." Her eyes lit up. "I'm so stupid." She called her father. "Hi, Dad. I'm going to stay over at Joanne's tonight. We're having too good of a time to break it up just yet. Okay. Yes, sure. Love you, too."

She came back around the couch and sat down. "That was way too easy. I feel so much better." She snuggled in beneath his arm. "It's crazy to think I'm a grown woman and I need to check in with my father."

"He loves you, Jade, and that's a good thing." He ran his hand through her hair, thinking about what his father had said to him. "You know, if you were Savannah, you'd have more trouble dealing with me, Treat, or Dane than our own father. He's protective, but we're the ones who always kept our eyes on her." He had an overwhelming urge to share with Jade—his life, his thoughts, his touch, his beliefs.

"I remember. You beat up Steve one time because of something he said about her."

"Yeah, and I'd do it again now if someone bothered her. Family knows no boundaries." *I'm breaking everything I believe in with Jade, but she feels like family to me—or like she should be family.*

"I love that about you. My father says that same thing—*family knows no boundaries.*"

"I thought my father made that up," Rex admitted.

"They were so close when they were younger. It probably came from one of their fathers. I know my father loves me, but he can have a heavy hand when it comes to his kids, and I guess I've been staying there because it's easy and safe."

"Safe from what?" he asked.

When she didn't answer, he moved a little closer to her.

"Safe from what?" he asked again.

She dropped her eyes. "Don't you know why I came back home?"

"I heard rumors, something about a breakup, but that was the extent of it." Now he wondered what would possibly have scared his strong, capable girlfriend. *Girlfriend. God, that feels good.*

"That's true. I did break up with my...the guy I was dating."

"And?" The muscles in his neck tensed.

"He turned out to be a bit of a stalker. He went nutty after we broke up, and he wouldn't stop calling and coming by my house. It just got to be too much. She shrugged. "So, I packed up and came home, where it was safe. He'd never follow me out of Oklahoma. He's not that brave."

Rex pulled her close again. "You must have been frightened."

"I wasn't at first, because I just thought he wasn't over me, you know. But then he'd show up at all hours, and when I went out, he'd be there, in a dark corner of the restaurant, waiting in the parking lot. It was pretty creepy."

His mind was running down all sorts of protective paths.

"I know that look. Listen, Superman." She splayed her hand on his chest. "You've already saved me once from the guy in the parking lot. There won't be a reason to save me again. Let's talk about something else. Tell me about your mom."

He touched the charm beneath his shirt. "My father says he still talks to her. Actually, he even argues with her. I'm not so sure he isn't really talking to her."

"He could be," she said. "I believe that those that are really, truly loved never leave us completely."

He kissed her head, chalking her belief up as just another thing to love about her. "You're just like my mom. My father told me today that she was worried about me. And then he said something to me that worried me a little."

"Dads always do that."

"He told me to be careful where I tread. I had the feeling he knew about us, but for the life of me, I can't figure out how he could." He took off his boots and set them beside the couch, then removed his belt and loosened his shirt.

"Striptease?" Jade asked with a flirty smile.

"Comfort," he answered, also with a flirty smile. He sat

beside her. "You've already stripped me bare and made me obey your commands." *Let me.* Just thinking about it gave him chills.

"You call that a command? Where have you been all my life?"

"Hiding from you, so I wouldn't have to live inside a cold shower."

"Oh, let me tell you something, Mr. Braden." She scooted up on her knees, running her fingers beneath the open buttons of his shirt, and touched his chest. "There are so many things I've wanted to do, but I've never trusted any man enough to do them."

Jesus. He shifted, trying to alleviate the pressure beneath his zipper. She planted soft kisses on his chest.

"Don't you have anything you've been dying to do with a woman?"

Hell yes. He could think of a million things. He told her what he felt was the most pressing. "Yes, wake up with you still in my arms."

"That's a given," she said.

He'd tried all night to keep himself from fulfilling his carnal urges, and now, smelling her, feeling her tender lips on his skin, he knew he wasn't going to last. He remembered the taste of her on his fingers in his truck, and he'd wanted to taste the rest of her ever since. He knew if they started, he wasn't going to be able to stop until he'd tasted every bit of her, touched her, probed her, and God knew what else. His appetite for Jade was insatiable.

"Anything?" she asked again, unbuttoning his jeans.

"I'm really trying to restrain myself here, to make sure you know that I love you for more than sex, and you are making it immensely difficult." He felt his biceps twitch as she unzipped his pants. "Jesus, Jade."

She unbuttoned the rest of his shirt and ran her tongue down his belly, then pulled down his boxers and licked the tender tip of his arousal. He groaned, and she teased him, putting just the tip in her mouth and then drawing it out again. She came back up his body and licked his lower lip.

"Is this your version of getting to know each other?" he asked.

"I can't help it if you drive me crazy. I want to talk with you, but I can't with all these raging hormones between us." She kissed his collarbone. "Anything?" she repeated.

In one swift move, he took her head in his hand and kissed her hard, until their teeth knocked and his tongue reached the back of her throat. When she moaned into his mouth, he slid from the couch and stripped off his jeans. She began taking off her dress, and he shook his head.

"Don't." The idea of taking her while she was still dressed so prettily made his blood simmer.

Fire shone in her eyes. She stood on the couch and reached for him. He couldn't control his need for another second. She pushed him to the edge—talking could wait. He picked her up with one arm and ripped her thong from her body with the other. He kissed her again, then backed her up against the wall.

"Take me," she said. "Yes, take me," she begged.

He put his hand beneath her dress, and her wetness was too big a temptation to turn away. He lifted her easily, and she wrapped her legs around his neck and he feasted on her. God, she was sweet. He probed her with his tongue as she dug her nails into his scalp, pulling him deeper. He eased his touch, licking her in long, slow strokes. His arms began to tremble, and he lowered her down the wall until her legs wrapped around his waist, and he thrust into her, deep and hard as she clawed his shoulders. He lowered his mouth to hers, still wet with the taste of her, expecting her to push him away. A new surge of need pushed through him as she sucked his tongue and drew every ounce of her own sweetness from his mouth. Jesus, she was every man's dream come true. He couldn't get enough of her against the wall. He had to have more, to go deeper. Still entwined, he carried her to the bedroom and stood above the bed.

She looked at him with hunger in her eyes as he lowered her to the edge of the bed and lifted her dress from her body.

"I just want to hold you and kiss you. I want to touch you and love you," he said. The feelings of wanting to cherish her competed with the desire to devour her, to flip her over and drive himself into her from behind. He looked down at her, and the desire to love her took over. His needs were pushed away.

She reached between her legs and began stroking herself, teasing him. He gritted his teeth. Her lasciviousness was beyond anything he could have imagined. She bent her neck back and began to moan, soft, like a purr, as her finger ran up and down her silken flesh. He dropped to his knees and licked between her legs. She pulled her finger away and he drew it back, licking along her slender finger as it touched and probed her beautiful flesh. He took her clit in his teeth and sucked until he felt her muscles tightening, then lapped beneath.

"Oh yes," she moaned.

He slid two fingers into her, and she writhed against him, raising her hips and wrapping her feet behind his back, pulling him deeper. He replaced his fingers with his thumb, just enough to dampen it, then teased her tightest orifice. Again she pulled him deeper, silently willing him on. He slid his thumb into the tight spot while at the same time he licked her sensitive folds, and seconds later she bucked beneath him, shuddering and tightening around the tip of his tongue. With her in mid-orgasm, he pulled away. She cried out for him, and he plunged himself into her center. Her orgasm heightened, pulsating so hard it drew the come right from his shaft, every deep thrust pulling more from him, sending his pulsating heat into overdrive. He couldn't stop the loud moans that shot from his lips. The pleasure was too immense, the need too greedy, as he rode their love to the crest. Until finally, achingly, their bodies began to descend from their peaks, and he lowered himself against her glorious body, kissing her slightly parted lips. Her eyes fluttered open, then closed. Her breasts rose and fell in time to each breath as he slid beside her, laced his fingers into hers, and closed his eyes. Content for the second time in forever.

Chapter Twenty-Four

SOMETIME DURING THE wee hours of the morning they made love again, and when Jade woke up, with the sun barely brightening the cloudy sky, she lay perfectly still, wrapped in Rex's embrace. She felt safe and warm, and as she closed her eyes, she had a momentary flash of embarrassment over the things they'd done the night before.

"No need for that embarrassment," Rex whispered in her ear.

She felt her face flush. "How could you possibly know?" She reached for the necklace lying against her breastbone and held the charm between her fingers.

"Your heartbeat sped up and your body went stiff."

She groaned.

"Nothing we do together will get to the Weston grapevine. I can swear that to you. I have never talked about my private life, and I don't intend to. What you do with it is up to you. I'm not embarrassed by any of it. I find you dangerously provocative and deliciously libidinous, and I might just be the luckiest man on earth to have all that in a woman that I'm crazy about."

She turned to face him. "I swear, you always know what to

say. It's like you studied how to say all the right things."

"Nope. I speak from my heart, and I was brought up to be honest and loyal. That's what I'll always be with you."

Her smile faded as she realized that their relationship would cause him to deny the things he believed in most when it came to his family. He must have noticed her facial features change, because he drew her eyes to his when he lifted her chin with his finger.

"We'll figure out the family stuff. Give it a little time. This isn't a race, and we are keeping this from them only until we figure out how best to handle it."

She nodded, knowing he was right, but sometimes doing what was best felt very wrong.

Rex leaned on his elbow and ran his finger along her jawline. "Tell me what you eat in the mornings. Are you a coffee fanatic? Do you have a morning routine? I don't want to get in your way."

"Ice water with lemon in the mornings with a bowl of fruit and Greek yogurt, usually, and when I'm feeling like a rebel, I add granola. How's that for a dullard?" She laughed.

He picked up the bedside telephone and requested everything she'd mentioned, including granola, egg whites and turkey sausage with toast for himself, and toothbrushes. He walked naked to the bathroom and returned a minute later with a thick robe for Jade. She could hardly pry her eyes from his gorgeous physique.

"And?" he asked.

"Oh, I don't really have much of a morning routine. Shower, brush my teeth, breakfast, and I usually just do some stretches. Sometimes I go for a run, but I haven't lately."

He sat on the side of the bed and smiled. "I'd like to run with you sometime."

"Yeah?" She thought about what it might be like to wake up with him and move through their days side by side. Kissing each other goodbye when they had to run errands or when she had to see clients, taking walks, going for a morning run. It all seemed so reasonable—until she remembered that he was a Braden and she a Johnson. She pushed the thoughts away.

"Wanna shower with me?" she asked.

"More than you could know, but I respect your space. I don't want you to get too sick of me too fast."

She slipped into the luxurious robe. "So getting sick of you slowly would be okay?" She kissed his chest.

"It's preferable to too quickly," he joked.

Jade took his hand and they went into the bathroom to-gether, then she turned on the warm water. Steam fogged the mirror, and she thought of how natural it felt to be with Rex. She'd never showered with a man before. The thought had crossed her mind more than once, but Kane was not a very prurient man, and her other boyfriends hadn't been the shower-together type. As they stepped beneath the warm water, she knew that moment had been saved for Rex.

"This is a first for me," she said.

"I was hoping to make your list," he teased.

"Oh, you already made my list of firsts in about five differ-ent places."

He lathered his hands and ran them over her shoulders, up her neck, and down her arms in slow, careful strokes. The familiar tug began down low and tickled her senses up through her chest. He ran his soapy hands over her breasts. She tried to keep her eyes from continually dropping back to the heated rod bobbing between them, but it was difficult to ignore.

She took the soap from him and took the length of him between both hands, mimicking his slow strokes, feeling him swell within her palms. He lowered his lips to hers and took her in a mercifully long kiss. The water rained down on them, wetting their lips and washing the soap from their bodies.

"I just can't get enough of you," he said as he lowered his mouth to her breast. Then his hand went to her wet curls and cupped her sex. "You're so wet already," he said, sending a shudder through her body. He pressed her against the tiled wall, and she gasped at the cold ceramic against her back as he probed her with his fingers and took her other breast into his mouth. Oh God, she was so close so fast. She felt her muscles tense around him and clenched her teeth, trying to hold out for just…a little…longer. When he moved his mouth to her neck and sucked like a high school boy, it sent her nerves into a titillating frenzy.

"Oh God. Oh God." She sucked in air between her teeth and curled her toes under. Steam filled the shower as she came around his hand again and again, and he moaned into the curve of her neck.

"God, I love it when you fall apart in my hands."

"Jesus, Rex." She panted as he slipped his fingers out and sucked her juices from them. She groaned. His dirtiness only made her want him more, and as he sank to his knees on the shower floor and pushed her legs apart, that was just what she was going to get. More. The minute his tongue touched her, she was already climbing that peak again. She clawed at the wall as she lifted to her toes, and her body pulsed again, tight and hard. In the next breath, his mouth was on hers, and he was inside of her, holding her against the wall with his weight alone, his hands caressing her breasts. She couldn't breathe. She was going to die right then and there from the sheer eroticism of it all. The water, the steam, his teeth on her neck.

"Come with me," he said as he pumped harder. With one hand, he held her under her thigh and wrapped the other beneath her, teasing her flesh as he pumped and thrust into her.

She closed her eyes and leaned back against the wall, squeezing her legs against his back as she came again. He swelled within her, sending her into another wave of shocks and pulses as he exploded inside of her, each thrust accompanied by a visceral groan, until, once again, they clung together beneath the water, satiated and whole.

Chapter Twenty-Five

WEDNESDAY MORNING ON the Braden ranch arrived under a cloud of worry and avoidance. Rex hated lying to anyone, much less his family, and when he arrived home Wednesday morning, after the glorious night with Jade, Treat was waiting for him at the kitchen table with a cocky ass grin and a shake of his head.

"What's that for?" Rex challenged him.

"You tell me," Treat answered, taking a sip of his coffee.

"Dad around?" Rex wasn't intent on dodging the question so much as finding out if his father was in earshot.

Treat nodded toward the barn. "He's with Hope. I'm worried about him. He's back to arguing with the wind."

"Mom."

"Right. He's back to arguing with Mom. I don't want him to end up in the hospital again." Treat handed Rex a to-go cup of coffee.

"Thanks." He sat at the table and wrapped his hands around the tall cup, staring at the table rather than his brother, concentrating on how to tell Treat what was going on.

"What's around your neck?"

He reached up and touched the necklace. *Damn it.* He'd forgotten to tuck it beneath his T-shirt. He did that now and let out a long breath.

"Dance of two lovers." He held Treat's wide-eyed gaze.

"How?" Treat drew his eyebrows together.

"Mom's favorite, right? How many times had she told us about her and Dad being created in the image of the lovers? I always thought it was a load of crap, you know, just a…a fantasy or whatever."

"Not following you here, Rex. So you went out and had that made?" Treat asked.

He shook his head. "I wish it were that simple. We went into Allure, into the Village, to a shop called Jewels of the Past."

"The one with that loony, albeit sweet, woman?" Treat asked with a smile.

"That's the one. Turns out she's not so loony. When she saw us, she said she had just the thing for us, and she came out with the necklace."

"So? She saw two lovers and made an assumption, grabbed a necklace. That might even make her more loony." Treat stretched his long, jeans-clad legs out to the side with a stretch.

"Dance of two lovers, Treat. Do you really think anyone other than our family knows about that? She said she got them from Mom. Well, she said Adriana, a girl she'd known in high school." He shook his head. "You gotta admit, there's something weird there. I mean, she had no clue who we were, and before I got there, man, all sorts of weird shit went on in my head." He ran his hand through his hair and felt his jaw begin to twitch.

"I gotta admit, that's a bit spooky. Good shit or bad shit?"

"Good, but it got me thinking about Dad talking to Mom. Before we got to the shop, as we were just walking along, not really talking or anything, I got this overwhelming feeling of…"

Treat's eyes flew open wide. "Shit. That happened to me, too, with Max. I know what you're going to say, that suddenly you felt like you loved her, that you knew that every second you were apart was going to kill you." He shot to his feet. "Damn, I never thought I'd see the day that my cold-ass brother fell in love."

"Shut up and sit down. Yes, it was all of those things. Damn it, Treat, what about all this Mom stuff? Is it a crock of shit or what? Are we fabricating what we think we need? What the hell? I'm so damned confused."

Treat sat back down, his legs bumping up and down. Rex wanted to take his brother's exuberance over his finally falling in love and toss it out the window until he figured all this stuff out.

"I never told you this, but when Dad had that heart episode, it was because of me. I put two and two together. He kept fighting with Mom, or whatever, whoever he talks to out there by the barn, and he made a few comments to me about Mom wanting me to fix things with Max and even give her the ring. So, who knows? Maybe we aren't giving Dad enough credit."

Rex stood and paced. "Great, so now our lives are being led by our dead mother? You know how strange that sounds, right?"

Treat shrugged. "I don't know what I believe, but I know Dad believes it, so what's the harm in letting him—unless it gets him so riled up that it lands him back in the hospital again."

Rex crossed his arms. "I think he knows about Jade. He said Mom wanted him to tell me something, but he wasn't going to do it. Instead, he pointed at me. You know how he does that death stare? He said, *You be careful where you tread, son,* in that voice that used to send us running for the hills."

Treat checked his watch. "We gotta get moving. The Tates are coming to pick up Brownie today."

"Shit, I forgot about that. I gotta finish grooming Hope for the show, too, but I can do that tomorrow."

Treat motioned to Rex's neck. "Keep that shit tucked away before Dad sees it, unless you want to start answering some god-awful questions. And don't forget, Josh and Savannah are arriving Thursday night to watch Hope in the show. I'm looking forward to seeing them. I miss them."

"You know, that's another thing. Hope probably has another eight years or so. Why does Dad act like she's failing fast? She could show for the next few years if he really wanted her to."

"I have no idea, but then again, I've never tried to figure him out. The man gives sound advice, though. He was right on target with Max."

Just as Rex's stomach took a nosedive thinking about his father warning him about Jade, Treat added, "But I'm not so sure he's right about you and Jade, if that's what he meant by watching where you tread. You've been in love with that girl for more years than I can remember."

Rex shook his head.

"Oh, bullshit. When you were a teenager, you'd practically drool over her when we'd see her around town. I thought that after I went to college you might have hooked up with her without Dad knowing." Treat searched Rex's eyes.

"I never would have done that to Dad," Rex admitted.

"So my baby brother's growing up?" Treat draped his arm around Rex's shoulder as they headed outside. "It's about damned time. One thing I've learned is that you can't control who your heart falls in love with, and once it does, there's no changing its mind. So you'd better figure out a way to dance that dance, or you're going to be one miserable dude for the rest of your life."

Chapter Twenty-Six

JADE RODE RUDY hard, working out all of her frustrations about her family, the feud with the Bradens, and her worry about her father selling off part of the ranch.

When she'd arrived home that morning, her parents had already left for town, but she'd found papers on the table from a local surveyor. A quick snoop revealed that the idea of selling off pieces of the ranch wasn't new. Some of the documents were dated as far back as five years. Had they always been hanging on by the skin of their teeth, or was he really trying to set things up so that her mother could stay in their home without worrying about taking care of the land if something should happen to him?

She rode along the tree line, her mind running in endless circles. She felt the charm beneath her shirt bouncing against her skin, and it brought a worried smile to her lips. After the night with Rex, her mind kept taking her down paths that led to a life with Rex, and she knew that was dangerous territory to hope for. He was protective, but not possessive, as she'd thought. The way he loved her was passionate and pure. From his touch to the love in his eyes, she knew she was anything but a cheap thrill for him. But what would it be like to *be* a Braden? Could she ever fit into their family without the feud hanging over her head? Were his brothers and sister as loyal to their father's ideals as he was? What was it like for Savannah to grow up with all those brothers watching out for her?

Steve and Jade had been close growing up, but he wasn't a protective brother in the sense that the Bradens were. The Bradens were all brawn and loyalty. Steve had always stayed out of Jade's private life, other than asking about a date here and there. She didn't love him any less for it, and it wasn't until now that she'd even thought of the way the Bradens took care of one another. She'd seen Rex's protective side when he'd knocked the snot out of Steve. All that childhood crush and adoration for the way Rex had protected his sister coalesced with the shame of liking a boy she knew she shouldn't, one who had hurt her brother. The conflicting emotions had poured out in the form of tears on the very same comforter she currently used every night.

She rounded the front paddock and slowed Rudy to a trot. Jade had a full afternoon ahead, and at some point she'd have to face her father. She just hoped he wouldn't see past her lie.

BERLE HANDLED HIS therapy well, and Jade was pleased that he seemed to be over all of the discomfort he'd been having. Now, if she could only do something for her own discomfort.

On the way back home, she stopped at the library to do a little research on the dance of two lovers—anything to delay seeing her father. The Weston Library was a historical stone building with two-story ceilings and cherry shelves that lined the walls of the large structure.

"Hey there, Jade. So great to see you. How's your mom?" Polly Wright asked from behind the desk by the door.

Jade had gone to school with Polly's daughter, Krista. Krista had gotten pregnant right after high school and had married the father, Tom Hardwick. Last Jade had heard, Krista had a house full of children and an unhappy marriage. She was careful to avoid that topic.

"She's doing great, thanks for asking. I just came in to use one of your computers."

Polly leaned over the desk and spoke in a hushed tone. "I'm really sorry to hear about your family's troubles. With the price of things these days, it's amazing any of us can stay afloat."

Jade tried to hide her surprise. *Does the whole town know?* If her father was just posturing with the whole financial demise aspect in order to create a safety zone for her mother as she grew older, then he was doing it at the expense of his own reputation. She didn't know what to think anymore. What if she'd chosen to believe the wrong explanation and they really were having financial troubles?

"We'll be fine. Thanks, Polly." She headed to the computers by the back window with her head down.

She did a quick library search on the dance of two lovers, and nothing came up. Not a book, a movie, or a myth of any kind. *How could both Rex and the woman from the shop know what the dance of two lovers meant?* As much as she wanted to avoid any further discussion about her father's decision, she needed some answers. Polly was on her computer when Jade approached the desk.

"I'm really sorry to bother you, but I'm looking for information on a myth, the dance of two lovers? Have you ever heard of it?"

Polly blinked without answering, then squinted like she was thinking. Finally, she said, "Why, that's one I've never heard of."

Great.

"Catherine, have you heard of the dance of two lovers?" Polly called into the office.

Catherine had been the head librarian forever. She had to be at least seventy-five years old by now. Her shaky voice called back, "I haven't heard that in forty years. Who's asking?"

"Jade Johnson."

She heard Catherine's chair scoot across the wood planks. Then her slow footsteps approached. Catherine was a tall, large woman. She filled the doorframe between the office and the large desk, one hand gripping the edge of the frame. Her gray hair had always been cropped into a short, layered style, and as Jade looked at her now, she noticed that nothing had changed. Catherine's sense of style remained constant: polyester slacks, jacket buttoned up to her neck, and flats that looked as tired as the wrinkles on her face.

"Jade Johnson." Catherine smiled, exposing her impeccably straight yellowish teeth. "I hear you're working wonders on the animals around here. It's good to have you back in town."

"Thank you. I'm glad to be home again," Jade said with a smile. She had many fond memories of afternoons spent in the library studying while other kids were out on dates or with their friends. Catherine had supported her efforts by bringing in veterinary articles she'd cropped from magazines and newspapers.

"What is this about the dance of two lovers?" Catherine's face grew serious; the lines around her mouth appeared more pronounced.

Without thinking, Jade reached up and touched the charm beneath her shirt. Careful among the eyes and ears of the library, she made up a story to back up her question. "I was in town the other day and heard someone say something about it. It was intriguing, so I thought I'd look it up."

Catherine's lips turned up into a curious, careful smile that did not reach her eyes. "Mm-hmm. Well, I doubt you'll find anything on the dance of two lovers in any book. You could go ask Hal Braden about it."

Polly snapped to attention. "Oh, no, no, Catherine. She couldn't do that."

Jade cringed at the truth of her situation.

"No, I guess you really can't, can you?" Catherine narrowed her eyes in a way that made Jade's nerves sting.

What the hell is going on? "Yeah, I can't really do that. It's not a big deal. Thanks anyway."

Jade hurried out the front door and into her car, where she rested her forehead on the steering wheel and closed her eyes, wishing she could talk to Rex. She hated the situation they were in, and as she drove home, that hatred grew. It was her own damned fault. What kind of educated woman runs home to Daddy when there's an issue? She could have relocated anywhere in the world. Why did she have to come back to the one place where she'd fall in love with the one man she knew she could never really be with—at least not publicly? Maybe she needed to take this horse by the reins and find another place to live—another state altogether. Someplace where her heart wouldn't break every time she thought of seeing Rex. Someplace where everyone didn't know everyone else's business. Someplace where she could stay up all night with a man and not feel guilty. The real problem was, the only man she wanted—she'd ever want—was Rex.

She stormed into the house and stomped up the stairs to her childhood bedroom, slamming the door behind her. She paced the small space as tears welled in her eyes. Jade fell across her bed and buried her face in her pillow, crying, much like she had when Rex had punched Steve when they were kids. *I'm such a loser!*

"Darlin'? Is something wrong?" her father asked from behind the closed door.

She bit back the urge to scream, *Go away! This is all your fault! If you were a* man *instead of a* child *none of this would be happening!* Instead she said, "I'm fine. Just tired. I'll be down later." *After you're asleep and I don't have to see your face.*

"Was everything okay with your girlfriends?" he asked.

She sighed. He was so good to her that it made it hard for her to capture the spears of anger and keep them alive.

Chapter Twenty-Seven

BY THURSDAY AFTERNOON, Rex was a nervous wreck. He hadn't had a chance to get a message to Jade the day before, and it had taken all of his willpower not to drive over to her house and confront her father. Thankfully, he'd listened to the sound of reason echoing in his head and had kept his cool. He'd gotten up early this morning and left a note in her car, but the whole situation sucked, and Treat was right. He had to find a way to make it work. Running from his feelings for Jade was not an option. He'd spent too many years denying any thoughts of her. He wasn't used to lying—especially to his family—which meant that, as far as he could see, he had one option. He had to find a way to convince his father to fix the feud, and he fully expected his efforts to fail, which put him right back to where he'd started: trimming Hope's muzzle whiskers, bridle path, ears, and fetlocks in preparation for the show, knowing there was no solution to the only issue he cared about.

"How long are you going to avoid me?"

Normally, his father's pat on his shoulder was reassuring. Now it made him feel rebellious.

"I'm not avoiding you. Just taking care of business." He felt his father's eyes watching him and clenched his jaw harder.

"Family's coming in tonight. You going to show up for dinner?"

"Don't I always?" Rex felt guilty, speaking to his father so harshly, but he was roiling inside, and he knew that if he gave his voice an inch of slack it would lash out in a way that he might not be able to recover from.

"We missed you the other night."

Rex closed his eyes, stifling the urge to say what he felt. *I was out with the woman I love. I didn't even know I could love a woman, but I do. Be happy for me. Fix your shit so we can be together.*

"Son, you can't avoid me forever, and you surely can't avoid yourself. Guilt is a terrible enemy. She'll eat you up and spit you out, then stomp on your writhing body until there's nothing left but a broken shell of a man."

Rex faced his father. He felt his nostrils flaring with anger, his hands fisting by his sides. "What are you saying, Dad? Just come out and say it. Don't play these stupid games with me, all right? I've got a lotta shit to take care of."

A slow smile spread across his father's lips. "I think you're the one who's playing games, son," he said in a calm voice. "You just gotta decide if the game you're playing is worth risking the reality you know."

What the fuck is that supposed to mean?

His father shook his head and headed for the lower paddock.

JADE NEEDED TO ride. She'd spent all afternoon with clients, the last of whom was a nasty man who treated his horse like crap. He yelled and tugged and generally showed no respect for the animal. It had taken all of Jade's willpower not to haul that horse back to her own barn and nurture it properly. All afternoon she'd craved the thundering beat of a galloping horse beneath her and the feel of the wind in her face as she crouched down low and let him carry her away. She saddled Flame, skipping his usual calming massage. He was feisty, but she didn't care. She wanted danger. She'd finally found a note in her car from Rex, and it appeared he was having the same trouble she was, which made thinking about moving away even harder. And she'd never expect Rex to move away with her, no matter what he might say he'd do. She ached to see him, to hold him, to be safe in his arms again.

She mounted Flame and trotted around the edge of the property. The sun was just beginning to set, making it difficult to see into the woods. She found herself searching for Rex even when she knew he wouldn't be there. When they reached the back of the property, the long stretch of pasture called out to both her and Flame. One light tap of her heel sent him cantering at a fast pace. She squeezed his muscular body between her thighs. She knew she shouldn't make Flame push too hard, even if his leg seemed fine. All she needed was a few minutes to relieve her mounting stress. She lifted her weight off the back of the horse and shortened the reins. Flame did the rest. In perfect balance, they bulleted forward in the evening light. Jade's heart slammed against her chest. The muscles in her lower back and legs tightened and pulled. Her long dark hair lifted from her back, whisking away her stress and worry with it.

When she no longer felt like she wanted to climb out of her own skin, she lowered her body down to Flame's back, and he slowed his pace.

She stroked his warm, thick neck. "You are such a good boy."

They were heading toward the woods that separated the Braden ranch from theirs, with the unoccupied land in between. Jade guided Flame down one of the narrow trails.

She heard the laughter before she reached the edge of the woods. Clear joy sifted through the air and drew her forward. She guided Flame toward the road, leaving the woods behind, the same way she had so many months ago when she'd come upon Rex and his family in the driveway.

They walked past the driveway, in the direction of the voices, and she brought Flame to a halt just above the barn, giving her a clear view of the family gathered around a long table. She counted three dark male heads and a woman who she assumed was Treat's girlfriend. Her heart kicked up a notch when Rex walked out of the house toward the table. She'd recognize his formidable gait anywhere. His dark brown Stetson made him appear even taller than she knew him to be. Oh, how she longed to be at that table. *No, not just* at *the table. I want to be* welcomed *to the table.*

She watched as Savannah stood and brushed her hair from her shoulder, then scooped something from a bowl and put it on the plate of whichever brother was beside her. Then she reached across the table and did the same for her father, but he knocked the ladle just as she was putting it on his plate, and the plate tumbled off the table. Jade bit her lower lip through her smile as Hal Braden shot to his feet, his hands out to his sides. All fell quiet, and just as quickly uproarious laughter filled the air. She picked out the cadence of Rex's hearty laugh, wrapped it up, and tucked it away next to her heart. Then, fearful of being seen, she guided Flame home.

SEEING HIS BROTHERS and sister was just what Rex needed—and just what he didn't. Anytime the Bradens were together, there was laughter and love, and tonight was no different, even without Dane and Hugh, who were unable to clear their schedules for the weekend.

"Josh, tell me what's going on in New York these days," his father said, slinging an arm over Savannah's shoulder.

"I've got a new fall line coming out, and so far the critics are loving it." Josh's brown eyes were smaller, more almond shaped than Rex's, and ever since he was a little boy, they'd told the story of his emotions. Now Rex saw delight as Josh spoke of his fall line. He ran his fingers through his closely shorn dark hair just above his ear, a mannerism as familiar to Rex as the silence Josh kept regarding the women he dated.

"I saw something about it in *People* mag. Someone wore one of your gowns to something," Savannah said. "Very impressive."

"Someone's always wearing something of mine," Josh teased. "Other than that, not much is going on."

"You seeing anyone special?" Josh never talked about the women he dated, and though his father would never push any of his children for information, he held Josh's gaze until Josh turned away.

"Nah, Dad." Josh slugged his beer and began to choke.

As Rex patted him on the back, he caught sight of Jade passing their driveway on Flame, and his chest squeezed tight, stealing the laughter right from his throat and replacing it with a longing so present it inhabited every inch of him.

Rex lowered himself to his chair across from Max and Treat. Max reached over and wiped the edge of Treat's mouth with a napkin, then kissed him on the lips. His father reached out and draped his arm across the back of Max's chair. The tug on Rex's heart spurred his jealousy. He narrowed his eyes, watching his father whisper something in Max's ear. He yearned for his father to accept Jade in the same way.

"Rex, hello?" Savannah tapped his arm.

"Sorry, what?" he asked.

"Ketchup, can you pass it, please?"

He handed her the ketchup while looking up toward the driveway again, feeling Jade's absence like a missing limb.

"Hey, what's that?" Savannah said, touching the chain around Rex's neck.

He swatted her hand away and rolled his shoulders forward. "Nothing."

"Oh, come on. Let me see. You never wear any jewelry. What is it?" Savannah was being her normal teasing self, and if she'd have done that two weeks ago, he'd be laughing right alongside her, tickling her ribs until she stopped badgering him. But tonight he was all kinds of stressed out.

Rex's biceps flexed, and he gritted his teeth. A hush swallowed the din of his family, and he felt five sets of eyes on him. "It's just something I bought in town," he said gruffly.

Savannah reached up again, and his father growled, "Savannah, leave the man alone."

She arched a brow. "O-kay then." She picked up her fork and stabbed a piece of broccoli.

Treat caught Rex's eyes and held them. Rex read his brother's message loud and clear: *Stupid shit. Are you trying to get caught?* At this point, he wasn't sure that wasn't exactly what he was doing. He pushed away from the table. "I'm going to get some water."

"Actually, that sounds good to me, too." Treat rose to his feet.

"Me too," Savannah chirped.

Josh was right behind Treat, leaving their father and Max alone at the table.

Rex stood in the kitchen against the counter, drinking a glass of water, one ankle crossed over the other. He watched them file in and knew he was in for an inquisition.

"Too bad Hugh and Dane couldn't make it. We could have had a full house," Rex said in a serious voice.

"Hugh had a race, and Dane got some lead on a major funding initiative for the whale sharks. Max'll keep Dad busy. She knows how this goes by now," Savannah said, winking at Treat. "So, what's the scoop? And what's around your thick neck?"

Rex shook his head.

Josh leaned against the fridge next to him. His black slacks were perfectly pressed, his white dress shirt pristine. He was narrower than all of his brothers, as lean and sleek as they were thick and rippled, and every bit as handsome. His dark hair was just as thick, though he kept his much shorter. As a fashion designer, Josh was more interested in his appearance than any of them. Treat used to rival him with his Armani suits, but now that he was spending more time back home, Rex noticed that Treat rarely broke out anything more formal than a pair of jeans or dress slacks.

"Anything I can do?" Josh asked.

Rex shook his head. "Not unless you can end a forty-year battle," he said honestly. It felt good to get it off his chest. What had his father said? *Guilt'll eat you up and spit you out, then stomp on your writhing body until there's nothing left but a broken shell of a man.* Rex wasn't about to let that happen.

"You mean the Johnsons? What's going on with them?" Josh asked.

Savannah grinned mischievously. "Josh!" she said in an excited whisper. "Jade!"

Rex lifted his eyes to his sister and couldn't keep a smile from his lips. He'd expected a modicum of support, but he'd also expected a rage about his breach of loyalty.

"Jade Johnson? She was eyeing you the day of Max's accident in the driveway." Understanding dawned in Josh's eyes, and he cracked a smile and elbowed his brother's ribs. "You dirty dog, you. Did you eat the forbidden fruit?"

You could say that. "Hey, let's keep it clean," Rex said. "Aren't you guys going to ream me out for going against Dad?"

"Ream you?" Savannah asked. "I've known you were in love with Jade since high school when I caught you staring at her during that 4H auction. Remember?"

He hadn't remembered until now, and now he couldn't believe he'd forgotten. Jade and her girlfriends were hosing down the animals in skimpy little bikini tops and cutoff jeans, and her father was standing guard with a scowl so deep, Rex thought he'd stab anyone who came near her.

"I do," he answered Savannah.

"How come I'm always the last to know these things?" Josh asked.

"You're not. Hugh and Dane will be," Treat said, leaning against the kitchen counter. "The question is, how do we convince the old man that this is okay?"

Savannah laughed. "You're on drugs if you think that's ever going to happen." She put her hand on Rex's arm. "Sorry, Rexy, but short of eloping and living several states away, I can't see how you can be together and live through it."

"You're a lot of help, Vanny," Treat said.

She reached into Rex's shirt for the chain, narrowing her eyes at him when he reached for her hand. "The cat's out of the bag now, so I'm looking whether you like it or not."

He watched his sister roll the little silver naked woman between her thumb and forefinger. Her smile lessened, and her eyes darkened.

"What is this? It reminds me of a story Treat used to tell me. Remember, Treat? You said the symbol was a naked woman and man twisted around each other. It looks like half of the dance of two lovers," she said with wonder.

Rex set down his water and wrapped his arms around his sister, feeling her heart beating against him, knowing she was missing her mother as much as the rest of them were at that moment.

"It is," he said softly.

"I thought it was a myth," she said.

"We all did," Treat said. "I used to tell you guys that story all the time, to keep Mom's memory alive, but I never really meted out the truth of it."

Savannah pulled away and tucked the charm back into Rex's shirt. "So, what does this mean? Where did you get it?"

Josh stared at his feet, and as Savannah moved away, Rex wrapped his arm around his shoulders and pulled him against his side. "You okay?"

"Yeah," Josh said quietly. "I don't think about Mom all the time. It's too hard. I always feel like she's right out of reach. I can't really see her face anymore, or hear her voice."

Rex bit back the well of sadness that was slowly filling his body. "I know. It's been a long time."

"Where did you get it?" Savannah asked.

"A woman in the Village in Allure. She knew Mom in school, and she said it was just the thing for me and Jade. I have no idea why or how. I'm just as baffled as you are."

"Fate," Savannah said. They all rolled their eyes. "Come on, Treat. You believe in fate. Look at you and Max."

"You have a point there," he said with a nod.

When Treat and Max were still trying to figure out if they

should be together or not, Treat disappeared, and Max went to Wellfleet, Massachusetts, his favorite place, hoping to see him. It was the first time he'd been there in more than a year, and that's when they finally came together. Max had never been a believer in fate either, and that weekend had changed her view completely.

"Wait. So you and Jade were together in Allure? How long have you been seeing her?" Josh asked. "How serious is this?"

Treat smirked, and Rex shot him a harsh glare. Treat knew that Jade and Rex had been together only a few times, and he also knew that Rex's heart already belonged to her.

Rex drew his brows together and lowered his chin, hoping Josh would understand his silent message: *Don't even think about questioning my sanity.* "We've only been together a few times."

"But he's loved her forever," Savannah said, sticking her finger on the edge of the chocolate cake she must have brought with her and licking the frosting from it.

"Rex, do you really think this is smart? I mean, a few times?" Josh asked.

Josh had never been very good at reading him. "It might not be smart, but it is happening." Rex pushed away from the fridge.

"I have to assume you know what you're doing, but…a few times? I mean, I go out with women a few times and know absolutely nothing about them. I can't tell you what we talked about, and I'm a good listener." Josh shook his head.

"Yeah, so have I. All I can tell you is that this is different. When I'm with Jade, I hear everything. It's like…" He reached for the right words, and the only thing that came even close was, "Everything else in the world falls away, and all that exists is me and Jade." He wasn't taking any chances with Josh. "One word of this to Dad and I'll personally rip you to shreds. Even you, Savannah."

"Oooh, I'm scared," she teased.

"We gotta get out there before Max feels left out," Treat said, heading for the door.

Rex was dying to be able to say something similar about Jade at their family dinner table. The idea of Jade being included in his family stewed within him. He envisioned her beside him, tossing snarky comments at his brothers and whispering with Savannah, like Max did. He touched the charm beneath his shirt and watched his family settle back around the table. "Mom, if this is from you, then I need a little guidance here," he whispered before heading back to the table.

AFTER DINNER, HAL took Rex aside. "You okay, son?"

His father seemed to have a sixth sense about his children. He always knew when their minds, or in some cases, their hearts, were tied in knots. It pained Rex not to be able to tell his father the truth.

"Yeah, just sidetracked with the horse show."

His father's eyes narrowed, and Rex watched him search his own. His stomach clenched, feeling as though his father could see right through his evasion. He had the urge to just spill it all, lay it out on the table, but he knew that would open up a can of worms that nobody was ready for.

If his father saw something in his eyes, he didn't let on. "If there's anything you want to tell me, I'm here. You know, your mother used to call you Rascally Rex."

Rex smiled at the memory. "I remember."

"I don't know what's going on, Rex, and I don't expect you to tell me, but you and I…" He put a hand on Rex's shoulder. "We've had our share of going head-to-head with the ranch. This feels different. I don't expect you to talk to me until you're ready, and your gut will tell you when that's right. Just know that I love you."

Rex had never doubted his father's love. Everything his father said rang true in his heart, momentarily curbing his anger about the feud and soothing the hurt he'd been carrying about the increasing rift between him and his father.

"Thanks, Dad. I love you, too."

His father pulled him into a warm hug, then headed down to the barn. Rex touched the necklace beneath his shirt and wondered if, just maybe, his mother had had a hand in that out-of-the-blue conversation.

REX AND THE others did the dishes and put away the leftovers.

Josh peered out the glass doors toward the barn. "I worry about him. He seems like he's all tied in knots again, like he was before he had that heart issue. He's usually much warmer, and he didn't say two words during dinner."

Treat and Rex exchanged a knowing look.

"He's fine. You know how Dad is. He goes through moods, like we all do. Right now he's dealing with something in that big old head of his." Rex knew his father wasn't fine. His comment about being careful where he tread, coupled with Rex's growing anger about the feuding families coming between him and the woman he loved, had caused a fissure between the two men, and the brief conversation they'd just had still had him reeling with conflicting emotions.

Ever since he'd been given the necklace, he found himself believing more and more that his father remained connected to his mother. Whether that made his father delusional or spiritual, he had no idea, but he wasn't there to judge him. He was trying his best to be there to love and support him, just as his father had done for him his whole life. He knew he was falling short as he questioned the value of his loyalty to his father against his loyalty to Jade.

"He was fine when you guys were in here passing secrets like children," Max said with a smile. She pulled the elastic band out of her long dark hair and rewrapped it, then helped Treat dry the dishes while Savannah put them away.

"Are you going to clue me in? I know I'm not a Braden yet, but almost…"

Treat dried his hands and pulled her close. "You're a Braden, whether we're married or not." He kissed her so tenderly that Rex had to turn away.

When they drew apart, Treat answered Max's question.

"Jade," he said.

"The dark-haired beauty from Fingers?" Max asked with a smile.

"Yup," Rex said, turning to face them.

"Yay! So you finally asked her out?"

"Something like that," he said. Rex wasn't really listening. He was biding his time until his father went to bed so he could go over to Jade's and see if he could catch her in the barn. He just needed to see her. The longer he waited, the more anxious he became. He grabbed his keys.

"I'm going to the store. I'll be back in an hour," he said.

"I'll go with you. I want to get—" Savannah lifted her eyes as she grabbed her purse and saw Rex's stare, the shake of his head. "Oh. The *store*. Got it. Have fun!"

He laughed on his way out the door. As he climbed into his truck, he heard his father's voice down by the barn, and guilt tightened around him again. He pushed it away and drove toward Jade's.

Chapter Twenty-Eight

JADE CALLED RILEY from the safety of her bedroom. She needed to share what she was feeling. Holding it in was making her feel like a balloon ready to pop.

"Hey, Ri," she said when Riley answered.

"Well, if it isn't Ms. Sneakaround. What's up?"

Jade sighed, her lips lifting to a smile. "That's what's up, actually. This is proving to be much harder than I thought it was going to be. Am I doing the right thing, sneaking around to see Rex?"

"You know, I never really pegged you for such a straitlaced worrywart. Since when do you worry about following your heart—or lips—or whatever it is that's drawing you toward Sexy Rexy?"

"See, I knew you'd make me smile." Jade lay back on her bed. "I care because of the crap between our families." She thought about what she'd said and knew there was more that she needed to get off her chest. "Ri, I love him, and this is so impossible. I mean, our families hate each other. It's not even realistic, right? Tell me I'm right, because I can't stop thinking about him, and I'm not sure I can stop myself from wanting to be with him, either. Tell me I should, make me turn away or something."

Riley sighed. "Girlfriend, you know that's not happening. You have fallen so hard for him. Hell, you fell for him too many years ago to count. You need to pull up your big-girl panties, suck up the sneaking around until you figure it out, and go with it. What kind of friend would I be if I let you turn away from the love of your life?"

Jade smiled and closed her eyes, knowing Riley was right and also realizing that Riley's response was exactly the reason why she'd needed to call her.

"Thanks, Ri. I'm just so tied in knots right now."

"I know you are, and that's okay. Somehow, some way, this will all untangle and you'll be stronger for it. I just know you will." Riley blew out a long breath. "I love ya, Jade, but sheesh, I need to charge you a therapy fee or something."

Jade laughed. "Do you charge by the minute? I'd better get off the phone."

After hanging up with Riley, Jade felt better, but she still had too much energy to relax. Her mother was sewing, and her father was practically asleep in his recliner in front of the television. Jade stole into the barn to spend a little time with Flame. She gave him a nice rubdown. Every stroke of his muscles beneath her hands reminded her of Rex, the way she'd kneaded and worked his muscles by the creek.

She'd just locked Flame's stall when she caught a flash of something by the back barn doors. She watched the doors for a minute, and when there was no more movement, she wrote it off to her nerves and went to close the doors for the night.

Out of habit, she glanced into the woods, nearly screaming when she saw Rex standing there. He broke through the trees and wrapped his arms around her, picking her right up off the ground in a deep and tender kiss.

"God, I've missed you," he said, nuzzling into her neck.

"I can't believe you're here," she said as he set her back down on the grass.

"I love when you smell like the barn." He kissed her neck.

"I'll have to roll around in the hay more often," she teased. "Come here." She dragged him around to the far side of the barn, where they were hidden from the house and the street.

"I couldn't wait until tomorrow at the horse show to see you," he said, running his hands up and down her bare arms.

"We're on gate patrol together," she said.

"Gate patrol, sounds hot," he joked. "Listen, Jade. I'm sorry to risk coming by, but I had to see you. I'm not sure I can do this," he said.

Her heart nearly stopped. "What?"

"Hide from everyone. Jade, I'm not giving you up either way. Whether they get over their feud or not, I'm with you. If you're with me," he said.

She watched him search her eyes. She took his cheeks between her hands and said, "It's the dance of two lovers, not one."

He lowered his mouth to hers, and she stood on her tiptoes to kiss him deeper. His hands wrapped around her waist and she pushed him back until he was leaning against the siding of the barn.

"Hey, I'm supposed to do that," he teased.

"I didn't know we had rules," she said between heated kisses. She put her hand between his legs and cupped him through his jeans.

"Jade," he whispered. "Your family is right inside."

She stroked him slow and hard, feeling him swell beneath his jeans. She couldn't help it. She hadn't planned to touch him, and now, when she thought about pulling away, she didn't want to. He pulled her closer, and she ground her hips into him.

"Jesus." He kissed her neck, sucking and licking, drawing her need closer and closer to the surface.

She licked her lips.

"You've gotta stop doing that," he said.

"Okay," she lied. She guided his hand down between her thighs.

"This is dangerous," he said with a coy smile.

"I know. Just for a minute. We won't do much."

"That's much," he said as he slid his finger under the edge of her shorts and found her wet and ready. "Mmm."

She kissed his lips lightly.

"I didn't come here for this," he said.

"You tell me that so often that I'm starting to get a complex," she said, her knees growing weak.

"Maybe you just want me for sex," he said with a grin.

They slid down against the barn. Jade lay on the grass, her arms locked around Rex's neck.

"I feel like I'm in tenth grade," he said.

"Good, then do what you might have done with me in tenth grade." Her father could come outside at any minute, and it only made what they were doing more exciting. She wiggled out of her shorts and tugged at his jeans.

"Jade, this is hardly not doing much," he said between kisses.

"I can't help it. I've gone thirty-one years without you. I don't want to waste a second of our time together. Besides, just look at you." She pulled him against her.

When he slid inside her, the illusion of driving away from Rex and living someplace else disappeared completely. This was the man she wanted to be with. This was the man she loved.

He moved in slow, deep strokes. "Am I hurting you?" he asked.

She shook her head and pulled him deeper into her. The air around them was still, broken only by the sounds of the horses milling in their stalls.

They heard the house door open, then close. Rex froze.

"Hurry," she whispered.

"Hurry? What if that's your father? We're in a compromising position here."

"Just do it," she said with a smile, then licked his lower lip.

"I've said it before, Jade Johnson, and I'll say it again. You're killing me." He pumped harder and faster, until each thrust was met with a groan and she was clenching her teeth and calling out his name.

"Shh," he warned.

She dug her fingers into the grass against her own quaking body.

They dressed quickly, kissing as she hopped on one foot to pull up her shorts.

Rex shushed her giggle.

"Whoever opened that door didn't come down to the barn. We're fine," she said.

"You just might be too much woman for me."

"What's that supposed to mean?" she asked.

He put his hands on her hips and kissed her. "How can I keep up with you?"

"You came to me, remember?" she teased.

He took her face between his hands. "I love you, Jade Johnson. I really, truly love you."

He loves me. Loves me! Jade's heart swelled as he kissed her again. When he released her, she was breathless—from his words as much as the kiss.

"I'm not a guy who goes around disrespecting other men. I'd never have done this, here," he said, his eyes dancing over hers.

"You just did."

"Yeah, because you reeled me into your devious world," he said.

She knew he was teasing, but she had no idea how to respond. Had he not wanted to do it? Had he not enjoyed it? What was he telling her? Instead of asking, she held her breath, contemplating how to respond.

"Don't get me wrong. I want to be in your devious world." He ran his hands beneath her hair at her temples and pulled it from her face, then held on tight, so her neck craned back and her chin tilted up. "I'm a thirty-four-year-old man you are turning into a seventeen-year-old bundle of hormones. I barely lived through those agonizing years. How am I going to live through this, with you so…?" He raked his eyes down her body. "Supple and frisky?"

She wiggled out of his grasp and snuggled into his chest. "I think you'll figure it out."

They sat in the grass, side by side, beneath the moonlight.

"I had dinner with my brothers and Savannah tonight, and all I could think about was how much I wanted you there," he said.

"I came by."

"I know. I saw you riding away on Flame. How's his leg?"

She loved that he remembered to ask about Flame, but she loved even more that he'd wanted her there with him when he was with his family.

"He's good. Better, actually."

"I told Josh and Savannah about us. Dane and Hugh weren't there, but I would have told them too, if they'd been there. I just haven't figured out how to tell my father."

Her breath caught in her throat. "You told them? I thought you told me not to tell anyone. You said—"

"I know what I said, but Treat already knew, and they're always there for me. I figured they'd ride me about not being loyal to the family a bit, but instead they supported me. They supported *us*."

Jade blinked away tears. She laced her hand into his and wondered what his family had said to him, if they thought he was crazy, falling for a Johnson.

"So, what now?" she asked.

"I don't know. I need to figure out a way to get through to my father about the feud, but I still don't really understand what happened. He's pretty tight-lipped about it all, so it's hard to decipher what really went on."

Rex leaned his arms on his knees, and she put her head against his side.

"All I know is that there was some kind of a deal that went bad, but I got the feeling that it didn't have to do with the land at all, that the land was just a product of whatever the other thing was. I can ask my mom, but I'm not sure my dad is being honest with her about things. He says he's downsizing so that if anything happens to him, she won't have as much land to look after, but she thinks they're doing it for financial reasons. I don't know what to believe."

He kissed the side of her forehead. "I'm sure we'll figure something out, and if we don't, then we have some decisions to make."

She pulled back from him. "What do you mean?"

"The way I see it, if we can't get past this with them, then we have to decide if we stay here in Weston and build a life together and hope they come around, or move out of town to escape their scrutiny." He shrugged.

Jade was at that point—hell, if she'd been more in tune with her heart and less dedicated to her studies, she would have realized it long ago about herself—but she hadn't been sure that Rex was thinking that far into their future.

"You're thinking about our future." She wasn't asking, just stating a fact.

"Shouldn't I be?"

"I don't want you to do anything to drive a wedge between yourself and your family, but selfishly, I don't want to live without you, either." She gathered her courage and told him the truth of what she'd been debating. "Before tonight, I was playing with the idea that maybe I should move away so you can live your life with your family without the weight of me around your neck. I have to find a place to live any—"

Rex shot to his feet. "You were going to leave? Just like that? Jade…"

The hurt in his voice was palpable.

She rose to her feet. "No, I wasn't going to leave just like that. I was just thinking through what was the smartest thing to do. I know how close you and your family are, and I don't want to be the one to ruin that for you."

He pulled her closer, searching her eyes with his. "The only way my life could be ruined would be if you weren't in it. But if you would be happier without me, I'm a big boy. I can understand not wanting to battle your family for a man."

"No," she said quickly. "That's not what I want at all. I want to be with you. I just hate the hiding, the lying, the inability to pick up the freaking phone and call you."

"I'll get a cell phone," he said. "Easy. I'll do it tomorrow before the horse show."

"You hate cell phones."

"So what? I'd hate losing you more. Now that I know what it feels like to love you, it would be like ripping my heart out and shredding it apart to lose you."

God, she loved how dramatic he was. Most guys hid their emotions so well, and from what she'd witnessed of Rex, he was good at presenting himself as a tough cowboy. But when he was with her, all those facades went down, and he became transparent, revealing his soft edges and tender undersides.

"You said the other day that maybe we're victims of circumstance. Do you really believe that?" she asked.

"Of course not. But I wasn't going to run home and profess our undying love after one night together."

"But you will after three?" she challenged him.

"I want a few days to figure out how to do this tactfully, and hopefully, to work toward our families selling that plot of land so your family doesn't lose theirs."

She shook her head. "You've been thinking about that?"

"Of course. It's your family." He looked at her like she'd lost her mind.

"But our fathers hate each other. It's one thing to want to be with me, but another to want to help save my father's land—after he's been so atrocious to your father all these years." Rex was really too good to be true. His loyalty ran deeper than she'd imagined. She felt the same way about his family, and she knew she'd do the same for him.

"You and I both were brought up to believe that family knows no boundaries. He's your father. That's all that matters."

Chapter Twenty-Nine

FRIDAY MORNING BEFORE the show, Rex headed into town to buy a cell phone. He'd made it thirty-four years without one, and he couldn't imagine what he'd do with it besides talk with Jade, but if that's what she needed, then he'd go along with it. Hell, he'd wear it around his neck if she needed him to.

The Sprint store was empty, as he'd expected. The horse show brought the entire community into town. The young guy behind the counter asked what he was looking for, and Rex was so technologically unaware that he told him that he had no clue.

"So, you've never had a cell phone before, I take it?" the short, lanky boy asked. He looked like he was in eighth grade, all pimples and uncomfortable in his own skin.

"Nope, sure haven't."

"Do you want an Android or an iPhone?"

"You're speaking Greek to me, kid. I really have no clue. I want a phone so my girlfriend can call me." He shrugged. How difficult could this be?

"Okay, do you have a budget?"

Rex laughed. "How much can a phone cost?"

The boy walked him over to a display of phones. "Let's see. I take it you don't have a phone plan yet, so you can get a good deal on a phone with a plan."

Phone plan? Rex was beginning to feel like he'd been living in a cave. The boy explained how phone plans worked, and he attempted to show him the difference between an Android phone and an iPhone. Rex tried to be patient, but when he began talking about windows and social media, things that Rex didn't give one hoot about, he gave up.

"Listen, all I want is a phone to make calls or send a message from. I'm a rancher. I can get onto a computer and order what I need to, but other than that, I have no interest. Can you find me the best phone for that?"

"O-kay." The boy looked at him like he *was* a caveman.

An hour and a half later, he walked out with a cell phone, a case to hook to his belt, Jade's and his family members' numbers programmed in, and a modicum of understanding about texting. He was a happy man. He strode to his truck and had just opened his door when he felt a tap on his shoulder and heard a woman's voice behind him.

"Rex Braden?"

Jade's mother, Jane Johnson, stood behind Rex with a serious, nervous look on her face.

Shit. He smiled and extended his hand. "Mrs. Johnson, it's nice to see you."

"I'm sure it's nerve-racking to see me, Rex."

"Yes, okay. That's fair." Rex's pulse sped up.

For a minute she just looked at him. She was an attractive woman with the same dark hair as Jade. The fire in her brown eyes had his nerves twitching.

"I'd like to talk to you."

He nodded, ready to take whatever she might want to give him. He wasn't going to hide how he felt about Jade. "That'd be nice," he said.

"Given our families' history, I don't think it's a good idea to talk here in the parking lot. Perhaps we can cross the street to the park?"

The park. Of course. It was open, safe. No one would think they were having an unpleasant discussion. This was Weston after all. The last thing that either of them needed was to start the grapevine ringing.

"Yes, ma'am." He closed his truck door. "Is Jade all right?"

"I think you'd know better than I," she said.

He swallowed the shock of surprise that ran through him. If she knew, what did her husband know? And if her husband knew, what was Jade being put through right then?

They went into the park and sat on a bench that looked over a small pond. He noticed that she sat a good distance from him. To a bystander, they might look like they'd just happened to share the bench.

"What are your intentions with Jade?" she asked.

He needed to know what she knew before he gave away their entire relationship. Maybe she was just fishing for information. "Ma'am? I'm sorry, my intentions?"

She pursed her lips. "Rex, come now. Jade doesn't stay out all night with girlfriends. She doesn't come home at two a.m. after swimming in the creek alone, and she sure as heck doesn't make those kind of noises behind the barn without a man involved."

He kept his voice calm despite his thundering heart. "I'm sorry, Mrs. Johnson. Our intent was never to hurt anyone, and we surely didn't know...Well...to answer your question, I love her. I love your daughter." He felt as though an enormous weight had been lifted from his shoulders. He turned to face her then, and the pain he saw in her eyes tore at his heart.

She nodded, rolling her lips into her mouth. He could see she was holding back tears.

"I'm really not a bad guy. I would never treat Jade badly or hurt her in any way." His explanation did nothing to ease her pain. A tear dripped from the corner of her eye.

"I'm not sure what else you want to know. I'm sorry we didn't tell you right away, but given the situation between our families, we just didn't see how we could. We're trying to figure out the best approach, but I guess that doesn't matter now."

She put her delicate hand on top of his, and with a trembling voice, she said, "My husband doesn't know, and I don't advise you to tell him right now."

"Ma'am?"

"Jade doesn't know that I know either."

"I don't understand. Why did you come to me instead of Jade?"

A half smile graced her lips. "I'm her mother. I had to know if you loved her, or if you were just, you know, having fun."

"Ma'am, I'm not a having-fun type of guy."

She nodded. "I know, Rex. I've known you since you were an infant, and I've watched you grow into a fine, strong gentleman. All of you Braden boys have kept your noses clean.

And Savannah, what a doll she's grown up to be."

"I thought—"

"The feud has always been between your father and my husband. Your mother and I never let on that we remained friends. Rex, your mother and I had always hoped our families would remain close. When that fight first started between them, we thought it would just blow over. But when you put two stubborn, competitive men in a cage, someone has to win." She drew in a deep breath, then blew it out slowly. "It might not be good timing, but I couldn't have asked for a nicer man for Jade."

He took her hand in his. "Thank you. That means a lot to me." He released her hand and thought about what she'd said. "How did you and my mother remain connected? I'm not sure what your husband is like, but my father wouldn't allow the Johnson name in our home. No offense, of course, and if it helps to know, my siblings are very accepting of Jade."

"I had no doubt they would be. Your parents raised you right, even Hal. He's a good man. Earl's a good man, too. They just got a little lost and they've never found their way out of the woods." She folded her hands in her lap and let out a slow breath. "Your mom and I used to meet for picnics on the property between yours and ours, sometimes down at the ravine, when the men were out, of course. Oh, we were master schedule manipulators. Somehow Earl would have a dental appointment when Hal was picking up feed, or your mom would conveniently be too tired to run an errand at the same time that my kids needed to go to an event somewhere. We found ways." She wiped her eyes. "As you kids got older, it became more difficult, of course, so mainly we talked on the phone and occasionally met while you kids were at school. Even that became difficult. There were so many of you, and babies eventually learned to talk." She smiled. "I miss her, more than you can know."

"And you've had to mourn her in silence." Now he understood where Jade got her strength and courage. The woman before him risked everything for a friendship with his mother, and today she risked it all for her daughter.

"Mrs. Johnson, can you tell me anything that might help us bring this feud to an end? I want nothing more than to be with Jade out in the open. I want to build a life with her, and I want to make her proud. And I'm very sorry about being close to your daughter behind the barn. We got a little carried away."

"I'd say," she said with a grin. "You'll have to speak with your father about what went on between him and Earl. I believe your father was fighting for your mother's honor, but that's all I can say about that. Just know, Rex, when all this comes out, I'll be standing behind you and Jade, and so will your mother."

Chapter Thirty

JADE DIDN'T CONSIDER herself a jealous person, but watching every woman between the ages of eighteen and forty-five ogle her boyfriend was starting to rouse the green-eyed monster. He was so damned nice to them all, too. He smiled that killer smile of his, and when he ran his hand through his hair—just one of his habits Jade had come to love—it made her warm all over. Surely it had the same effect on other women.

The horse show was in full swing. The loudspeaker chimed, announcing the children's halter classes. Smells of barbeque, popcorn, and hay flittered through the air. Children wearing their cutest Western shirts, boots, and show pants giggled as they ran toward the small petting area, while mothers trailed behind with shouts to stay out of the dirt. Jade loved the feel of community horse shows. Somehow, the dress pants and hats amped up the women's sexiness, prompting them to swing their hips a little wider and throw their shoulders back, all dolled up and feeling special. The men looked so handsome in their best Western wear. She especially loved the vests that many of the men wore, and the string ties and bandannas were an added flair. But the sexiest thing Jade had seen, and what she couldn't help but envision Rex in, were leather chaps. She looked at him now, handing a ticket to a heavyset man in a gray Chevy truck, and she imagined his bare chest easing down to that dip below his hips that she loved to touch—the one that drew an instant shiver from him—and soft, worn leather covering his—

A honk pulled her from her fantasy.

"Sorry," she said quickly, taking the woman's money and waving her on to Rex.

Twenty minutes later, there was a lull in the incoming traffic. Rex looked over and blew her a kiss. She snagged it from the air and slapped it on her cheek with a grin. They sauntered toward each other. She could tell he was taunting her as much as she was him.

"How's the prettiest girl in all of Weston?" he asked.

"I don't know, there were some pretty hot women strolling by you." She hated herself for saying it aloud, but she was powerless to stop it.

"Really? Huh, I didn't notice. I'll pay better attention next time."

She punched his arm, and he started to pull her into a kiss. Her heart roared to life. Then he looked around, and with a disappointing frown, he released her and took a step back, leaving her wanting him even more.

"I have eyes for only one woman. You're pretty well stuck with me, so get used to it. Women can look all they want, just like the men who have been eyeing you all day. None of it matters. It just makes me proud to be with you."

"There you go again, Mr. Smooth."

"I'll show you Mr. Smooth." He stepped closer, narrowing

his dark eyes and looking as if he might take her right there and then.

She could feel the heat of him; every breath ratcheted up her pulse a little more.

"I need to check on Hope when things slow down more," he said. "She wasn't herself this morning."

She wasn't sure if he was saying he had to check on Hope to dissipate the rising sexual tension, or because something was really going on with Hope. She erred on the side of caution. "Is there something I can do? Maybe I should check her out?" Jade knew she couldn't check on Hope. Rex's father would never allow it. He'd have to call Dr. Baker. Her mind switched to veterinarian mode, and instead of thinking of the pulse of Rex's heart, her mind was wrapped around Hope's health.

"Dad thinks she was just a little out of sorts. I'll check her out and let you know if she's doing any better." His face grew serious and he reached for her hand, then drew back again. "Everything okay at home?"

"Yeah, no one said anything, if that's what you mean." She hated their inability to touch in public. Rex was a salacious person, comfortable and demonstrative in his love. It was one of the things she loved most about him. Every time he pulled back from her, her anger at their families multiplied.

"Good," he said.

Jade noticed that he had a sharp edge to him, and she wondered what he wasn't telling her. Another grouping of cars came through the gate, and Jade took their money while Rex handed out tickets, but she couldn't stop worrying about Hope. A horse's health could go downhill fairly quickly if they were dealing with something serious. When the cars slowed, she asked Rex to go check on Hope.

REX HURRIED TOWARD the ring, where he saw his father having a hell of a time walking Hope, while Hannah, wearing an adorable pink Western shirt with black and white embellishments and black jeans, her blond curls surrounding her fair cheeks beneath her felt hat, watched on.

"How're you doing, Hannah?" Rex asked with a smile.

"I'm fine, but I'm not so sure about Hope. She keeps pacing and pawing, like she's really nervous." Hannah still had the soft, innocent face of a child, and the makeup she'd worn for the show made her look a little like a Kewpie doll.

Rex saw a strain on his father's face as Hope arched her neck back, like she was looking for something. His boots thudded against the dirt with each determined step toward his father.

"What are you thinking? Colic?" Rex asked.

"She's got plenty of gut sounds, but let's get the vet over here and have her checked out." His father looked sadly at Hannah. "Son, tell Hannah we're going to have Hope checked out. The poor girl. She's been looking forward to this for so long."

"I'll tell her, and track down Dr. Baker."

By the time Rex reached Hannah, she'd figured things out on her own.

"She's not doing well, huh?" she asked in a disappointed

tone.

"We don't really know. She might just be nervous. I'm going to get the vet and have her checked out. Do you think you can hold on a bit? Maybe notify the judges for us and ask her to be called up last?" Rex knew just how difficult it was for kids not to be able to lead a horse after practicing and getting all psyched up to be in front of a crowd. He watched her head toward the judges, and for the first time ever, the thought of having his own children rolled through his mind. He asked himself what he would do if Hannah were his daughter. He didn't have an answer, but it was another first for him to even have such a thought, and he chalked it up to Jade.

Rex's stomach rumbled as he passed the concession stands and headed for the house to call Dr. Baker, the town veterinarian. Then he remembered that he had his cell phone hooked to his belt.

Rex broke clear of the crowds and called information. He stole a glance at Jade, leaning down by a car at the gated entrance to his left. As he dialed Dr. Baker's office number, he wished he could ask Jade to examine Hope. This whole mess with his father was like an octopus, and the deeper he fell for Jade, the more he felt the tentacles of the feud strangling them.

Twenty minutes later, Dr. Baker was examining Hope.

"What's going on with Hope?" Savannah sidled up next to Rex with a big pink fluff of cotton candy.

"That's what we're trying to find out," Rex answered.

Josh appeared beside Savannah. "Did you guys see how proud Hannah's little brother was when he won his halter class? Remember that feeling?"

"I remember feeling like a girl in my outfit," Treat said as he tugged a piece of cotton candy from Savannah, ignoring her smirk.

"You did not. You begged me for a new vest and hat. You thought you were John Wayne," his father said.

"Dad, really? You want to kill my image?" Treat teased.

"Your image is still pretty hot, if you ask me," Max said. "I'm sorry Hope isn't feeling well. I heard you down at the barn this morning, Hal. You seemed upset. Was she sick then?"

Rex shot a glance at Treat.

"No, she seemed fine, just didn't eat much. I was just mumbling to myself," he said, but his children knew the truth. He was no more mumbling to himself than Treat hadn't loved his cowboy costume.

"Well, her temperature is fine," Dr. Baker said. "I'm not hearing anything concerning in her gut sounds, but her pulse is slightly elevated, and given her behavior, with the pawing, the way she's watching her flank, I'm concerned that we might be looking at a mild case of colic." Dr. Baker had been the Weston veterinarian for the past forty-five years. Rex appreciated his calm demeanor. His careful nature had always led to solid treatment results as far as their horses were concerned. He trusted the pasty-skinned, bald-headed man's judgment completely. A pang of sorrow passed through him at the realization that Jade couldn't have looked over Hope instead.

"She's not showing today, Rex," his father said. "We need to break the news to Hannah." Hal took off his hat and held it against his chest as he stroked Hope's side.

"I'll do it after Dr. Baker's through talking," Rex offered.

"Now, Hal, you've been moping about Hope for half a year or more. You're a bright man. You know she's got plenty of years left in her, so why are you looking so gloomy?" Dr. Baker had never minced words with Hal before, and Rex was glad to see him asking what everyone was wondering.

"Maybe she does, but maybe she doesn't." His father set his hat back on his head with a firm nod, indicating that he was not going to go down that line of questioning with Dr. Baker.

"So what's the plan, Doc?" Treat asked, taking the attention off of his father.

"Well, given that she's never been a colicky girl before, I want you to keep a close eye on her." He scratched his head. "You said she hasn't been eating well, so I'm going to give her a shot of Banamine to try to alleviate any discomfort she's feeling. I'd take her home. Let's keep an eye on her. No food or water. You know the drill."

"Yes, sir, we'll keep a close eye on her," Rex said.

After Dr. Baker left, Hal and Josh headed home with Hope. Max, Treat, and Savannah were going to stick around the show for a while and enjoy the afternoon, and Rex had to remain until four o'clock to tend the gate.

Rex approached Hannah with a heavy heart. He hated to let her down after she'd worked so hard to prepare to show Hope.

"Hannah, Hope isn't doing very well. We're going to have to take her home." Rex watched her swallow hard.

"That's okay. I hope she feels better." She tried to smile, but fell short.

Rex watched her walk away with her head hung low, and he ached for her, but he couldn't get too caught up in that now.

He had to get back to the gate.

JADE WATCHED MR. BRADEN'S truck and trailer drive off of the show grounds, and she knew something was wrong with Hope.

"What happened?" she asked as soon as Rex appeared.

"He thinks she has a mild case of colic. He gave her Banamine, and Dad's taking her home."

"Banamine will help, but how mild? What was her temperature? How about her pulse?" Jade had nothing but respect for Dr. Baker, but he didn't work with, or necessarily believe in, massage the way she did.

Rex filled her in on the particulars and eased Jade's mind. Dr. Baker had taken the right course of action—but still, she knew how much good a hands-on approach could be for horses.

"I'd love to get my hands on Hope," Jade said. "I can do massage to ease her discomfort."

Rex reached out and touched her cheek. "That's what I love about you. You're so caring." He moved in closer, and Jade shot a look to their left, then right.

"Sorry." Rex took a step back. "I hate this."

"Have you come up with any ideas on how to handle all of this? I think, given Hope's health, that we shouldn't push things right now. If your father's upset, he's not going to be receptive to something like us." She tried to smile, but her heart broke just a little at the thought of waiting even longer to be able to touch him in public. She didn't really believe that they could do anything to change the situation, but she was more than willing to try.

"Hey there, girlfriend!" Riley came up from behind Jade and hugged her. "Sexy Rexy," she teased.

Rex arched a brow, and Jade cringed.

"Sorry," Jade said to Rex. Then she turned back to Riley. "I thought you were coming with that guy from the tack store. Where is he?"

Riley tucked her hair behind her ear and rolled her eyes. "The guy's a loser. All he wanted to do was get me into the sack." She smiled at Rex. "Sorry, girls are crude, I know, but it's true. Why do all men just want one thing?"

"I can listen to you call me silly—and maybe true—names." Rex looked serious, but Jade could tell he was fighting to hide a smile. "And I can even understand when you have a hard time with the way a guy treats you, but please don't lump us all together. Not all of us are that way."

"Yeah, well, you're already spoken for." She winked at Jade.

"So you ditched him?" Jade asked.

"Yeah, I didn't want to waste a day on him. One day, I swear I'm going to meet a nice guy who isn't so caught up in sex that he can't see me for the great gal that I am." Riley put her arm around Jade. "Right? Tell me I'm right, please. Just lie to me."

Jade laughed, a little embarrassed that Rex was witnessing them at their most comfortable, and private, interaction.

"You know it, babe," Jade said, planting a kiss on her friend's cheek.

"What are you doing these days, Riley? Didn't you study fashion? What are you doing back here?" Rex asked.

Riley groaned. "Do you have any idea what it's like to break into the fashion industry? It's harder than finding a worthy date."

Jade liked that Rex was taking an interest in her friend, and she imagined what it might be like to have joint friends. They had so much to look forward to—she was afraid to think that far ahead.

"Did you do well in school?" Rex crossed his arm, studying her with a serious gaze.

"Are you kidding? I graduated with a three-eight GPA and won two design awards while I was there," she said with pride.

"The field is really competitive," Jade added.

"It's really more who you know than what you can do, and coming from Weston, Colorado, knowing ranchers and horse breeders didn't carry much weight in the fashion industry. So, here I am. I've been working at Macy's doing menial work for menial pay, good discounts, you know. In other words, I'm doing all the things I could have done without a college education." Riley pulled her arm from around Jade's neck. "I know I'm not destined for greatness," she said.

"She's an amazingly talented designer," Jade added. "Remember the white dress I wore on our date?" She saw the dirty memory pass through Rex's narrowing, appreciative eyes. "Riley made it. She designed it and made it."

"That was a killer dress," Rex said with mischievous smile.

"Nah," Riley said with a wave of her hand. "That's not my best work. I have tons of designs that I haven't had time to make, but I have them all laid out. They're not really Weston Western wear, so..." She shrugged.

"I don't know if it will help or not, but my brother Josh is a designer. Why don't you give me your portfolio and I'll get it to him. He might have some suggestions."

Jade wanted to jump into his arms and thank him, but she didn't dare.

Riley, however, did. She jumped right up and kissed his cheek. "Are you kidding? Even if he doesn't like them, which he probably won't, he might have ideas of what I can change and what I need to work on. I know Josh from school. He was always nice to everyone, and everyone in Weston knows he's only about the best designer ever. Gosh, I haven't seen him in years. I'd give anything for more direction, but my parents and I kind of ran out of funding for extra stuff."

Riley was beaming, and Jade felt her chest swell with pride that Rex would even think to offer a hand to Riley. Even if Josh hated her stuff, Rex had still tried, and to Jade that meant more than any job ever would.

"Are you guys going to the concert tonight?" Riley asked.

Jade shot a look at Rex, knowing that his family was in town and they'd be worried about Hope.

"Jade?" he asked.

He always seemed to think of her first, which was just another reason Jade had fallen so hard for her sexy cowboy.

"I'd love to go, but I know you have family to tend to, and it's not like we can go together anyway." His jaw began its clenching dance—confirmation that he hated the deception as much as she did.

He stepped closer to Jade and softened his voice. "I'll check and see what my family's doing, but I'll be there one way or another. Call me and let me know when you're going."

Riley shook her head. "I get why you guys have to do this secretive relationship thing, but can I just tell you that anyone who would stand in your way is out of their minds. I mean, just look at you two. It's like you were made for each other. He looks at you like you are the very oxygen that allows him to breathe, and she looks at you like all googly-eyed, like you're Brad Pitt or something. And you both look like you're ready to pounce on each other."

"Riley!" Jade gasped.

"The girl's got a good eye," Rex teased.

Chapter Thirty-One

REX'S PHONE RANG at seven fifteen, after he and his family had finished dinner. He was surprised at the surge of adrenaline that ran through him. He hadn't been excited about a phone call for as long as he could remember, and as he spoke softly into the tiny, strangely shaped phone, he was glad to hear Jade's voice.

"Hey, babe," he said.

"Hi. How's Hope?" Jade asked.

Her voice was so sweet and she was asking in such a tentative fashion that he had to sit down on the grass and just drink it in. "She's not herself, that's for sure. Dad's going to stay with her." He and the others had discussed staying around in case his father needed help with Hope, but his father had waved them away. *I've been taking care of horses all my life. Go to your silly concert. Have some fun.*

"Is she lying down? Because you can't let her y—"

"Jade." He smiled at her caring nature. "Dad's been breeding horses since he was a kid. He knows what to do."

"Right. I'm sorry," she said. "So, you're coming tonight?"

Why does that word coming from those lips get me hard? "If you mean to the concert, yes. If you mean that some other way, not unless it's with you."

She was silent, and Rex worried that he'd overstepped their playful bounds. He had no idea what would be considered appropriate cell phone etiquette, and going with his feelings had seemed right at the time. Now he worked to cover his tracks.

"I'm sorry; that was crude."

"No, it was sexy," she said in a hushed tone. "I just...You always take my breath away. I feel like a fifteen-year-old when I'm with you, even on the phone. When I dialed your number, my heart was racing. I swear, Rex, it's so weird."

"I know, babe. I feel it too, and I have no idea how I'm going to stay away from you tonight, but I still want to be there and see you." Could he do it? he wondered. Could he see Jade at the concert and not be with her? Not hold her hand or put his arm around her? Not talk with her alone in a dark corner, lest someone see them and their fathers get wind of their relationship? Hell, at this point, he wondered if he even cared. Then his loyalty rose to the surface, and he knew he did.

"Me too. Maybe we shouldn't go."

"No, not seeing you is worse than seeing you. Besides, Max's friend Kaylie is singing tonight, so everyone is psyched to go. We'll just be careful. Are your parents going? Your brother?"

She laughed. "My brother hasn't been to a community event in years, and my parents are too wrapped up in their own stuff right now to want to go, so no, they won't be there. Meet me by the entrance?"

"Yeah, I'll be there at eight. Jade?" he asked. He debated telling her about the conversation he'd had with her mother about how she and his mother had remained close and that she supported their being together and finally decided to do it when they were face-to-face.

"Yeah?"

"I miss you."

A simple, quick intake of breath told him that she was feeling the same longing as he was. "Me too," she said.

"Jade?"

"Yeah?"

"I love you." Telling her he loved her was still so new to him that he held his breath until she said it back.

"I love you, too, Rex."

TREAT AND MAX sat in the back of the SUV, snuggled against each other like they were keeping warm during a winter storm. Rex tried not to keep looking at them, but how could he not? The way Max gazed into his brother's eyes and touched his cheek, like the sun rose and set around him, made Rex long for Jade's touch.

"Savannah, what's happening with Connor?" Rex asked, to distract himself from Treat and Max.

Savannah made her living as an entertainment lawyer, and she'd been A-list-actor Connor Dean's attorney for the past few years. She'd also been his on-and-off-again lover for the past several months.

"Nothing's happening," she answered.

"Are you still dating him?" Rex asked again. He'd always been protective of Savannah, and even now, as an adult, he liked to be sure she was okay.

"We're...It's complicated." Savannah turned toward Rex and asked, "What's the plan tonight with Jade? I mean, how do you do this not-tell-anyone thing in public?"

"Hell if I know. This is all kind of new to me," Rex answered. He pulled his hat down low, wondering the same thing.

"I think you should just go for it. What's the worst that could happen?" Savannah flashed a mischievous grin.

"Savannah, don't stir the beehive," Treat warned.

"What? He deserves to be with the woman he loves, just like you did." Savannah winked at Max.

"She's right, you know," Max said. "I can't wait to hear Kaylie sing tonight. She's amazing. Hey, Rex, can you dance with Jade, or do you have to be totally hands-off?"

Josh laughed from the driver's seat. "That's like asking an alcoholic to hold your beer at a party."

Rex leaned forward and punched Josh's arm. "Hardly," he said in a stern voice. "What am I, an animal?" *I am when it comes to Jade.*

"I saw the way you looked at her when she rode by the day Max crashed her car in the driveway." Josh flashed him a challenge in the rearview mirror.

Rex stewed. Being near Jade without being able to touch her was going to be difficult enough. He didn't need his brother egging him on, but silencing a Braden brother was never as easy as he wished.

"We'll be fine. It's not like we have a choice. Max, it's probably not a good idea for me to dance with her. No need to create an issue. If word got back to Dad that we danced…He's a smart man." He shook his head, knowing it was time to make some hard decisions—tonight. There was no way he'd be able to act like a kid on restriction forever.

Chapter Thirty-Two

"YOU'RE A CRUEL girl," Riley said as she eyed Jade in her short jeans skirt and sexy Rogue boots.

"What?" Jade fingered the plunging neckline of her nearly transparent silky blouse. She might not be able to be with Rex in public, but she sure as hell could keep his mind on her and her alone.

They stood by the busy concert entrance, waiting for Rex and his siblings to arrive. Half the town was already there, and Jade was nervous about being there with Rex. She was sure her feelings for him were written all over her face. She plastered a smile on her lips and hoped that no one would notice how her smile changed when Rex arrived.

"Oh, there they are!" Riley pointed to the Bradens walking across the parking lot. "Wow. It's like watching the opening of a movie, when the actors all walk out. Damn, they really are the hottest family around."

"Stop drooling," Jade said as she licked her lips. Rex walked between Josh and Treat, his eyes locked on Jade. His arms arced out to his sides from his glorious muscles, and every step of his thick, powerful thighs straining against his jeans made her heart thump a little harder. Savannah bent down to pick something up, while the others continued forward. Max reached for Treat's hand, and Treat pulled her close. Rex hung back with Savannah. He touched her shoulder lightly, saying something that Jade couldn't hear. Savannah looked up and smiled. She got up and hugged him, and Jade felt her restraint falling away. The way Rex loved resonated in everything he did, not only with his siblings, or the way he said all the right things to Jade, or the perfect specimen of a man that he obviously was. Those things were only part of the equation. His desire not to hurt his father by rushing to disclose their relationship was also the way he loved. Seeing him now, waiting for Savannah, walking with his arm around her, Jade knew she was a goner. She thought she'd fallen for him before. Now, she realized, she hadn't fallen; she'd tumbled head over heels, and there was no righting herself.

Chapter Thirty-Three

"I THINK YOU should stop worrying about Dad and just go for it," Savannah said as they neared the gate.

"Is that why you picked up that quarter? So you could try to convince me without Treat and Josh around?" Rex asked.

Savannah raised her eyebrows with a smile.

"Do you have any idea how difficult this is already going to be? You know me, Savannah. When have I ever told all of you about a girl? Huh?" Rex's voice was harsh, but not because of Savannah's pushing him toward doing something that he knew would hurt his father. It was because Jade stood by the gate looking sexier than ever before in those boots she'd been wearing down by the ravine, with a goddamned see-through shirt that already had his blood pumping when he wasn't even close to her yet. She looked at him with an innocent smile he was sure was meant to fool everyone else, but one glance into those blue eyes and he knew differently. He was only a handful of steps from her, and when they reached the gate, he had to put his hand on it to steady himself. If his hands weren't busy, he'd pull her close and answer every lusty desire that pooled in her eyes.

"Hi," she said, licking her lips.

Rex swallowed a groan and a long breath. "You look gorgeous."

She ran her eyes up and down his body. "So do you."

Savannah barged between them. "Jade, hi! So good to see you. Hi, Riley."

"Hey, Savannah. Great to see you again," Riley said.

Rex and Jade's eyes hadn't strayed, but he knew that if he didn't move now, he might never let her get away from the gate.

"Riley, this is Max, and you know Treat and Josh, of course," he said.

"I hear you're a clothing designer now?" Josh said as they headed into the gate.

Riley and Josh talked about fashion on their way through the crowd.

Rex's senses were heightened. He felt Jade beside him and desperately wanted to reach for her hand. He clenched his fists instead.

"How's Hope?" she asked.

"Our father's with her," Savannah answered. "He's got our numbers, and he'll call if he needs us. She was still acting different when we left. She's not rolling or biting or anything, but she's not exactly calm, either. I thought that medicine would help her pain."

"It should have," Jade said with a worried tone.

"Look!" Max's eyes lit up at the sight of the band on a makeshift stage, where her boss's wife—her best friend, Kaylie Crew—stood front and center, singing into a microphone. Max turned toward a pretty, curly-haired woman and squealed.

"Danica! I didn't know you'd be here, too!" Max embraced Danica, and Danica's husband, Rex's cousin Blake Carter, appeared behind her.

"Hey, cuz," Blake said to Treat.

Treat hugged him with a wide smile. "Blake, so great to see you again."

"Kaylie is my wife's sister. Do you really think we'd miss this one? A chance to see my cousins and my sister-in-law sing all at once?" Blake answered.

Blake looked very much like his Braden cousins—tall, darkly handsome, and well built. Rex pulled him in close and gave him a brotherly pat on the back, then put his hand possessively on Jade's lower back and felt her flinch beneath his touch.

"I'm sorry we missed your wedding," Savannah said, kissing Blake's cheek. "Josh is around somewhere. He disappeared right after we got here."

"Blake, this is Jade." God, he wanted to claim her as his. Just two simple words. Would that be so hard? *My girlfriend.*

"Hi, Jade," he said. "You're here with Rex?" His eyes darted between the two.

Savannah came to their rescue. "Jade Johnson," she said, like that explained everything.

Blake opened his eyes wide as Rex removed his hand from Jade's back. "Ah, got it." He moved close to Jade. "Forbidden love?" He winked.

JADE HADN'T EXPECTED her stomach to clench the way it did, or the hurt that stirred in her heart. She didn't want to be forbidden. She wanted to be on Rex's arm, showing all the women who were watching the handsome Bradens that she was his, and he was hers. Instead she smiled at Rex's cousin.

"I guess you could say that," she managed.

Rex looked at her with a silent apology in his warm gaze, but even that didn't lessen the pain she felt, or the way she felt dirty for being hidden.

She spotted Riley dancing with Josh, and jealousy spiked something akin to anger within her.

"Excuse me. I'm going to grab a drink," she said, wanting to get away before she said or did something stupid.

"I'll come with you," Rex offered.

"No. Stay here; visit with your family. I'll be back." She felt Rex's hot stare on her back as she made her way to the concession stand.

"SORRY, MAN," BLAKE said to Rex. "I didn't mean to upset her."

"It wasn't you," Rex said. "It's the whole family feud thing. There's no way to rectify it and…"

"And you want to be with Jade. I get it. When I met Danica, she was my therapist. Talk about forbidden." Blake turned and looked at Danica. "Best damn apple I've ever eaten."

Rex shot a glance at the concession stand, where Jade was

laughing with Jimmy Palen, who owned a large auto-repair and body shop in town. Jimmy leaned against the edge of the concession stand, one hand grasping a beer bottle. Rex couldn't see his green eyes, but he'd bet they were focused on Jade's chest.

Jade threw her head back with a laugh, and Jimmy reached out and touched her arm. In the next breath, they were heading toward the dance floor.

"Wanna dance with me, big brother?" Savannah knew how to create a distraction. She wasn't one to wear Western style clothing. Instead she had on tight jeans and a black spaghetti-strap blouse. The contrast of the black against her radiant auburn hair was stunning, and her eyes danced with happiness—or a devious plan. Rex wasn't sure which.

"No, thanks," he said.

"Oh, I think you do." She took his arm and dragged him onto the dance floor.

At six foot three, he was not an easy man to drag, but his feet would not obey his mind. He wanted to stay put and stew—or stalk—Jimmy and Jade. The last thing he wanted to do was dance with his sister, but there he was, on the dance floor, moving to the music.

"Look at you go," Max said as she and Treat sidled up beside them. Danica and Blake were right behind them.

Rex fixated on Jimmy and Jade. His body might not want to cooperate, but his head was right in the game and getting angrier by the second, watching Jade's hips sway beneath Jimmy's hungry gaze. Oh yeah, he could see the bastard's eyes now, and they hadn't left her breasts once since they'd begun dancing.

"Rex, you okay? They're just dancing." Savannah touched his biceps, and he was so tense that he instinctively flexed.

He barely registered her next comment beyond the blood thundering in his ears.

"Treat? We might have a problem."

"Rex, we can't have any trouble here," Treat said in a low, firm voice beside his ear.

"Oh, don't worry, big brother. I'm not about to make any trouble." *I'm just going to claim my woman.*

Jade shifted her eyes to his, and in that brief glance, he saw hurt so deep it was like she reached into his gut, grabbed his organs, and twisted. How could he have not recognized how much she'd be hurt by the same things that angered him? This situation was untenable, and even as Treat put a stabilizing hand on his shoulder, Rex knew there was no way that he'd be the cause of any more of her pain. This madness had to stop.

He looked into his brother's eyes and asked, "Could anything have kept you from Max?" It wasn't a challenge; it was a question—one to which Rex already knew the answer. Before Treat could answer, he asked Blake, "Would you have let anyone come between you and Danica?"

"Not on your life," Blake said, pulling Danica close and wrapping his fingers beneath her wild, dark curls.

Rex ran his eyes over his family's faces. Their worry was quieted by their support for him. Rex nodded, coupling their strength with his.

"The hell with this. Dad's not here, and her parents aren't here. Even if they were, I can't live a lie. It's not who I am. It's time to end this shit."

Rex took a determined step forward and was pulled back by

Treat's strong grip on his arm.

"The minute you do this, you have to be ready for the fall-out back home," Treat warned.

Rex's eyes didn't waver from Jade.

"Rex, look at me."

He shifted his determined eyes.

"I'll stand behind you—we all will—but are you one-hundred-percent sure that she's *the one*? Because if you're not, you're going to dig a ditch that you might be buried in, and it might not be worth it."

The flash of rage happened so quickly that Rex couldn't buffer it. "She's the one, and if I'm buried because of it, as long as she's with me, it's worth it." He yanked his arm from his brother's and stalked over to Jade and Jimmy. He had no intention of causing a scene. Jimmy was a nice enough guy, and the only thing he was doing wrong was ogling the wrong woman.

"Rex." Jade centered him, dulling the sharp edges of his anger.

"Hi, babe," he said. "Jimmy, you mind?" He draped his arm around Jade's shoulder.

"A Johnson and a Braden?" Jimmy lifted his eyebrows in surprise. "You gotta be kidding me." He laughed under his breath.

"Jimmy, I've lost my dance partner. Dance with me?" Savannah, in her typical manipulative, flirty fashion, pulled him alongside of her, then flashed a wink at Rex.

The music slowed, and Jade wrapped her arms around Rex. He guided her chin up so he could look into her eyes.

"I'm sorry. I wanted to tell Blake you were my girlfriend,

but I was afraid of people finding out."

She blinked several times, renewed worry shading her eyes.

"What?" Rex asked.

"And you think dancing with me isn't going to cause a stir?"

His heart swelled with love. Everything about Jade fed him in some way; her sensuality fed his sexual desires, her thoughtfulness fed his heart, the way she worried about animals, and the way she loved Riley and her family, fed his loyalty. It killed him to know that instead of feeding her right back, he'd been souring her with hurt.

He lowered his mouth to hers in a greedy, possessive kiss. She smelled sweet and familiar, and the press of her breasts against him warmed him with need as he pulled her closer, covetously deepening the kiss, until they parted with the need to breathe.

"I can't hide anymore," he said. He took her mouth again, there, in the middle of the dance floor, with his family beside him and half the town watching.

Jade splayed her fingers on his stomach as their lips drew apart. He could feel her trembling against him. Her eyes darted around the crowd, a flush rising on her cheeks. He wrapped one arm around her lower back; the other gently held the back of her head as he pulled her close and whispered in her ear, "I'll never hurt you again. I'm telling my father tonight, and I'll go with you to talk to your family when you're ready."

She looked up at him, the hurt in her eyes replaced with love. "I'm ready," she said.

Rex's world had never felt so right. He was in for the fight of his life with the man who gave him life—for the woman who would give that life meaning.

Chapter Thirty-Four

REX TOOK JADE'S hand, and together they forged forward on a path to change the course of their lives. The thundering in his heart was no longer weighted by anger or longing. It was pushed and thrust by the knowledge that after tonight, the world would know about him and Jade, and they'd no longer have to hide. He wouldn't have to replay their morning together over and over. He would relive it for years to come.

His brothers, Savannah, Max, and Riley all hurried behind them as each determined step brought them closer to the gate.

"Where are you going?" Savannah asked, out of breath from jogging behind his long strides.

"We're going to tell Jade's parents before her dad hears it from someone else," he called over his shoulder.

"Her parents?" Savannah said. "Treat?" Her phone rang. She hung back as the others raced forward.

"I'm here." Treat caught up to Rex. "I'm coming with you," he said. He asked Max what she wanted to do, and Max said she'd stay with Riley, Blake, and Danica.

Rex stopped at the gate. Josh and Treat stood beside him, adrenaline causing their chests to heave with every excited breath.

"I can do this alone," he said.

"No way. This feud is bigger than you, Rex. I know how much you feel for Jade, and, Jade, I know how much you love my brother. But I also know how things can get out of hand too fast to comprehend. We're going with you." Treat left no room for negotiation.

Rex pulled Jade forward. "Fine."

"Wait!" Savannah yelled, jogging to catch up to them. "Dad just called. Hope is going nuts. He can't keep her from rolling, and now she's trying to bite her stomach. He can't reach Dr. Baker."

Treat and Rex exchanged a glance that held an entire silent conversation.

"Josh, you go with Rex. I'll go home and see what's going on," Treat said.

"She needs a vet, Treat, not us," Savannah said.

"I can go," Jade offered without a moment's hesitation.

"What about your parents?" Rex reminded her. "Someone might say something. I don't trust Jimmy not to try and cause a ruckus."

"Oh, I think Jimmy'll be fine," Savannah said with a confident smirk.

"Your father wouldn't call if Hope didn't need help, right?" Jade asked.

She was right, but there was no way his father would let her anywhere near Hope. "Jade…"

"Jesus, you guys. Do I have to figure everything out?" Savannah barged between them. "We'll all go to Dad's. Josh and I will get Dad sidetracked and back up to the house. Rex, you and Treat take over for him with Hope; then Jade swoops in when Dad's safely inside." Savannah nodded at their contemplating eyes. "Well, come on. Let's go."

Rex put his hands on Jade's shoulders. "Are you sure you want to do this before we settle things? I'm sure I can find another vet somewhere."

"You can't find another vet fast enough. If her stomach twists, she could die, Rex. We have to do this. I *want* to do this." She put her hands on his arms. "Besides, I'm not afraid of any of this. Love conquers all, right? Isn't that the way things are supposed to work?" She withdrew the charm from beneath her shirt and held it out for him to see.

He touched his finger to the lump beneath his own collar. God, he loved her. "It is," he said, thinking of all the signs that had blessed them in the last few days. From his mother's charms miraculously finding them at just the right time to her mother seeking him out. What were the chances? Now he could only hope that love could conquer the most difficult road block of all. His father.

HOPE WAS SLAMMING her body against the stall walls when they arrived. Her nostrils flared and her neck flailed forward and back. They heard their father's voice before they saw him. He came in the back door shaking his head, his face a tense mask of worry and irritation.

Treat and Rex stood by the stall. "What happened?" Rex asked.

"It's gotta be colic. She was fine for the past few hours, but then she began rolling and craning her neck. I brought her in, and she's been doing this since. I tried Dr. Baker, but he was out on an emergency over in Preston."

"Dad, let Treat and Rex take over. Come with us, and we'll look up other vets." Savannah took her father's arm and tried to walk with him, but he stood firm.

"Dad." Josh's eyes opened wide. His eyes darted between Rex and his father, and before he could stop himself, "Jade Johnson is a vet," fell from his lips.

Treat and Rex burned stares in his direction. Their father did the same.

"No Johnson is touching your mother's horse," he said in a firm tone.

"She might be Hope's only chance if this is really colic. Did you take her temperature?"

"Since when did you become a horse expert?" his father asked. "She has no other signs. She was rolling, craning her neck, and snapping. I'm no vet, but I think we're looking at some kind of stomach issue."

Rex shot a hot stare at Josh. "Dad, you've been at this all day. Go with Savannah and Josh. We'll sit with her and see if we can calm her down."

"Go on. We've got this," Treat said.

With Savannah's persistent yank on his arm, their father reluctantly went toward the house.

Rex grabbed Josh's arm. "What the hell was that all about?"

"I thought maybe he'd make it easier for everyone and just let Jade help." Josh shrugged.

"Whatever. Just keep him in the house." Rex heard Jade's car pull up behind the trees along the road. He pulled out his cell phone and called her.

"He's inside," he said when she answered.

A few minutes later, she entered the back door of the barn, carrying her medical bag.

JADE'S NERVES FELT like wires that had been pulled too tight. She kept looking at the barn doors, waiting for Hal Braden to storm in and throw her out.

"What can we do?" Rex asked.

"I'm fine with Hope, but I'm really nervous about your dad. Can you guys just give me space to work and watch for your dad?" she asked.

Rex kissed her lightly. "Thank you. I know this is a lot to ask."

"Nothing is too much for an animal." She watched them go to the barn doors, two strong sentries allowing her to do the thing she loved most next to being with Rex.

Jade closed her eyes and breathed deeply for a few seconds. She inhaled the smell of moist hay, leather, and the unique scent of hot horses, and when she opened her eyes, Hope was looking right at her.

"Hi, sweet girl." She calmly stroked the side of her jaw.

"You're not feeling so well, huh?" Hope stopped throwing her body from side to side. She nudged Jade's solar plexus over the gate of her stall. "That's a girl," she said.

She unlatched the stall and opened the gate.

"Jade, be—"

She cut Rex off with a silent palm in the air. Hope walked out of the stall, and Jade tried to ignore Rex's eyes watching over her. She focused on leading Hope toward the back of the barn, where she tied her lead to another stall. The center of the barn stretched about twelve feet wide between the stalls on the left and the ones on the right. Jade moved with slow and careful steps to Hope's side, speaking in a soothing voice.

"I'm just going to do a quick exam, Hope." She rested her ear against Hope's stomach, relieved to hear plenty of stomach noises. She took the horse's temperature, her pulse, and when she moved to Hope's head to check the mucus membrane in her mouth, she was drawn in by the sad look in Hope's eyes. Jade pet her muzzle gently.

"It's okay, sweetie. I'm just going to open your mouth, okay?"

Hope neighed and pushed her nose into Jade's chest again. Most women would worry about their blouse or the wetness that brushed their skin, but to Jade, the feeling of the horse against her body was a blessing. It meant that Hope was comfortable with her, which was half the battle when examining a horse.

She checked Hope's gums and her capillary refill time.

"I'm not seeing anything alarming here, Hope. What's going on in that pretty head of yours?" She stroked Hope's side and checked her eyes and skin for dehydration.

Jade glanced at Rex, who was still watching every move she and Hope made. She wanted to tell Rex that she wasn't concerned with her findings, but she didn't want to break the bond she and Hope had established by hollering to Rex. Instead, she spoke to Hope.

"Okay, sweetie, I'm just going to give you a bit of a massage. This will help ease whatever is going on in your belly." She rested her palms on Hope's body until she found her rhythm. Then she worked her way along her stomach meridian.

She heard Treat and Rex approach before she saw them. They watched in silence as she inched her fingertips along Hope's body, feeling for abnormalities beneath her fingers. Hope was no longer cranking her neck. She was still and calm as Jade took extra time around the same point where she'd massaged Berle, and so many other horses, to alleviate stomach discomfort.

REX'S ADORATION FOR Jade multiplied just watching her put so much love and energy into Hope. He was mesmerized with the care she took, every ounce of her focus on the horse, and as she spoke to Hope, her voice was soothing and calm, as if she were talking to a child or a lover. Despite himself, he began to picture her with a child. With his child.

"She's doing fine," Jade said a few minutes later. "I don't think you're looking at colic. She's too stable for that. The exam showed no indication of colic other than what your father said about her behavior, and that could just be stomach discomfort. She might have become stressed over the show today, and that alone could have sent her tummy into distress."

"What the hell is she doing here?"

They all spun around at the sound of Hal's voice. He stood at the barn entrance, his wide shoulders and height accentuated by the moonlight.

"Dad," Rex said. He looked between the woman he loved and the man whom he also loved, feeling the pull of each in his chest.

"Don't you *Dad* me, Rex Braden," he said as he neared. His father narrowed his dark eyes, which had gone almost black. "You step back from Hope," he said to Jade.

"Dad, Hope's fine," Rex said.

His father wasn't listening. He was staring at the necklace that hung around Jade's neck, exposed for all to see. His chest rose and fell with each breath as he stepped closer to Jade.

Rex stepped between them just as Treat came to his side.

"Hope needed a vet. Jade's a damn good vet," he said.

"Step out of my way, son," Hal ordered in a deep, cold voice.

Rex crossed his arms. "I'm not moving until I know you are going to be civil to her."

His father put one strong arm out and pushed his son aside. Rex turned to retaliate, and Treat gripped his arm—hard— restraining him.

"What the hell?" Rex said angrily.

"Where did you get that?" his father asked Jade.

She brought a nervous hand up to her necklace and fingered the cool silver.

"I asked you a question, Jade Johnson."

Savannah and Josh flew into the barn.

"Son of a bitch," Josh said. "He said he was going to lie down. I didn't think anything of it until I went to check on him and found his bed empty and the door cracked open."

"It's okay," Treat said.

"Dad," Savannah said, coming to his side, "Jade's helping Hope."

One look from her father sent her two steps backward.

Rex yanked his arm free from Treat and approached his father. "Dad, you want to give someone hell, you give it to me."

"I plan to," he said, his eyes never moving from Jade's. "Just as soon as she answers my question."

"I…We…" Jade began, then swallowed hard.

Rex wasn't going to let Jade flounder at the hands of his father, no matter what trouble it might cause. He loved her and he was done pretending he didn't. She was his to protect. What kind of man let their girlfriend go up against his own father alone?

He stepped between them again, and his father pulled himself up to his full height; the three inches that separated them allowed his father to look down upon him. The loyal man in Rex almost relented. He almost lowered his eyes and stepped aside, but Jade's whisper of a touch, a quick brush of her fingertips on his back, was enough to give him the courage and strength he needed to confront his father.

"You want to talk to Jade, you do it with respect." He

crossed his arms to keep them from shaking. "I gave her that necklace. You got a problem with it? You take it up with me, not her."

There was a direct line of tension from his father's dark eyes to his. His siblings watched on, but Rex barely registered them. He had tunnel vision, and all of the recent tension and the hiding came rushing back to him, with the last fifteen years close on its heels. His father was at one end of the dark tunnel, and protecting Jade was the light at the other end. The space in between was thick with tension and matters of the heart that were too magnanimous to be defined.

"Step aside, son," his father said.

"I'm not moving, Dad." He reached into his shirt and pulled out his own necklace.

His father drew in a sharp breath and blew it out his nose. "I asked once, and I'm not fixing to ask again. Where did you get that necklace?"

"I'll tell you anything you want to know. I've got nothing to hide, and I'm not ashamed of anything I've done—except hiding my relationship with Jade." Rex took a step to the side and wrapped Jade's trembling body within the safety of his arm.

His father shot a look at Treat. "You know about this?"

Treat looked dead center in his father's eyes. "Yes, sir, I did."

"So did I," Josh said as he stepped forward.

"Me too," Savannah added.

His father stood surrounded by them, breathing hard, his face growing redder by the second, and for a beat, Rex felt sorry for him.

"I never thought I'd see the day that a Johnson would turn my own children against me."

"Mr. Braden, I'm not turning—"

He interrupted her with a gruff demand. "I want to know one thing and one thing only." He looked at Rex. "Where did you get those necklaces?"

"I'll tell you that just as soon as you apologize to Jade." Rex knew he was playing with fire. No one challenged his father, especially not one of his own children.

His father crossed his arms. Rex did the same.

Suddenly, Hope whinnied and threw her body from side to side. Rex swooped Jade out of her reach.

"You're upsetting her!" Jade broke free from Rex's grasp with a fire in her eyes and heat in her voice. "He got the damned necklace at Jewels of the Past. The woman there said she knew Adriana in high school and that it was meant for us."

His father clenched his jaw, and his biceps were right behind.

Hope was becoming more agitated by the second. Her neck flew hard from side to side.

"What else do you need to know?" Jade spat. "Because we can deal with this crap later or someplace else, but this horse is in distress, and the more you boys fluff your feathers, the more upset she's going to get."

"She's got colic," his father said adamantly.

"No, she doesn't. She has no medical signs of colic other than behavioral, and she responded to a stomach meridian massage. She's probably just upset over all the stress around here lately, and the show just threw her over the edge."

As his father approached, Rex stood between him and Hope. "Let her take care of Hope, Dad. She fixed her right up before."

"No Johnson is going to touch my horse."

"Too late," Savannah said, and nodded to Jade, who had her forehead resting against the tender spot between Hope's nostrils.

Treat stepped between Rex and his father. "The important thing right now is to get Hope well. Let's give her some space to do that, Dad. We can talk outside." He took his father's reluctant arm and left Rex guarding Jade and reluctantly building a wall between his father and himself.

Chapter Thirty-Five

"I'M SORRY. I know I shouldn't have opened my mouth, but when Hope reacted, I just flew into veterinarian mode. I'm so sorry. I don't want to make things any worse with your father." Jade had tears in her eyes, and her body shook.

Rex took her in his arms.

She felt his heart pounding against her ear, and she knew the depth of the trouble they'd started. Why had she opened her big mouth? There was no way he'd ever accept her into their lives. His brothers and sister made her feel welcome and she liked them—really liked them—but how could they ever get past Hal's hatred of her family?

"This wasn't how I had planned to tell him," Rex said. "But the truth is, there's no easy way, so this was as good as any. Are you okay? I'm so sorry about the way he treated you."

"I'm fine. I kind of expected worse. He's very focused on the necklace, so I felt bad for him, especially if it really did come from your mother."

"It did. There's no doubt in my mind that it did. I'm going to talk to him. Do you need me here with you and Hope?"

Hope had already calmed down.

"I'm fine." Jade vacillated between telling him to just let it drop with his father and wanting to kiss him hard to give him the courage to fight harder. She didn't know the right path to take. She'd never come between a father and son before. In the end, she did neither. She watched him walk out of the barn and put her faith in him.

REX WAS HEADED around the barn toward the others when Josh pulled him aside.

"I gave Riley my number at the concert, and she just texted me," Josh said. "Apparently, word got back to the Johnsons about you and Jade dancing together, and Earl Johnson showed up at the concert madder than hell."

Josh was the quietest of the Braden boys, and he tended to stay out of trouble and away from anywhere it might be brewing. For him to support Rex the way he had tonight meant a lot to him.

"Great. Thanks, buddy." No sooner had the words left his mouth than Earl Johnson's car came to a screeching halt in the driveway.

The burly man stepped from his car and called out, "Hal Braden."

His wife hurried after him down the driveway. "Earl, please. Please, Earl, don't do this."

Rex, Treat, and Josh made a beeline for him, with their father and Savannah just behind them.

"I believe it's me you want to talk to," Rex said, crossing his arms and planting his feet in a wide, stable stance. Treat and Josh flanked his sides, with the same guarded posture and confident stare.

"Dad?" Jade yelled from down by the barn.

None of the men turned away from their competitors.

"I heard you were dancing with my daughter," Earl said to Rex.

"Yes, sir, I was." Rex spoke with strength and confidence. He was done messing around. If they had to move out of Weston, then so be it, but he was done being strangled by a feud that wasn't his in the first place. "I love your daughter, sir, and I'll dance with her again and again." Rex nodded at Jane. "Mrs. Johnson."

"Hi, Rex," she said in a thin voice.

"Daddy, what are you doing here?" Jade asked in a curt voice as she approached. She didn't go to her father's side. She didn't reach for Rex. She stood between the two families, her eyes bouncing between them.

"I got a call from Maggie Strong. She was concerned about how things looked between you and Rex Braden," he said.

"How things looked?" Jade spat. "Really? Do you not remember that I'm thirty-one years old? What is wrong with you?"

"Jade." It was a *stand-down* command that every one of them understood, but Jade ignored it.

"Don't *Jade* me. This foolishness between you and Hal Braden is crazy. I've spent my entire life avoiding this family like the plague, and all that while, my heart was so wrapped up in the thought of Rex Braden that it's a wonder I could function at all." She crossed her arms like the angry men, then dropped them to her sides and went to her father.

Rex watched as she touched his bulbous arms, and her voice came out as a loving plea.

"Dad, I love him. If you want me to be happy, then be happy for me. Rex is a good man."

"Rex is a Braden."

Hal Braden pushed between his sons. He put his hand on Rex's shoulder. Rex snapped his head toward his father. He didn't know what to expect after the words they'd exchanged in the barn.

"These boys are the finest in all of Weston. Your daughter can't do any better and you know it." He looked at Jane. "Jane here knows it. Don't you, Jane?"

Rex had had enough of the posturing and enough of the games. He wanted honesty and he needed clarity.

"What the hell is going on?" Rex asked. "You just threatened me in there, and now you're supporting me?"

"I'm supporting your mother's wish, son." Hal walked up to Jade and nodded at her necklace. "Show that to your mother."

Jade's eyebrows drew together as she nervously turned toward her mother and lifted her necklace.

Her mother gasped a quick breath. She covered her mouth with her hand and reached a trembling hand toward the silver charm. "Wh-where did you get this?"

"A woman in Allure said she got it from Rex's mom when she was in high school," Jade answered.

Jane's eyes welled with tears. "That's hers," she whispered. "She used to talk about this dance of two lovers." She looked at Hal. "Remember?"

Hal nodded; his eyes were also damp.

Jane continued. "*Everything in their lives was meant to keep them apart, and against all odds, they found their way to each other.*" She looked up at Rex. "Your father had that necklace made for your mother for her fifteenth birthday. She treasured it, wore it every day. One day she didn't have it on, and when I asked her why, she said she'd put it in a safe place for someone who would need it more than she and your father."

Hal lowered his eyes.

"Dad?" Rex watched his father close his eyes and rub them with his thumb and forefinger. He saw so much of himself in his father's mannerisms that his heart clamped down, dislodging the simmering anger that had settled there only moments before.

"Her father didn't want us together either," his father admitted.

"I don't understand any of this, but, Dad, Mr. Braden, what do we have to do to get past this family feud?" Jade asked.

Rex stepped forward and took Jade's hand. "If we can't resolve this, Jade and I will be forced to build our lives without you. The choice is yours." She squeezed his hand and leaned in to him. Rex put his arm around her. "I love your daughter. Let me love your daughter."

Earl Johnson stepped forward, eye to eye with Hal. "You know that I'm not buying any of this necklace bullshit, so if this is your way of having our children mend the miles of broken fence between us, you're barking up the wrong tree."

Hal shifted his eyes to Rex and Jade, clinging together in a bubble of love so thick, Rex knew they all could see it. He brought his eyes back to Earl.

"You screwed Adriana over. All those years ago, you threw loyalty out the window and threw us both under the bus at the same time," Hal said.

"I had no choice. I know we agreed not to do business with the worthless son of a bitch, but I had no choice. I'd have lost everything." Earl's harsh tone carried angrily into the night.

"Bullshit. I could have given you enough money to carry you over a few months; instead you went and dealt with the devil," Hal accused.

"Damn it, Hal. You're the most stubborn, bullheaded man I know," Earl snapped.

Treat and Josh stepped up and flanked their father, chins held high.

"No, he's not, Earl. Have you looked in the mirror? You're every bit as stubborn. Yes, you needed the money, but you knew that selling horses to that man was wrong. You admitted as much then, and you did it anyway," Jane said.

"I was building a life with you. Without that money, we'd have had to sell the ranch altogether." Earl looked from Hal to Jane and then to Jade.

Jade and her mother were looking at Earl with serious eyes, almost cold. Rex felt badly for him. "I can't even pretend to understand what this is all about, but my best guess is that you broke some time-honored loyalty to my father, and my father, being the honor-driven man he is, tossed you aside for it." He shot a heated stare at his father. "I can think of only one solution to your mess. Forgive and forget, or kick us out of town. The ball's in your court."

He took Jade's hand and pulled her toward the driveway, then turned back to the stunned faces of his siblings. "I'll do that one better. If you two can grow up, I'll buy that patch of land between your two ranches and build a house there for me and Jade. Cash deal, but only...only if you two make up, because I'm not going to have my children feeling the stress of grandparents who can't communicate."

"Children?" Jade asked as they headed up the driveway toward her car.

"Son!" His father's voice stopped him in his tracks. Every muscle clenched. This was it. No one challenged Hal Braden. He dropped Jade's hand and faced his father.

"Yes, sir?"

"You know what you're asking me to do. This family lives by three steadfast beliefs: a strong work ethic, family loyalty, and honesty. If you don't believe in family honor, then you're the not man I thought you were." Hal held Rex's stare.

Treat walked up behind his father and said, "What happened to *family knows no boundaries?*"

Hal spun around and looked Treat dead in the eyes. "You stay out of this, son."

"It's okay, Treat. I understand his feelings." Rex wasn't about to beg for his father's forgiveness for falling in love with a wonderful, intelligent, beautiful woman. He turned to leave. Each painful step as he moved away from his father felt like a knife in his heart.

"Son, I'm talking to you, and when I'm talking to you, eyes remain on me." His father's commanding voice boomed through the night.

Rex took a deep breath and turned around. He crossed his arms. He'd known it would be hard to stand up to his father, but he hadn't anticipated the gut-wrenching agony of a slow departure. He wanted to flee, get as far away as quickly as possible and pretend the man he'd built his life around hadn't tossed him aside like he didn't matter. He wanted to wrap Jade in his arms and feel her love so he would know he'd done the right thing. He didn't want to look into his father's dark eyes and say goodbye, but for Jade, he would do just that.

His father walked closer, until they were less than a foot apart and he could see every whisker, every wrinkle, on his father's face.

"I hate the way you handled this," his father said.

No doubt. I should have told you fifteen years ago. "Yes, sir. So do I."

"But I hate how I handled it even more. This crazy-ass feud took over, and when your mama died, I let that feud run all kinds of crazy into my head. I had so much anger inside me, son. I needed an outlet."

A lump lodged itself in Rex's throat. He felt Jade slide her hand into his, and he drew strength from her touch.

"I had six kids to raise, and I couldn't take it out on each of you, but damned if I didn't need a place for it. And that feud was a solid outlet. I didn't think it would hurt anyone, and what he did was wrong. He sold horses to a man who caused all sorts of hell for your mother when she was younger." Hal lowered his gaze, then looked back up at Jade and shook his head. "Rex, you're more of a man than I could ever be. You were loyal to me for far longer than I probably deserved. I knew how you felt about Jade when you were younger, and I should have released you from my grip back then, but I couldn't. Every time I thought about your mother and the way that old neighbor, Joe Richter, treated her, how he tried to stand between us, how low he made her feel, I saw red. Your loyalty lasted thirty-four years, son, and now it's doing what it should. It's shifting to the woman you love. It's shifting to your family."

Rex looked at Jade and wiped the tear that slid slowly down her cheek with the pad of his thumb. Then he turned to his father, but words eluded him. He stepped forward and embraced the man who'd taught him how to be a man.

"I'm sorry, son. We do the best we can in this world, and sometimes that's not quite good enough."

"You did fine, Dad. Thank you for your support." When they pulled apart, Rex bit back the tears that threatened to fall as his father approached Jade.

"Jade, you're a feisty, beautiful woman, and you did not deserve our family's back turned on you for so long. I hope you'll accept my apology. I'm truly sorry."

"Of course," she said as he scooped her into his big arms and held her close.

Rex barely heard his father whispering in her ear.

"That boy of mine has never had eyes for any other woman, and damn if his mother didn't know that you two were meant for each other. Hell, even Hope knew it." He looked at Rex and shook his head. "Son, one thing you need to know. As much as we hate to admit it, women are right most of the time." He turned back to Jade. "Now, don't you let that go to your head, because I'll deny ever saying it." He winked. "And another thing, don't you hurt him, ya hear?"

Jade cracked a wide smile. "Not on your life."

His father pulled away from Jade and said, "Now we gotta talk to that stubborn mule of a father of yours."

Chapter Thirty-Six

THERE WAS SOMETHING different in Jade's mother's eyes. In the space of ten heated minutes, the subservient softness had been replaced with confidence and an underlying beat of disturbance. Jade stood before her now and wondered if her mother was going to stand up and fight for her and Rex, or if she was going to be up against them both.

Under the light of the moon, the Bradens stood on one side of the driveway and the Johnsons on the other, with the exception of Rex and Jade, who stood in the space between.

Savannah and Josh came to Jade's side. Savannah set her hand on her shoulder. All the wonder that Jade had felt about being accepted into Rex's family was replaced with gratefulness, and as she watched her father's clenched jaw and furrowed brow, she still had no idea how to soften his resolve.

"Jade Johnson, this is the position you put me in, after all the years of love I've given you?" Her father's desultory tone told of his own wavering surety of the accusation.

Jade drew her shoulders back and opened her mouth to speak, but her mother stepped in, cutting her off.

"How dare you thrust this on Jade! Jade isn't putting you in any position. She's fallen in love, Earl. Do you even remember what that feels like? Remember how you used to call me at night and never want to hang up? Or all the walks we took in the moonlight? Don't you have any memory of holding my hand those first few dates and telling me how it was all so new to you? Remember how much you ached when we had to say goodnight and go our separate ways?"

Jade couldn't even imagine her father doing those things. She watched her mother searching her father's eyes. Savannah squeezed her shoulder, and without thinking, Jade covered her hand with her own. She saw Treat walk up behind them, and she felt his hand on top of hers. Rex's family was every bit as loving as he was. She felt safe with them as she watched her mother drawing emotion from her father's stoic gaze.

"Earl, Jade can't have that. She can't have any of it. They have to go to another town just to spend time with each other. She has to lie to her own father to see the man she loves."

Shit, how did she find out? Rex squeezed her hand and Jade held on tight, bracing herself for her father's harsh reaction and for possibly losing him altogether.

"Earl." Jane softened her tone. "Your daughter can't love the man she should because you are too scared to say you made a mistake. I lost my best friend and never got to mourn her or hold her children while they grieved for her. I never got to tell them how much she loved them. I was never able to help Hal with all those hurting babies because of your childish behavior. I can't get those years back, and neither can they. When I think of all the promises I made to Adriana, all those previous years that I swore to Adriana I would share with them. They're lost,

Earl. Lost!"

"Mom." Jade reached out to her.

Her mother kept her eyes trained on her father. "No, Jade. This is between your father and me. Damn it, Earl. I love Adriana's family as much as I love our own family. I'm with Jade on this. If you want to keep us together, you need to apologize to them—all of them—and move forward. Hal has done his part. He's accepted Jade into his family. Please. Rex is a good man." She turned tear-filled eyes toward Rex. "He's a wonderful man, and he loves our daughter very much."

"Damn it, Jane. I was trying to save our property and allow us to have a future. All we had was what we made on the ranch. We didn't have any money to fall back on. Hell, we didn't have money to start breeding horses, which is why I bought from someone other than the guy Hal recommended in the first place, but it turned out to be too good to be true. I wanted to make something of our ranch for you. I wanted to be successful so you could be proud." He turned away and rubbed his chin, then brought his attention back to his wife and spoke with a softer tone. "I failed at horse breeding because I tried to buy the horses for less than the normal price. I didn't know they weren't real thoroughbreds."

Jane gasped. "Oh dear."

"It's not an excuse, Jane. It's the truth. I was tricked, and it ruined me. Do you know what that felt like, to admit defeat? Do you have any idea what it felt like to fail so badly that I had no choice but to sell all those beautiful horses and go to work at that goddamned company? That wasn't our plan." He turned to Hal. "Remember, Hal? Our plan was to be ranchers, breed horses. Well, no one wanted my damned horses because they weren't thoroughbreds at all."

Hal's jaw clenched; his eyes narrowed.

Earl continued. "I'm not proud of what I did, but what choice did I have? I either had to admit that I'd been hoodwinked—which would only prove to you that I was cheap in the first place—or try to cheat the system once I realized that I'd been tricked. You know I'd never do that. I'm not that kind of man. My only other option was to do what I did and sell them to that bastard Richter. He was the only one who would buy them, and the only way I could keep the ranch was to do just that. Hal, it's true that I knew what he'd done to Adriana, and I'm not proud of my decisions. But I couldn't have looked you in the eye—or, Jane, God knows I couldn't have looked into your trusting eyes—and told you what had happened. I couldn't lose you both, so when it came down to it, I knew I couldn't lose the woman I loved. Hal, this was the only way I could figure to at least keep my marriage alive."

"Earl," Jane said, "I've never cared about material things. We could live in town, or in an apartment, and I never would have cared. Even now, we're having financial issues again. So what? Sell it all off."

Earl grew silent. He took his wife's hand in his. "We're not having financial trouble, Jane. I told you that because I knew if I told you the truth, you'd fight me on it. I want to sell some of our land so that if something happens to me, you can remain in our house without needing to do anything more than have someone tend the yard. I'm tired, Jane. I want time with you. More than anything in this world, I want to spend less time worrying about horses and property and more time enjoying your company." He held his hands out to his sides. "Look at me. I'm not going to live forever."

"Oh, Earl." Jane wiped a tear from her eye. "You make the worst decisions, for the best reasons." She drew him into her arms.

Jade watched her parents change right before her eyes. Her strong, self-assured father, the man she both feared and loved, approached her, looking deflated and relieved.

"Darlin', obviously I'm in the wrong here. I'm often in the wrong, though I am terribly embarrassed that my little girl has to know that."

"Daddy—"

"Let me finish, please, before I lose my nerve. I've always tried to do the right thing by you. And now the cat's out of the bag. Your daddy is not the man you thought he was, but my love for you and Steven and your mother is more real than the mud on my shoes. If you love Rex Braden, well, hell, then I'll love Rex Braden. If your heart hurts, my heart hurts." He looked at Hal. "Ain't that right, Hal?"

Hal nodded.

"Family knows no boundaries," Earl said.

"Family knows no boundaries," Hal repeated.

"Hal, I'm sorry about disrespecting Adriana by dealing with that thief, but if I was going to keep up with you and make a go of the ranch, I had no choice. It was the only way I could afford the horses—and, it turned out, I'd have been better off not having a ranch at all."

"I could have fronted you the money. Hell, Earl, you didn't

need to breed horses at all," Hal said.

"That was our plan. I wanted our plan to work. Then one thing led to another, and suddenly I was trying to save my family. I wasn't trying to cause any more hurt to her. Treat, Rex, Savannah, Josh, your mother loved you more than life itself, and I'm sorry that your father and I stood between my wife and each of you." When he looked into Jade's eyes, tears welled in his. "Darlin'…"

Jade jumped into his arms. "It's okay, Daddy. I love you." She hadn't realized how much anger she'd been carrying about the feud, but suddenly she felt lighter, even with the tears in her eyes and the discomfort that wrapped around each of them, tying them all together, pulling them down while they tried so hard to stay above the surface.

Chapter Thirty-Seven

LATE SUNDAY AFTERNOON, after the horse show had ended, the Bradens gathered for their typical afternoon barbeque. Josh manned the grill while Treat and Max stood arm in arm beside him, teasing him about adding too much pepper to the chicken. Treat pulled Max into a deep, passionate kiss, and this time, when Rex watched them, he didn't experience the familiar flash of jealousy. He pulled Jade closer to his side and lowered his mouth onto hers. She leaned in to him, and he wrapped his hand beneath her long, dark hair and kissed her. He could kiss her forever and never tire of it—and he planned on it.

Savannah came out of the house. "Get a room!" Her cell phone rang, and she looked at the number, then said, "I'm going to take this over there." She walked back toward the house.

Rex finally let Jade up for air. He loved the rosy flush that covered her cheeks and the breathless way she tried to recover from their kisses. "I love you," he said to her.

She touched his cheek. "Those words…that kiss…you're just trying to get into my pants," she teased.

Their families were just beginning to clear a path toward each other. It would take time, but they were making strides, and Rex wasn't going to stop pushing until the path was no longer hidden beneath the brush, but cleared and lined with olive branches.

Hope had been fine ever since their families reconciled, although, when Rex noticed the parallel, Josh was quick to correct him. *You mean since Jade gave him that massage.*

He watched his father leaning against the fence, and for the hundredth time that day, was thankful for their reconciliation.

"I'm going to talk to my dad for a sec." Rex kissed Jade and went to his father's side.

"Hey, Dad." He leaned his forearms on the fence, just as his father did.

"Son."

"I'm sorry about lying to you. I never meant to hurt you or to disrespect the family." He touched the silver charm that he now wore above his T-shirt.

"I know you didn't, son." His father looked out over the pasture, and after a minute or two, he said, without looking at Rex, "You know how I told you that your mother wanted me to tell you something?"

"Yeah."

His father nodded, then put an arm around Rex. "She said you were doing the right thing."

Rex looked into his father's eyes. "I don't know if you're delusional or not, Dad, but right this second, I'd like to believe you're the sanest man alive."

His father let out a laugh and slung an arm over Rex's

shoulder as they walked toward the driveway, where Earl and Jane were stepping out of their car.

"Thank you, Dad. I know it's not easy to welcome the Johnsons back into your life. I don't know what that Richter guy did to Mom, but I respect your need to protect her, and I'm sorry to have put you on the spot like that with Jade."

"You know I'll love Jade as much as you do. She made a difference in Hope's health, and I appreciate that you cared enough about Hope to risk our relationship and bring Jade by to help her." They walked in silence for a minute, and then his father stopped walking and looked into Rex's eyes. "Son, you've never let me down a day in your life, and I wish I could say the same for myself, but I can't. Fifteen years is a long time to wait for the woman you love. I'm sorry."

Savannah charged up the driveway with a suitcase in her hands. Treat, Max, and Josh were right behind her. "I have to leave earlier than anticipated."

"Oh Jesus. Don't tell me you're running back to Connor Dean," her father said as he took her into his arms.

"No, Dad. That was a call from my office. There's a new client coming into New York City, and they need to meet me tomorrow afternoon," Savannah assured him.

"Before you go, Vanny, Max and I have an announcement." Treat stood arm in arm with Max, both flashing enormous smiles.

"She's pregnant?" Savannah asked.

Max put her hand on her stomach. "No. Gosh, way to make me feel self-conscious."

Treat and Rex laughed. They pulled Earl over to where they

stood. "We came to a deal that we think will work for everyone. Earl has agreed to sell Max and me the parcel that he's selling off, and he's offered us first right of refusal for any other parcels that he might want to sell."

"And last night Dad, Earl and Jane, and Jade and I came to an agreement about the unoccupied property, which will no longer be unoccupied. When Treat and Max build, Jade and I will be building our home as well." Rex kissed Jade's forehead.

Savannah jumped up and down. "So I'll have two sister types living right by Dad that I can visit? This gets better by the second."

"Give them your biggest news, Treat," Josh urged.

"You suck at keeping secrets," Treat teased.

"What? I didn't tell them."

Treat put his arm over Josh's shoulder and pretended to punch him in the stomach. "I love you, bro."

Max sighed. "I'll tell them." Her eyes lit up. "We're getting married! We finally set the date for next spring!"

"Yes!" Savannah yelled, and hugged Max.

"And Josh is designing my wedding dress. Nothing too fancy," Max said.

"Of course not," Josh said, winking at Savannah.

"Oh, Max! I'm so excited for you." Jade hugged Max.

In the past few hours, Rex had watched Jade and each of his siblings, as well as his father and Max, get to know one another, and he could tell by the smile on her face that Jade was just as thrilled about being included in their family as he was.

Hal slung an arm casually over Jade's shoulder. "Now let's see if Rex'll make an honest woman out of you, too."

Rex beamed. "One day. You'll be the second person to know." He blew a kiss at Jade.

Riley's red Camry pulled into the driveway. She stepped out with a wide smile. "I'm sorry. I had no idea that there was a family gathering going on. Josh asked me to bring by my portfolio."

Rex cast a curious glance at Josh.

Josh leaned in close to him. "I learned from your mistake." Then louder, he said, "Riley, welcome to our home. Come on into the yard."

Rex and Jade laughed. "What have we done?" he asked.

Ready for more Bradens?

Fall in love with Josh and Riley in Friendship on Fire!

Chapter One

RILEY BANKS HURRIED down Thirty-Seventh Street in her red Catherine Malandrino dress and Giuseppe Zanotte leopard-print, calf-hair pumps. It was the week after Thanksgiving, and Manhattan was buzzing with the feverish zeal of the holidays. Riley slowed her pace to catch her breath. *Tomorrow I'll find the courage to take the subway. Maybe.* She tugged her coat tighter across her chest to ward off the chilly air and silently hoped that nobody would figure out that she'd purchased her outfit on Outnet.com, an online designer outlet store. She felt like such a hypocrite, heading to her first day at her new job as one of world-renowned designer Josh Braden's assistants wearing discounted clothing. The thought turned her stomach—but not as much as showing up in her hometown jeans and cowgirl boots would have. She was a long way from Weston, Colorado, and she'd spent the last few weeks gathering discount designer clothes and practicing omitting "y'all" from her vocabulary.

She stood before the thick glass door of Josh Braden Designs and took a deep breath. The sign above the door read, JBD. *This is it.* She closed her eyes for a split second to repeat the mantra she'd been playing in her mind like a broken record for weeks; *I'm educated, knowledgeable, and eager. I can do this.*

A warm hand on her lower back pulled her from her thoughts.

"Have any trouble finding us?" Josh Braden stood beside her with a friendly smile and perfectly shorn, thick dark hair. His black Armani suit fit his lean, muscular frame perfectly. A few years earlier, he'd been named one of America's Most Eligible Bachelors. Back then she hadn't given the magazine cover a second thought. He was in New York, and she was back in Colorado, so far removed from him that she'd still thought of him as Josh Braden, the boy she'd had a crush on for too many years to count. Now, standing on the streets of New York City beside the man whose name rivaled Vera Wang, she felt the air sucked from her lungs.

His deep voice sent a shiver right through her. Not only had she had the good fortune to be reconnected with Josh when he was back home visiting his family, but during his visit, the two of them had also spent a few days getting reacquainted. Riley hadn't been sure if it was her crush going haywire or if there was something more real blossoming between them, but those few days had each felt a little more intimate than the last. And while their lips never touched and their bodies remained apart, she'd felt like they were always one breath away from falling into each other's arms.

"Uh…ye…no." *Oh God, please kill me now.*

Josh smiled, lighting up his brown eyes. "Nervous?"

At five foot eight, she was a full seven inches shorter than him. She wondered what it might be like to stand on her tiptoes and kiss him on those luscious lips of his. *Stop it!* The way he held her gaze brought goose bumps to her arms. *Stopitstopitstopit.* She envisioned him at seventeen; he'd reached his full height by then, thin but well muscled, with testosterone practically oozing from his pores. She'd wanted him then, but those schoolgirl feelings didn't come close to the desire that begged to be set free now. She cast her eyes away and took a deep breath, trying to ignore her thundering heart. The last thing she needed was to become one of those girls who swooned every time her boss appeared. She was here to build a career, not a reputation.

"A little," she answered honestly.

He pulled the heavy door open and waited for her to walk through before placing his hand on the small of her back once again. Josh spoke softly, his mouth close to her ear as he guided her through the expansive lobby.

"Think of this as Macy's back home. There's the customer service area." He nodded toward the elegant mahogany and granite reception desk.

Her heels clacked across the marble tile as they passed the

desk.

"Good morning, Chantal." Josh smiled at the blond woman behind the desk, who looked like she'd come straight from an eight-hour session at a local salon. Her hair glistened, and her green eyes were perfectly shadowed to match her emerald-green blouse.

Riley reached up and touched her shoulder-length brown hair, feeling the little confidence she'd mustered being whittled away. *If the receptionist is that perfect, what are the other employees like?*

"Good morning, Mr. Braden," Chantal said with a practiced smile. "Good morning, Riley."

You know my name? Riley pushed past her rattled nerves, forcing her mouth to obey her thoughts, and felt the grace of a smile. "Good morning...Chantal." She pulled her shoulders back, reclaiming a bit of her lost confidence. *She knows my name!*

"Chantal is an assistant in the design studio. She fills in for our receptionist when she steps away from her desk. I'm sure you'll see her in the design studio later," Josh explained.

Riley felt like she was in a dream as she walked beside Josh through the elegant offices. She'd spent years dreaming of what it might feel like to work in New York City, and more specifically, in a design studio. After graduating with a degree in fashion design with a 3.8 GPA and winning two design awards, she'd longed to move to New York City and land a job in the design field. After several months of applying for positions and receiving enough rejection letters to wallpaper her bedroom, Riley had given up and settled into her life in Weston, working at Macy's and designing clothes no one would ever see. Riley had come to accept that working in the fashion industry had more to do with connections than skills. She'd given up that dream until Jade had begun dating Rex, one of Josh's older brothers, and she'd worn one of Riley's dresses on their first date. One recommendation from Rex, and Josh had eagerly reviewed her portfolio. A few days later, Riley was having lunch at his father's ranch, and the next thing she knew, she had a job offer and was packing to move to New York City. Now, as she walked beside Josh, Riley wondered if he was thinking about the time they'd spent together as much as she was.

They rounded a hall and Riley stifled a gasp. Racks of designer clothing lined the walls; dozens of fabric samples were strewn across long drawing tables, and sketches littered an entire wall. The combination sent her pulse soaring. Men and women milled about, talking quietly and fingering through the samples. A woman wearing jeans, her jet-black hair cut short, pulled a rolling cart filled with clothes across the floor. A man scurried around her with a notebook in hand, talking into an earpiece.

Without thinking, Riley grabbed Josh's arm—as if he they were back in Weston at a farm show and he were Jade. "Oh my goodness. This is amazing!" she exclaimed.

He laughed, and several eyes turned in their direction.

Riley cringed. She must have looked like an excited child seeing Santa for the first time.

"I'm sorry," she said, frantically patting down Josh's suit sleeve. "I just...I'm so sorry." *God, I'm an idiot.*

"That's the kind of reaction I'd hoped for," he said.

She let out a relieved sigh as a tall, auburn-haired woman

appeared at Josh's side and locked her green eyes on Riley, then drew them down her dress, over her curvy figure, all the way to her heels.

"This must be Riley Banks?" She extended a pencil-thin arm in Riley's direction. "Claudia Raven, head design assistant."

Claudia's forced smile and threatening gaze reminded Riley of Cruella De Vil. There was no mistaking the way she pressed her right shoulder into Josh's back. Riley thought she saw him flinch, but his eyes never wavered from her, his smile never faltered, and she realized that she must have been projecting her own bodily response onto him. Every ounce of Riley's cognitive thought screamed, *Run! Run far and fast.* She wanted to flee from the awful woman who, by the look in her evil eyes, already hated her. The woman who silently staked claim to Josh. Instead, Riley forced a smile and took her hand in a firm grip.

"I'm honored to be working with you," she said, and tucked away any lingering thoughts about Josh. She needed a career, not a *Fatal Attraction* situation.

JOSH STIFLED A FLINCH at the feel of Claudia against him. She'd made no bones about being open to sleeping her way to the top, and while at first he'd found her innuendos comical, recently he'd begun to loathe them. But she was a dedicated worker and had been with JBD for five years, the last two as the head design assistant. She hadn't slept her way to that position. Josh had better scruples than that, even if to an outsider Claudia might appear to be the "right" kind of woman for him. He couldn't deny that she was attractive, intelligent, and she knew the design business inside and out. But Josh had seen the other side of Claudia—the manipulative, competitive-to-the-point-of-nasty side—and those were qualities that Josh was not looking for in a lover. As the niece of one of his oldest supporters, Josh felt trapped by loyalty to keep her on staff.

He was impressed by Riley's steely, though professional, reserve. He doubted that Claudia or anyone else could tell that her smile was forced. They couldn't know that the way her lips pulled tightly at the corners was different from the casual, natural smile Riley usually possessed. And they wouldn't notice the underlying discomfort in her hazel eyes, the discomfort that Josh recognized and longed to soothe.

He couldn't seem to remove his hand from her back. The feel of her curves beneath his palm were refreshing. The women he'd dated were usually pencil thin. Going out to dinner equated to watching skeletons graze on leafy greens, with fake smiles plastered on their artificially plumped lips and dollar signs in their eyes. Then again, Josh's dates had primarily been setups from business colleagues who believe he needed to date the "right" women for his social status. Over the past year or so, he'd become disenchanted with those expectations, and he'd taken to dating fewer and fewer of them, but that was a thought for another time.

"I can take her from here," Claudia said, pushing between them.

Josh reluctantly removed his hand. He looked into Riley's eyes again, remembering how he'd been drawn to her when they were teens. The way her eyes had always been like windows to her emotions. Even back then he'd known when she was happy or sad, angry or bored. He had an urge to put his arm around her and soothe away the worry that lay there, but just behind that worry, he saw excitement mounting, and he knew she'd fare just fine—at least he hoped she would.

"Riley, I'm glad you're here." Josh ignored the narrowing of Claudia's eyes and the iciness that surrounded her like a cloak. "If you need anything, just let Claudia know. She'll take good care of you. Right, Claudia?" He took pleasure in nudging Claudia out of her villainous stare.

"Thanks, Josh. I appreciate everything. I won't let you down," Riley said.

"Shall we?" Claudia grabbed her arm and dragged her away.

Josh headed for his office, thinking about Riley. Her designs were damned good—fresh and stylistic in a way that was different from the typical New York trends. He'd have brought her on as a junior designer if he hadn't believed that she needed to first learn the down-and-dirty side of the business. Claudia's designs, on the other hand, left much to be desired, as did her people skills, but as head design assistant, he knew she was the cream of the crop. Organized, efficient, dedicated, and never missed a deadline. Claudia kept the staff in line, even if a little heavy-handedly. He hoped she'd put away her claws long enough to teach Riley the ins and outs of the fashion world.

If not, he thought, *I just might have to do it myself.*

(End of Sneak Peek)

To continue reading buy FRIENDSHIP ON FIRE

New to the Love in Bloom series?

I hope you have enjoyed getting to know the Bradens as much as I've loved writing about them. If this is your first Love in Bloom book, you have many more love stories featuring fiercely loyal heroes and sassy, smart heroines waiting for you. Characters from each series carry forward to future series, so you never lose track of your favorite characters (including engagements, wedding, and births!). You may enjoy starting at the beginning of the Love in Bloom series with SISTERS IN LOVE, the first book in the Snow Sisters trilogy. You will meet the Bradens in book 3 of the Snow Sisters. Below are links where you can download a Love in Bloom series checklist, and several first-in-series novels absolutely FREE.

Checklist:
www.MelissaFoster.com/LIBChecklist

Free eBooks:
www.MelissaFoster.com/LIBFree

More Books By Melissa Foster

LOVE IN BLOOM SERIES

SNOW SISTERS
Sisters in Love
Sisters in Bloom
Sisters in White

THE BRADENS at Weston
Lovers at Heart, Reimagined
Destined for Love
Friendship on Fire
Sea of Love
Bursting with Love
Hearts at Play

THE BRADENS at Trusty
Taken by Love
Fated for Love
Romancing My Love
Flirting with Love
Dreaming of Love
Crashing into Love

THE BRADENS at Peaceful Harbor
Healed by Love
Surrender My Love
River of Love
Crushing on Love
Whisper of Love
Thrill of Love

THE BRADENS & MONTGOMERYS at Pleasant Hill – Oak Falls

Embracing Her Heart
Anything For Love
Trails of Love
Wild, Crazy Hearts
Making You Mine
Searching For Love

THE BRADEN NOVELLAS

Promise My Love
Our New Love
Daring Her Love
Story of Love
Love at Last
A Very Braden Christmas

THE REMINGTONS

Game of Love
Stroke of Love
Flames of Love
Slope of Love
Read, Write, Love
Touched by Love

SEASIDE SUMMERS

Seaside Dreams
Seaside Hearts
Seaside Sunsets
Seaside Secrets
Seaside Nights
Seaside Embrace
Seaside Lovers
Seaside Whispers
Seaside Serenade

BAYSIDE SUMMERS

Bayside Desires
Bayside Passions
Bayside Heat
Bayside Escape
Bayside Romance
Bayside Fantasies

THE RYDERS

Seized by Love
Claimed by Love
Chased by Love
Rescued by Love
Swept Into Love

THE WHISKEYS: DARK KNIGHTS AT PEACEFUL HARBOR

Tru Blue
Truly, Madly, Whiskey
Driving Whiskey Wild
Wicked Whiskey Love
Mad About Moon
Taming My Whiskey
The Gritty Truth

SUGAR LAKE

The Real Thing
Only for You
Love Like Ours
Finding My Girl

HARMONY POINTE

Call Her Mine
This is Love
She Loves Me

THE WICKEDS: DARK KNIGHTS AT BAYSIDE
A Little Bit Wicked
Wicked Aftermath

WILD BOYS AFTER DARK (Billionaires After Dark)
Logan
Heath
Jackson
Cooper

BAD BOYS AFTER DARK (Billionaires After Dark)
Mick
Dylan
Carson
Brett

<u>HARBORSIDE NIGHTS SERIES</u>
Includes characters from the Love in Bloom series
Catching Cassidy
Discovering Delilah
Tempting Tristan

More Books by Melissa
Chasing Amanda (mystery/suspense)
Come Back to Me (mystery/suspense)
Have No Shame (historical fiction/romance)
Love, Lies & Mystery (3-book bundle)
Megan's Way (literary fiction)
Traces of Kara (psychological thriller)
Where Petals Fall (suspense)

Acknowledgments

There are so many friends I'd like to thank for reading the early versions of *Destined for Love* and helping me work out the kinks and assisting me with bringing my work to my readers. A hearty thank-you to Shanyn Silinski, who was an incredible resource for all things ranch and horse related. Shanyn, even though much of what we discussed did not make it to the page, know that it all helped me to define and refine Rex and Jade's world.

Hugs of appreciation to my generous bloggers, authors, friends and fans across social media, and readers for continuing to support my efforts, and to my always encouraging Team PIF members—y'all are awesome!

Behind every strong woman is a group of female friends handing them chocolate and wine, and I'd like to thank several of them; Amy, Tasha, Sharon, Lisa F, Lisa B, Missy, Shelby—sisters at heart forever, gals! I love you all, and thank you.

Loads of gratitude go to my editorial team, Kristen Weber and Penina Lopez, and to my proofreaders, Jenna Bagnini, Juliette Hill, and Marlene Engel. Thank you for helping my work shine.

And, of course, thank you to my family for your understanding, encouragement, and support. You amaze me on a daily basis, and I adore you.

Melissa Foster is a *New York Times* and *USA Today* bestselling and award-winning author. Her books have been recommended by *USA Today's* book blog, *Hagerstown* magazine, *The Patriot*, and several other print venues. Melissa has painted and donated several murals to the Hospital for Sick Children in Washington, DC.

Visit Melissa on her website or chat with her on social media. Melissa enjoys discussing her books with book clubs and reader groups and welcomes an invitation to your event. Melissa's books are available through most online retailers in paperback, digital, and audio formats.

CPSIA information can be obtained
at www.ICGtesting.com
Printed in the USA
BVHW030211060721
611227BV00010B/46

9 780989 050890